Hunter's Moon

THE LUNATICS ~ BOOK ONE

A M LEONARD

Raven Song Press
Freeville, New York

Cover design: Betty Martinez

Editor: Brendan Dabkowski

Raven Song Press

46 Hammond Hill Road

Freeville, New York, 13068

(607) 844-8706

www.RavenSongPress.com

Publisher's Cataloging-In-Publishing Data

Names: Leonard, A.M., 1956- author

Title: Hunter's Moon / A.M. Leonard

Description: Freeville, NY: Raven Song Press, (2024)

Series: The Lunatics

The Library of Congress LCCN Data is available upon request

ISBN 9798990754409 (paperback) ISBN 9798990754416 (e-book)

Printed in the United States of America

First Edition August 2024

10 9 8 7 6 5 4 3 2 1

One

My name is Raven Callahan, and I am 16 years old. At least my birth certificate says I'm 16. Right now, however, on my 16th birthday, I look like I'm TWO.

Let that sink in.

That's no exaggeration: I LOOK TWO. Literally. Like I ought to be wearing diapers. I can't even reach the sink faucet in the bathroom, for gosh sake. I'd say something stronger, but Mom is quick to respond to potty language with her favorite bar of soap.

Consider how YOUR mother would react if you walked into the kitchen on your 16th birthday as your two-year-old self. Assuming she doesn't jump to the conclusion that some dire and elaborate sort of kidnapping has taken place.

My Mom nearly passed out when she saw me, then she phoned my father in New York—we live in North Dakota—and told him I'd turned into a toddler, and that he needed to get his ass out to our place immediately. Now. No excuses. *OR ELSE.* In the tone she only uses on people —usually me—for severe screw ups. Which really doesn't paint a particularly nice picture of my mother, I realize, but you have to cut her a little slack under the circumstances.

After all, I am supposed to be 16. Instead, I'm two.

~

Imagine what you would feel like if one morning you woke up suddenly much smaller than when you went to bed? Think about it.

1. The bed is HUGE, and way off the floor. Mine's a full, so it's pretty roomy for me when I'm normal sized. But it's gigantic for my two-year-old self.
2. The PJs don't fit. Nope. Nosir.
3. And then there's that sink faucet problem, not to mention the toilet. And whose dumb idea was it anyway to put the toilet paper holder on the other side of the room from the pot, way out of reach of short people? Really, guys? Wow.

So when I walked into the kitchen, I had wrapped a towel around my otherwise naked self because—news flash!—I literally had nothing to wear.

One thing to be grateful for at least: I did not *sound* like my two-year-old self. I still had all my words. I still remembered that Bismarck is the capital of North Dakota and that $E = mc^2$. Dumb stuff like that. I just packed it all into the two-year-old version of me.

After Mom nearly fainted, and then oddly called my father FIRST, before she made a move in my direction, she finally came over to me, got down on her knees, grabbed me by the shoulders and asked, "Raven, are you in there?"

No, really, that's what she said.

And my response was "Mother, have you gone completely insane? Because if you have, it is totally not my fault."

"You're ... little."

"Kinda looks that way."

"This is a problem," Mom said.

"You could say that," I responded.

"What in the world are we going to do?"

"I haven't a clue," I said. Unnaturally calm, you say? Well, either I could go into a screaming panic, or I could try to stay calm for Mom's sake. I picked the latter option.

But we were going to have to figure this out ASAP, because life was going to get a whole lot more complicated in a hurry.

But first, a bit more about me and my family. As I mentioned, we live in North Dakota in a little town called Kestral. My Mom is Hidatsa Indian. My dad is an Irish American white guy she met in college. They fell in love and got married. After a bit of time together, Mom decided she'd made a mistake, but by then *I* was there, and they tried ... but things didn't work out between them. The one time I'd mustered the courage to ask her why they split up, she'd just looked miserable and told me that Dad hadn't been straight with her. She wouldn't elaborate, and when I'd tried to find out more, she'd gotten angry. Wasn't worth the extra chores I'd earned for asking.

My Dad lives in upstate New York near his mother, my Nan, not far from a little town called Teaburg. I only see my Dad in the summer for a few weeks every year. Crappy, but that's how it is.

My Hidatsa grandmother, my Iku, lives on the Fort Berthold Indian Reservation. She and Mom fight about it all the time. Mom thinks it's not a good place to raise a "mixed" kid, especially a girl. Especially since the oil boom hit. Iku says the res has a lot to offer. Me, I don't know. I know I don't like being treated like an outsider on my rare visits there to visit my Iku. I'd never felt awkward about being a "mixed" kid, but other people seem to struggle with it. Their problem, not mine.

I'm in tenth grade at Kestral High. Despite the fact we're only about an hour drive from Fort Berthold, which is the largest Native American reservation in North Dakota, the student body at Kestral is 94% white kids. The other 6% is a motley collection of Latinos, one Black kid, one Asian kid, and me. I'm OK with being the only kinda sorta Native American in the place, but if I get called Pocahontas one more time, *somebody* is gonna get hurt.

Other than that, school's fine. People mostly leave me alone. That's the way I like it. It's not that I hate dealing with other kids, I'm just not very comfortable in groups. Mom doesn't want me hanging out with the kids in my school either because they are mostly "oil people." She's got nothing good to say about the oil industry. She even protested at Standing Rock last year, even though those folks are Sioux, and, as she puts it, Sioux and Hidatsa have a "difficult history." She wasn't able to protest for long because she had work to do. She's a hotshot lawyer. She does a lot of her work remotely, via computer, because her job is in Bismarck and that's two hours away if you drive like my Mom does. It's more like flying low than driving, according to Iku. Mom doesn't appreciate the description, but, well, Iku is right.

When Mom has to go to Bismarck, Iku comes down from New Town to stay with me. Mom doesn't want me to go to the res that much. She says just hanging around my Iku gives me enough crazy ideas. And she's worried about me being attacked by some random stupid white guy, like nearly half the women on the res have been. That, at least, she and Iku agree about. I try not to think about that too much. It's pretty scary. Sometimes I catch myself wondering if guys on the street are following me.

I think Mom is not so crazy about me being around my Iku much because she is a shaman. Mom has a thing about that, as in, she doesn't like it one bit. Maybe because Iku is also an RN; the shamanism is in addition to her nursing degree. I tried to get Mom to explain why she feels the way she does, but she just says she has her reasons. When I press her, she gets all grim and tells me to go read or something. Make myself useful. I wonder what happened to make her feel that way. I wish she would trust me to be able to handle whatever it is she doesn't want to tell me.

So. Mom doesn't like the res. She has issues with my Iku's status as a shaman. All things I'd taken for granted my whole life, like water being wet. Which is why I was pretty shocked when Mom bundled me into her Land Rover and told me we were heading to the res. *Now.* Before breakfast, even. Plus, despite the Land Rover having heavily tinted windows, she warned me to keep my head down so as not to be seen by the cops—because she didn't want to get a ticket for failing to secure little me in a proper car seat. (The horror!) Then we laid rubber out of our driveway to Iku's place in Fort Berthold.

It was a dark, gray day, which meant the countryside wasn't as pretty to look at as usual. Yeah, there were open fields with a few dead wildflowers on the side of the road, but without the light shining on them, things looked empty. The late October sun was just beginning to peek through the clouds when Mom's cell phone rang. She punched a button on the dash. "What?" she demanded, not even bothering to say hello.

Dad's voice crackled over the speaker, bordering on incomprehensible even as Mom cranked the volume up. (Cell service stinks out here.) "Hello to you too, Margaret." He sounded really tense. I leaned forward, straining to hear him. "Where are you?"

"Halfway to New Town."

"Martha White Buffalo's place?"

"Where else?"

"I'm not a mind reader, Meg. How long until you get there?"

"Forty minutes. About." A longish pause. "I think your mother might have been right. About Raven ... and that moon stuff."

"Looks like it." Another awkward pause, like they were both censoring what they had to say because yours truly was listening. "Look, we have a plane; we're flying into Minot; we'll get to you as fast as we can. But I have no idea exactly when we'll reach you. Whatever you do, don't stop for anyone, and hunker down at Martha's until we get there. You have your satellite phone?"

"Yes."

"Turn it on and keep me on speed dial. Whatever you do, don't let Raven out of your sight."

Mom huffed in frustration. I might be sympathetic if I wasn't being kept in the dark, too. Bad enough I couldn't even see over the dashboard! "Why all the cloak and dagger talk, Michael?"

Another one of those long pauses. "Because they're coming for her, Meg. And if they get there before we do, Raven is in grave danger."

"Who the hell are '*they*'?" Mom demanded, her voice rising to a squeak.

"Just drive that damned gas hog of yours like Mario Andretti, Meg. We'll have answers for you later." He hung up without saying goodbye.

"Mario Andretti?" I asked, my voice flat.

"A really good race car driver," Mom replied grimly and stepped harder on the gas. I stopped watching the gauge as it crept up over 90 mph, closed my eyes, and started humming under my breath.

Mom swore. "Will you knock that noise off? It's making me crazy!"

I peeked at the speedometer: 110, and still rising. "Will you please slow down?!" I fired back with as much dignity as my two-year-old self could manage. "You're scaring me."

"Fine. We'll make a deal. I'll slow down and you stop droning like a bee with a head cold."

"Deal."

Funny how 95 doesn't feel nearly as fast after 110 …

We crossed the reservoir bridge and hung a right into the heart of New Town, driving south through town to the outskirts where Iku's small white cinderblock house squatted on the edge of the reservoir. Mom had forbidden me to play in the water long ago—far too polluted, she claimed. Never mind that it's the drinking water source for hundreds of thousands of North Dakotans, including Iku.

Mom pulled into Iku's dirt front yard in a swirl of dust, slammed the Rover into park, turning it off as she was climbing out. I unbuckled my seat belt and slid off the seat, wrestling with the door handle. Much to my dismay, it resisted my pudgy little hands' attempts to move it. Could not get it open. Just too stiff.

"Mom!" I yelled. She was already halfway to Iku's door. "Mom! The door!" Oh, the humiliation of it all! She looked back at the car and waved at me to hurry up. I fisted both hands, pounding my frustrations out on the tinted glass. "I. Can't. Open. The. Door!"

Mom suddenly realized what was going on, came back, and opened the door for me. She had the grace to look a little sheepish for a second, but that quickly vanished beneath her tense expression. "You haven't done that in years," she said as she helped me to the ground.

"Done what in years?" I grumbled.

"Window pounding."

"I guess you forgot about me then, too," I snapped.

"Possibly." As if Mom would ever accept the fact that she was often a bit absentminded about me. She grinned. "You got red in the face then, too."

I muttered something under my breath that would have had Mom reaching for the bar soap if she'd heard me, but by now, Iku had the front door open and was waving us inside. "Come in, come in. Coffee's on, and I've got breakfast cooking."

I was floored by Iku's complete underreaction. For a second, I thought she must not have seen me, but she gave me a wink before turning around and heading back into the house. Well! At least some-one's not fazed by this.

Mom shoved me ahead of her into the house, then swung the door shut and locked it emphatically before turning and glaring at her own mother.

"Coffee? Breakfast?!! Hidu! Look at Raven—did you not notice something just a little off, here?" Hidu is "mother" in Hidatsa ... about the only word of Hidatsa my Mom uses, that I've heard, anyway.

Iku just smiled in that gentle, slightly spacey way she has and turned back to her kitchen duties. "Raven looks like her two-year-old self. Guess Michael's mother was right after all. I thought she probably would be, which is why I am prepared for your appearance. Breakfast, anyone? I have oatmeal, scrambled eggs, toast ..." She looked over where Mom was nervously checking the front windows and drawing the curtains. "Never mind the doors and windows, dear. They're all closed and locked already and warded according to Amaris's specific instructions."

Amaris is my Nan's given name. Apparently, she and Iku have been communicating. I chose to focus on that instead of the whole "locked and warded" thing.

Mom swung back from the windows and stared at my Iku. "Excuse me? Warded? What do you mean by that? What secrets have you been keeping from me, Hidu?"

Iku took several bowls out of the cupboard, set them on the counter by the stove, and spooned oatmeal into them. "Just that Amaris had her suspicions and we made arrangements ahead of time, just in case this happened."

Wait. They've been *expecting* this? How do you *expect* a 16-year-old to suddenly turn into a two-year-old?

"In case *what* happened? You mean Raven regressing to two?"

Iku smiled vaguely, gathered up the oatmeal bowls, and carried them over to the kitchen table. "Mm hm! It's just what we thought might happen. Margaret, Raven is a lunatic."

Two

"That makes her special," Iku hastened to say, as Mom's jaw dropped. "Close your mouth, dear. You look like a beached fish."

"Raven is not crazy! She's two!" Mom protested.

Iku rolled her eyes. "Not crazy, a *lunatic*." As if that were obvious and people hadn't been using "crazy" as a synonym for "lunatic" for who knows how long. "Like her Nan, she waxes and wanes with the moon. She's a lunar child—what Amaris calls a lunatic. Tongue in cheek, you might say. It's a crazy way to live, but that's the way of it."

"Waxes and wanes with the moon," Mom repeated, a stunned look on her face. "I never saw that in Michael's mom."

"You saw what you expected to see," Iku said, fetching the sugar and a bottle of half and half from their places in the cabinet and refrigerator, respectively, and plunking them down on the table. "Eat. You're going to need the energy. Orange juice, Raven dear? Some ketchup for your eggs?"

I needed the *Webster's Dictionary* booster seat to get my chin up over the edge of the tabletop, a detail I distinctly remember from childhood, as the big book had the disconcerting habit of shifting and twisting under my weight as I was lifted onto it. I clutched the table convulsively, as my two-year-old self also had done.

"That old book still rocking and rolling on you, honey? I'd forgotten." Iku patted my head. "I'm sorry. It's that broken spine. Eat. Eat."

Oatmeal has never been a favorite of mine, but Iku always makes old-fashioned seven-grain oatmeal, adds little pieces of apple into it as it cooks, plus lots of cinnamon, brown sugar, and cream, so I always ate Iku's oatmeal. The familiarity of it was comforting, even in the midst of … whatever this is.

Mom scowled as she watched me dig in. I never ate Mom's oatmeal; it was instant, plain, made with skim milk and no sugar. Bleah. I just grinned, shrugged, and kept on eating. At 16, you tend to know what you can get away with. Iku's cooking beats Mom's six ways to Sunday, and we both knew it.

In addition to the oatmeal, I polished off three scrambled eggs with ketchup and downed a huge glass of orange juice before announcing I was full and sliding to the floor. I had to push a chair over to the sink so I could reach it, but I helped Iku do up the dishes while Mom paced back and forth in the living room, occasionally peeking out around the edge of the lace curtains at the hard-baked bare earth that was my Iku's front yard.

Iku had a brown thumb. Not much liked growing for her, not even grass, and she preferred it that way. It didn't matter that traditional wisdom said that White Buffalo women were amazing gardeners. Iku said she had answered a different calling and didn't seem terribly upset about tradition. At least not this.

"Expecting someone?" Iku asked as she plunked herself down on the bench in front of her loom and began tossing the shuttlecock full of yarn along its race, her feet dancing on the treadles. The treadles squeaked and thumped gently in a steady rhythm as she wove a pattern of diamonds in blue and white. After every few tosses of the shuttlecock. she pulled the beater bar toward her, packing the threads together, punctuating the squeak, the thump of the treadles making a deeper thud. "Michael won't be here for several hours yet, Margaret. You might as well take the weight off your feet for a while."

Mom shot her a dark look. "It's not him I'm watching for."

"If it's the trolls you're expecting, they'll be here soon enough. The wards will keep them back. Or should."

"'Trolls'?" Mom and I repeated in unison.

"Like movie trolls, or Grimm's fairytale trolls, warts and all? I demanded.

"Internet trolls, more like," Mom grumbled.

"More likely Bureau of Indian Affairs boys, I expect," Iku said. "Wearing uniforms and badges, toting guns, and driving white cruisers or black SUV's with BIA emblems on the doors."

Mom was back at her post by the front window. "Like that one."

Iku did not get up from her weaving, just bobbed back and forth, peering through the lace from where she sat. "Yup," she said after a pause, and went right back to her weaving. "Like that one."

Mom started for the front door. "I'm going to get rid of them."

"Don't open that door!" Iku and I spoke as one.

"Remember what Dad said." I was nervous and confused. Plus, I was starting to get scared.

"As far as they know, no one is home," Iku added. "As long as we don't open the door for them, they can't get in. Thank the wards."

Mom returned to her station at the window. "They're just sitting there."

"Possibly waiting for backup." Iku sounded calm, but there was an extra little bit of oomph put behind the beater bar this time.

I crawled up on the bench next to Iku and put one hand on her thigh. My hands were so impossibly tiny. Incredible that they belonged to me. Had to be a nightmare. I needed to wake up! I pinched my bare leg under the T-shirt Mom had found for me in the Sally's Army bag of clothes I'd outgrown. The smallest one in our house and it still reached to my knees. OUCH! Nope. Wide awake. This was real. Unfortunately.

Squeak, squeak, thump went the loom.

"Trolls?" I whispered.

"That's what your Nan calls them." My Iku said with that incredibly even calmness. "Anyone who's a mean, miserable son of a ..."

"Hidu!" Mom interjected, a warning note in her voice.

"Your Nan says sometimes they're really like that, and sometimes they're just possessed by a spirit that makes them act that way," Iku continued.

"Hidu!!" Mom was very unhappy now.

"Margaret!" Iku snapped back. I jerked backward a bit and looked between them. My Iku doesn't raise her voice much, even when she and Mom are arguing.

"No more 'Woo-woo,'" Mom demanded.

"The child has a right to know."

"It's fantasy, Hidu!"

"It's reality, Margaret."

"Your reality, maybe. Amaris's reality. Not *real* reality."

"Just because you refuse to acknowledge these things does not make them fantasy, Meg. As you are about to find out, sad to say."

Mom's attention was diverted outside again with the sound of tires on gravel. "Backup has arrived," she announced. "Two more trucks and a squad car."

Iku got stiffly off her bench and shuffled over to where she could see the backyard. "And there's a K-9 team out back." She came back into the living room and hefted me up in her arms. "Oof! You weigh a ton! OK, *itamapisa*, time to play hide and seek." She carried me into the spare bedroom, opened the closet, and lifted a trapdoor in the floor.

It led to my old hiding place in the crawl space under the house, which I'd discovered quite by accident years ago while playing hide-and-seek with my Dad. I'd been down there an hour and fallen asleep, while my parents frantically searched everywhere for me, until Iku had come home from one of her shaman visits and immediately had sussed out where I'd taken myself off to so handily. I'd gotten my ears pinned back for that one.

She lowered me into the crawl space. "There's crackers and cheese, a water bottle, and a blanket and pillow for you down there," she said as she handed me a flashlight from the pocket of her sweater. "Stay quiet and leave the light off as much as you can stand. I'm going to push stuff back into the closet over the trapdoor so you won't be able to open it, but as long as you stay put, the wards will keep your hiding place hidden. Be strong, Raven." She lowered the trapdoor, and I sat in complete and utter darkness. I heard her pulling boxes across the floor into the closet, then the closet door shutting and her shuffling steps slowly moving away.

Then nothing. Just me and the darkness. No idea what was going on, only that it was something truly bad. No idea what was going to happen to Mom and Iku. No understanding of *why* this was happening to me.

I stayed quiet, but maybe, just a little bit, I cried. Wouldn't you, if you were two, alone in the dark with the boogeymen outside your door? Sure, you would.

That's when they started in with the megaphone. "Attention, there in the house! This is the police! Come out with your hands up ..."

Three

Judging from the horrendous racket happening above my hiding space, the agents must have shot out all the windows and pock-marked the concrete block walls with hundreds of rounds of ammunition. Mom and Iku lasted 5 hours until a flash-bang smoke bomb finally forced them out of the house. What did the neighbors think was happening, I wondered. Would they do anything even if they knew something was wrong?

I cowered in the crawl space, safely below ground level near a small air vent that let in enough fresh air that I did not suffer from any of the smoke. Not much got down into the crawl space anyway. Just enough that I could catch a whiff of it. I was like a hunted rabbit in its hole, completely and utterly terrified, tears pouring down my face, not uttering a sound as heavy footfalls and men's shouts echoed throughout the house above me. It sounded like they were tearing the house apart—doors crashed, heavy furniture was thrown about, fragile things were smashed.

It grew dark as they rampaged through my Iku's house, somehow not finding my hiding place. I could see the light fading through the grate above my head. Finally, blessedly, things grew quiet in the house. I heard the trucks start up and drive away. The dark grew deeper, pressing in all around me.

Then, incredibly, a young girl's voice whispered through the grate. "Psst! Raven! I know you're in there. Psst! Say something!"

"Psst," I managed, too softly to be heard, then "PSST" just a bit louder.

"Terrific! Hang in there, I'll take off the grate; it's held on by four screws. It'll take me a couple minutes, but I'll get you out of there."

I could hear the girl working. "One screw," she whispered, and kept working. "Two!" a minute later: "Three ... oh, crap."

I heard soft footfalls running away. Shortly afterward, feet crunching on the gravel outside, and snuffling noises. Then WOOF! Pant, pant. WOOF!

"Good boy. What'd you find?" a soft groan as someone bent down near the grate. "Well, what d'you know. A ventilation grate! Wonder if you smell the brat down there, eh boy? I'll call it in." A staticky crackle as a walkie-talkie was fired up. "K-9 to base. You copy?"

Then all hell broke loose. There was a rush of feet, the thud of heavy bodies colliding and the snarling, barking, growling and snapping teeth of a dog fight in full swing, the man yelling, a sudden pained yelp, then dogs running away, the man in pursuit yelling, all fading into the distance.

"I'm back!" It was the girl again, scrabbling at the final screw, her breath coming in shallow gasps. Then the grate was torn off and she half crawled in, extending a hand into the dark. "C'mon! C'mon!"

I grabbed her hand and she pulled, and I pushed myself through the tiny opening to freedom.

"Run! Run!!" She dragged me across the dying grass as fast as my little kid legs could carry me, which did not feel nearly fast enough. She pulled me into the shrubbery between Iku's yard and that of the neighbors. "Bran will keep them busy for a while, but we must hurry. You with me?"

I nodded, unable to speak, as I was hyperventilating, scared sillier than when I'd watched *Carrie* at midnight alone in my bedroom at age 12. Dogs. They'd sent *dogs* to get a two-year-old ... and do what?

"Good. Let's go. Just not too fast because we have a way to go before we get to the nightmare. C'mon." She grabbed my hand again and we were off, darting through shadowed backyards, cutting across lots toward the edge of town. Toward the town barns, if I had my directions right.

Behind us, lights started flashing in all directions, and a dog was barking. Police sirens started wailing, and just as I thought I was going to die from hyperventilation, a shadow with glowing red eyes hurtled out of the darkness and sent me sprawling. I screamed the shrill, distance-defying, ear-drum-destroying squall of a terrified little girl.

A small hand clapped over my mouth almost immediately, muffling the sound, but I still wailed. "Shut it, or they'll find us!" the girl hissed in my ear. "Dammit Bran, it's Raven. You scared us! Where's that dratted police dog, anyways?"

A brief pause; I didn't hear anything, but then "Atta boy, good work. C'mon Raven. Run! Bran will help. Here, grab his collar."

"Who's Bran?" I squeaked. It was the only question I could manage, so sue me.

"The klutz of a hell hound who knocked you down. Here." The girl guided my hand to a furry neck complete with nylon web collar. Part of me wanted to demand to know how she could be so calm, but my throat was too tight. "Hold on, we're gonna make this." She grabbed my other hand. "Quickly now!"

Mind you, it's darker than the outside of an iron frying pan. I can't see a foot in front of me, and I'm being dragged by leaps and bounds, my feet sometimes hitting the ground, mostly not, willy-nilly, who knows where by an unknown girl not a whole lot older than me, and a massive black dog that stands as high at the shoulder as I was tall.

They terrified me, but not nearly as much as the sounds of the pursuit that echoed in the darkness behind us. Yes, it was shouting and sirens and the K-9 barking and all, but there was an unearthly extra *something* to it, an overtone of crazed laughter and banshee-like shrieking that turned my knees to water. If I'd had breath left to scream, I would have. This can't be real, how can this be real? Help me! I'm trapped in a nightmare and I can't wake up!

"Faster, Bran," the girl gasped. In her voice, I heard echoes of my own panic. Something very bad pursued us in the dark.

It felt like an eternity, but probably was only minutes when we finally burst into the town barn yard. A thin light lay about the concrete parking lot, cast by security lamps on the corners of the repair shop. My ribs hurt so badly from a side stitch I was gasping and crying with the pain. Everything hurt. I'd never been much of a runner, but even if I had been, two-year-old bodies aren't built for sprinting.

My saviors dragged me over to where the big plow trucks were neatly parked side by side along the edge of the lot. "Moon!" the girl called in a loud whisper. At her call, a white creature loomed out of the dark behind the truck parked on the end. It came swiftly over to us, immediately lowered its head next to mine, and blew hot sweet breath in my face. It had an odor I would know anywhere.

"A horse!" I wrapped my chubby baby arms around its long face. I knew horses. I loved them. Even without context for anything, just seeing one lifted my spirits.

The horse gently drew its head out of my embrace, very gently lipped at my hair, then blew more of that lovely warm breath that smelled of summer sunshine and freshly dried hay in my face. Oddly, I was no longer scared. There was, instead, a comforting sense of just … being okay. Not complete safety maybe, but perhaps I wasn't going to die today.

"C'mon, we need to get up onto Moon." The girl whose name I still didn't know was pulling me again, this time over to a dump truck and pushing me up on the front wheel fender. I struggled to climb up, forcing my exhausted muscles to *move*, and with her pushing me, we both made it up. The white mare sidled up close beside us, and the girl urged me onto her back.

As soon as I was on, she scrambled up and on behind me, wrapping her arms around my middle. "We're gonna ride Moon Dancer—Moon —out of here, but you hold on tight to the saddle, you hear? Don't let go even for a minute. This horse can fly."

I didn't get a chance to say anything in response—probably a good thing, because I would have yelped out something confused and probably dumb. A floodlight flashed across the yard, blinding us in its beam. "Bran, come!" the girl screamed to her dog, and urged the horse forward into a gallop. Moon Dancer bolted like she'd been shot out of

a cannon, gathered herself into a powerful leap, and sprang into
the air.

Once, when I'd been five or so, Mom and Dad had taken me to
Disneyland. I had been just tall enough that I could go on Space Mountain. At the time, I'd been obsessed with the solar system and the
universe, and had my parents read me every kid's book in the library on
the topic. I'd decorated the ceiling in my bedroom with glow-in-the-dark
planets and stars, with the planets in order, mind you, the light in the
center of the ceiling representing the sun. All the constellations I could
manage with the kit my parents had bought me too: Orion, Pegasus,
Ursa Major, the Pleiades, Cassiopeia, you name it, I had it stuck on my
ceiling. As you might guess, I was psyched about a ride through outer
space as only Disney could provide.

I was practically dancing with impatience as my mother paused to
read some signs along the way. I tugged hard on her hand, trying to
make her hurry up; I was irrationally worried about missing out on
securing a spot on the ride and didn't appreciate her sluggishness.
"Mom! They'll start without us!"

"People with heart conditions, or pregnant, or with bad backs are
strongly cautioned," my mother read aloud. "Honey, I don't think this
is the sort of ride you're going to like."

"It's *Space Mountain*, Mom! Space! Planets! Stars! Galaxies!
Come ON!"

On we went. The attendant strapped us in, smiling at my five-year-
old excitement, and moved on to strap the next family in.

The ride started slowly, then turned a sharp corner ... and the car
seemed to drop out from under us. Our seat belt gave way with an
ominous click. Mom gasped and went rigid, one arm clamped like a vise
around my middle, her other three limbs jammed up inside the roller
coaster car as we swooped and whirled through the dark, twinkling
lights sparkling around us pretending to be stars and galaxies, both of us
convinced that we were going to die very, very soon.

We didn't (obviously), but I have never gotten on another roller coaster, not even on a double dare, and I insisted that all the stars and planets on my bedroom ceiling be removed the very same day we returned home. I never checked another book on the universe out of the library. Not one. Perhaps that was a sad thing, but I just couldn't break the association of my bedroom stars with that terrifying ride.

My Dad? When we wobbled our way out of the ride, he took one look at us and said "That good, eh? I think I'll give it a try."

All Mom said was "You'll be sorry."

A bit later, when it was Dad's turn to come staggering out of the exit, Mom just lifted one eyebrow. (I wish I could do that, but I can't.)

"That was intense," he admitted as we walked away in search of something a bit tamer.

"Now try it without a seat belt," Mom retorted.

Here I was again. Without a seat belt. Careening madly through the sky among the stars, in the dark. On a flying horse. Literally flying. As in "like a bird" flying. Maybe I shouldn't have been surprised, at this point, but I was. As if I had not had a hard enough day already!

I had no idea how this would all turn out, or if I would live to see the sunrise, so I did what any toddler would do under the circumstances. I wet myself.

My unknown rescuer said something I cannot repeat in good company, so I won't repeat it here. Just let me say she was not exactly couth. She did not let go of me, however, and I did not fall off. After a while, I got so I could open my eyes for quick peeps—very brief—because it is crazy scary riding a flying horse through the night several hundred feet above the ground.

To my complete surprise, though, it gradually got easier and finally I was able to keep my eyes open and even turn my head from side to side a little bit.

"See, Raven? Flying is easy peasy! You'll get good at it really quick."

I must have let my breath out rather shakily, as she gave me a reassuring squeeze. "Next time though, don't pee yourself," she whispered in my ear. "Kinda nasty." If I'd had the wit, I might have reminded her that I was two ... Argh!!

We were fast approaching a city, its streetlights a pattern of gold and white sparkling on the ground up ahead. On the side we were approaching, a line of flashing lights raced on ahead of us, chasing each other toward a long strip of darkness outlined by white lights. "There's the rabbit," the girl declared, a note of relief in her voice. "Minot airport. Let's follow it in."

We coasted down, not unlike coasting downhill on a bike, and when Moon Dancer's galloping hooves touched tarmac, there was hardly any bump at all. Moon slowed her pace to a ground-eating trot and finally to a swinging walk as we approached a sleek, small jet parked at a private airfield area not far from the runway. I kept expecting someone to stop us—surely horses weren't allowed on the tarmac, after all—but it was like we were invisible. Maybe we were; that made as much sense as anything else that was happening to me. There were lights on in the aircraft, and a set of stairs led up and inside. Several people crowded the open doorway, backlit by the lights, then one hurried down the stairs as we halted at the bottom.

It was my Dad. I burst into tears and threw myself at him as he ran up to us. He caught me as I came off Moon's back and squashed me tight to his chest in the kind of hug you only give loved ones you think you might never get to see again. He was crying, too.

I'd never seen my Dad cry.

"Inside. Quickly!" the girl ordered as she jumped down from Moon's back. Dad turned and sprinted back up the stairs with me, the girl behind us. I saw her horse gather herself and launch into the air, gone in an eyeblink as if she'd never been there. A huge black shape shoved past us at the doorway; Bran had also arrived. With a whirring of machinery, the staircase folded up in on itself behind us, retracting into place, the airlock door making a solid clicking noise as it latched.

Were we safe? Were we truly, finally safe?

I buried my face in my father's shoulder, my arms locked around his neck, and I breathed his Dad smell, a musky, herbal smell he had from washing with his favorite patchouli-scented soap. I shuddered with cold and shock, hardly aware that the jet's engines were winding up and the plane was already slowly moving. A man's voice on the intercom instructed us to take our seats in preparation for takeoff.

My wet T-shirt was stripped off and I was wrapped up in a fuzzy blanket and cuddled close in my Dad's lap in a seat that bore more resemblance to a living room recliner than an aircraft chair. The engines pitched higher and the plane picked up speed, the cabin vibrating from all the power and the rough tarmac, until suddenly that stopped, and we were airborne—fleeing North Dakota, my pursuers, and the horrors of the day that should have been my 16th birthday.

October 31st. Halloween. No treats, all tricks. Really nasty ones.

Maybe someday I'll appreciate the joke.

Four

I wish I could say my first thought after being rescued was of my mother and grandmother, but it took until I had warmed up before I thought of them. I had long since stopped crying and nearly fallen asleep when the realization hit that I was safe, but they were not. I sat bolt upright on my father's lap and went into total toddler meltdown mode.

I'll spare you the details. Unlike when you are little, I was able to remember the meltdown later, and I am convinced I must have been the most obnoxious kid ever born. I'm embarrassed to admit it, but I was. The fact that I couldn't stop myself from doing it despite having a 16-year-old's brain made it even worse.

Strangely, no one else made much of it. Dad just sat there and took the worst I could dish out, and the girl merely rolled her eyes and left the area. I cried myself into hiccups, to the point where it was a struggle just to breathe, which pretty much rules out screaming.

At this point, the girl returned with two enormous ice cream cones thickly crusted with rainbow sprinkles. She fixed a calm gaze on me and took a big bite out of one. She made a big deal about savoring it, then extended the other one toward me. "Want it? It's yours. Bittersweet. Your favorite. Or I could eat it, I suppose."

I wanted to say something sassy to that, but I couldn't come up with anything. I took it from her with both hands and stuffed a huge bite into my mouth. Bittersweet is my all-time favorite ice cream, the one flavor I will never get enough of. Bliss in a cone. It will fix whatever ails you.

"Don't I get any?" Dad asked grumpily. It made me smile; that we could still be aggravated by missing out on ice cream meant we were all still alive, right? The girl laughed as she curled up in the seat across from us.

"It's coming," she assured him, and shortly thereafter it did, brought by a dark-haired lady in a neat uniform. She also brought napkins, which come in handy when you're eating ice cream with rainbow sprinkles because, no matter how hard you try to be tidy, some of those sprinkles are going to come off and they go all over the place.

I chowed down on my ice cream, occasionally picking dropped sprinkles off the blanket on my lap and stuffing them into my mouth, solemnly studying the girl. I hadn't really registered her appearance until now. She was not much older than my two-year-old self, maybe 7 or 8. Her hair was so pale blond it was nearly white, cut short in a spikey haircut. Her skin was translucently white, her eyes a vivid blue in a pixie-like face. She wore a black T-shirt emblazoned with a sparkling silver print *Where there's a Witch there's a Way* and faded blue jeans with holes in the knees. She seemed otherworldly, perhaps made a little less so by the way she obviously relished her ice cream. But she was not your run-of-the-mill kid. After all, she had a flying horse of her own and a dog that could scare the pants off anyone.

We munched in silence for a few minutes. I gave a practiced slurp around the edge of my cone to tidy up the drips, licked my hands where melted ice cream had run onto them, and then glared at the girl over the top of my cone. "Okay, I give. Who are you?"

An impish grin split her face. "Don't you want to guess?"

After the day from hell? Not even bittersweet could fix that. "No," I said flatly.

"You're no fun." The girl popped the remainder of the cone in her mouth, crunching it down noisily. Well, at least one of us wasn't fazed by what had just happened. "Um, yum!" she pronounced and wiped ice cream off her lips and fingers. Then a serious look replaced her delight in the ice cream, and she went quiet. "You've had a rough introduction to the moon crazies, Raven," she said at last. "I wish that had not been the case, but it's history now. So, here's one more shock to your system, but maybe it'll answer a few questions for you."

"And add infinitely more," Dad commented.

She looked at him and shrugged. "Probably. Here goes," she said, and with that, the air around her started to shimmer, rainbow light pulsing out like a halo. She seemed to fade, change shape, grow larger ... and the girl became my grandmother. My Dad's mom. The old lady I called my Nan.

"Surprise!" Nan said. "Now you know."

My eyes must have been bugging out of my head. I made a couple very embarrassing squeaking sounds before I could speak coherently. "How'd you do that?"

Nan shrugged. "It's a spell of seeming," she said. "In reality, I am that kid you first met, but I change with the moon. As it waxes, I grow older until the full moon, and then younger again as the moon wanes. At the new moon, my physical body becomes invisible. Then, once the moon starts to be visible again, I appear again as a very little kid. I grow older faster than you will because you're just 16 and I'm, well, a LOT older. Maybe you noticed I'm several years older now than when I first pulled you out of the grate, but maybe not. We were rather preoccupied."

"A spell of seeming," I repeated dazedly, sounding a lot dumber than I'd like.

She nodded, her smile patient. "It can be really challenging being a kid when you're *not*, really. So I put on this mask that makes me seem whatever age I need to be at the time. It's tiring when you first learn it, but soon it becomes second nature. Like riding a bike. You don't even have to think about it, really. You just are."

"Can you *seem* older than you are?" I wondered aloud, thinking *Hm! Useful trick at the liquor store!*

"Nope. You still won't be able to buy booze until you're 21." It was as though she'd read my thoughts. I can only assume that's a universal grandmother trick. The air around her shimmered in that rainbow manner again and the young girl reappeared. Now that I looked again, she did seem a bit older.

"Am I older too?" I twisted around and demanded of my Dad.

"A bit, fledgling," Dad grinned. "Maybe all the way up to two and a half now."

I slugged him in the chest, and he just laughed and tickled me. Darn it! I have not been ticklish since I was six.

"If you two are done being silly," Nan said, sounding like her older self, "it's really getting late, and well past Raven's bedtime, even if she weren't two. Plus, we lose two hours headed east. We'd best try to get a few hours of sleep."

I protested, not that it did a lick of good, and despite my declaration that I would not sleep a wink for nightmares, I was very soon in dreamland, snuggled up close to my Dad in the cushy chair that had converted quickly into an equally cushy bed. I did not have any dreams. That was my Nan's work, I'd discover later. But for now, at least, the nightmares left me alone.

Five

I awoke to the sound of rain on the roof, not heavy but steady; a soporific drumming that normally would have put me right back to sleep had I not abruptly remembered yesterday's events. I sat bolt upright with a gasp, briefly terrified, then recognized the loft bedroom in my Nan's house where I stayed in summer when visiting my Dad.

Nan's house is less a house than it is a hobbit home nestled rustically into the land surrounding it. At times it looked like it could disappear into the landscape entirely. I would learn later that this is precisely what it could do whenever deemed necessary. Meanwhile, it was just a nifty house.

The loft room itself was round with a domed roof held up by peeled and bent logs supported at regular intervals by tree trunks. Cut-off branches jutted out here and there, handy places to hang one's discarded clothing or other whatnot. The walls and ceiling were tongue and groove cedar plank. The walls were only about 5 feet high and punctuated every 4 feet by square awning windows. Off to one side of the room a circular staircase made of oak twisted its way up to the first floor. There was a peak in the roof to one side, making the ceiling jut out and the wall full height. A French door graced that wall, which, when you walked out through it, led to a small but wonderful aerie of a deck over-looking a long, narrow lake named after the Native American Cayuga tribe. I went out there now, opening both doors and stepping onto the deck. As the roof pitched out over the deck, I was getting damp but not poured on. The clouds were low and thick and gray ... dull and depressing, dampening not only with rain but also cutting the autumn colors with their gloomy forbidding light.

Shivering, because it was cold outside as well as wet and I wore only an oversized T-shirt, I ducked back inside and closed the doors.

"Raven?" Nan's voice echoed up the stairwell. "I heard you moving around. May I come up?"

I went over to the open bedroom door and looked down the stairs. Nan, now looking more like a young woman, was on the bottom step. "Sure," I said.

I turned away from the stairs and caught sight of myself in a full-length mirror on the other side of the room. I must have gasped, because Nan, having trotted up the stairs, made a sympathetic sound behind me. "It really is rough at first," she said.

We stood there staring at ourselves in the mirror. I was maybe 3 or 4 now. "Greeeaat," I said finally and turned away. Nan put an arm around my shoulders and led me over to the bed, where we plopped down side by side on the end. "Now what?" I asked dismally.

Nan shrugged. "Hey, new territory for me too, honey. But I think the sooner you get comfortable with this lunar stuff, the better."

"And how do you propose for me to do that? How am I ever supposed to get used to randomly regressing back into a baby?"

She shrugged again. "Pick something, I guess. Anything."

My stomach chose that moment to growl loudly. We exchanged wide-eyed looks, then burst out laughing.

"Maybe breakfast," I suggested. I am nothing if not practical.

Breakfast was crepes and bacon, made by Nan's "ummer." At least that is what Mom calls him, because he's not Nan's husband and they don't admit to living together. It doesn't matter a fig to me anyways. Elias is always around when I visit, and he's a really great cook. Plus, he treats Nan like she's completely special, which in my not-so-humble opinion makes for good man material. It's nobody's beeswax if they're married or not.

Dad wandered in looking bleary-eyed and sporting a five o'clock shadow as I was munching down my third crepe stuffed with strawberries and whipped cream and sprinkled with cinnamon sugar. He ruffled my hair as he passed by on his way to the coffeemaker. "Working on a sugar high, kid?" he commented.

"Yup," I mumbled around a mouthful. He shot me a half-smile and began pouring himself a mugful of dark brew. I swallowed my mouthful and gave him a hopeful look. "Me too, please!"

He hesitated as he resettled the carafe back in place and sent his mother a quizzical look. "Stunt your growth?" he asked, half serious, half in jest.

Nan snorted and I yelped in protest. "I'm really 16, Dad. C'mon!" This de-aging is going to get old fast if I wasn't treated like my actual age!

"It really doesn't matter, Michael; let's not make an issue of it," Nan said.

Dad shrugged, took another mug off a hook under the cabinet, and poured me some. He brought both mugs back to the kitchen counter bar where Nan and I were eating while Elias continued cooking crepes. Elias handed Dad a plate of crepes and bacon, and he settled down on the bar stool next to me as I happily doctored up my coffee with plenty of cream and sugar. He took a bite and chewed, contemplating his plate for a minute.

"I heard from your Mom early this morning," he said, and held a hand up as I started to exclaim. For a second it felt like my heart would explode out of my chest. "She's OK. She and your Grandmother spent most of the night in jail, but they're out now. They were headed back to Kestral after they talked to me. Apparently, Martha's house has been thoroughly trashed and is uninhabitable for now." He took another bite, chewing and swallowing before continuing in a wry tone. "As you might expect, your Mom is none too pleased."

"Lawsuit?" I supplied.

He nodded, as he took another bite. He finished his mouthful before continuing. "She said the strangest part was that no one at the jail seemed to know why the two women were in the jail in the first place and disavowed having anything to do with what happened. Margaret took the police chief out to see White Buffalo's house, and he was completely floored. Claimed it couldn't have been any of his guys. He had everyone accounted for, no one was anywhere near her house all day yesterday. And the neighbors seemed not to have heard or seen anything, either. It wasn't until this morning that anyone even noticed. No one heard shots, nothing. If it weren't for the damage to Martha's house, it would have been like it had never happened."

Nan and Elias exchanged meaningful glances. She nodded once and he set the frying pan to one side, turned the stovetop off and quietly left the room. I watched him leave with growing trepidation. "How could anyone not hear? How could they not have noticed? It was a war zone!" Nobody had heard anything? That made absolutely no sense.

Dad looked grim as he finished up his breakfast. "Your department, Mom," he said to Nan. "I need to go in to work but should be back about noon." He leaned over, kissed me on top of my head, and slid off his stool.

"Take Erin with you," was all Nan said. He nodded, pulling his sheepskin coat off the rack by the door and shrugging into it as he left.

"But what about Mom and Iku? Will they be safe? When am I going home? What if those ... those troll things come back?" I pushed the rest of my breakfast away, not hungry anymore, aware my face was crumpling up in a distinctly about-to-bawl toddler-like manner.

"Bring your coffee," Nan said, picking up her own mug and heading for the front of the house where the living room's floor-to-ceiling windows overlooked the lake below. She curled up on one corner of the huge leather couch and patted the cushion next to her. "Sit."

I sat down, drawing my legs up to sit cross-legged, wrapping my hands around my mug and staring blindly into it.

"First of all, your Mom and Grandmother will largely be ignored now that you are here. Your Iku and I have taken precautions to protect them in your mother's car, at home, and at work. Your Iku made an amulet for your Mom to wear that will give her additional protection."

I sent an incredulous look at Nan. "An amulet? For protection? What is this, fantasy land?" Ah. Way to make myself sound like my Mom. I don't think that flying horse was a dream ...

"It's life with the veil lifted, Raven," Nan retorted.

"What veil?"

"The veil between what you knew as reality and the rest of creation, dear. Think of it rather like the belief that the earth is flat and is the center of all God's creation."

I nodded. I'd had a class about that in history.

"People now know this to have been a very narrow and hugely distorted perception of reality, but we have all the advantages that science affords us that the flat-earth people did not possess. Now, your perception of reality has been astronomically expanded with the *admittedly challenging* gift of lunar power. The learning curve is steep, and you will feel overwhelmed much ... OK, most of the time. But you have one advantage that I did not possess at your age."

"What's that?"

"You have me," Nan said.

Six

She took a sip of her coffee and looked at me over the top of her mug. "You have questions, so ask them."

Where should I even start? My brain spun uselessly for a few seconds before the most important point struck me. "How do we know Mom and Iku are safe?"

"We don't. We only know that they are as safe as we know how to make them."

"Are we safe here?" I looked around nervously.

She nodded. "As safe as we can be. Which is fairly safe. Don't be imagining the worst, Raven. Imagine only the best possible things. There is true power in positive thoughts plus positive actions based on them. If you only stare into the abyss, you will fall in and be lost forever."

"Like the book *The Power of Positive Thinking*?"

She grimaced. "If only it weren't quite so tied to the Christian belief system, yes."

I blinked at her in confusion. "What's wrong with that?"

"Nothing, unless you're not Christian."

"Oh." I pondered that a bit. "I guess you're not Christian."

"Does that worry you?" She looked amused.

I shook my head. Other people's beliefs were their business. "No. I never really thought about it much though. Iku sure isn't! And Mom claims to be an atheist. Are you Wiccan or something like that?"

"I am what I am. We cannot pigeonhole ourselves like that, Raven. Others will try, because it helps them attempt to define us, but it doesn't work because they do not have a large enough framework of understanding. Like the flat-earth analogy."

My head was beginning to spin a little. "So, our definition of *anything* is ...," I waved one hand in the air, "bigger."

"More complex." She nodded. "By a lot."

"So ... say I want clothes. Something besides this dumb T-shirt, for example. How do I do that? I can't exactly go shopping at Target for clothes that magically fit me no matter what size I am. Unlike you," I added a bit grumpily, because Nan was still dressed in her worn blue jeans and "Where there's a Witch there's a Way" T-shirt, which somehow still fit her even though she was a good bit bigger now than she had been on the plane last night. "Is this a spell of seeming too?"

A huge grin split Nan's face. "You're a rock star, honey."

It surprised me. I hadn't said anything remotely amazing, and it must have shown on my face.

She chuckled at my confusion. "Your attitude, Raven. It's refreshing. You have a lot on your plate, but instead of trying to take it all on at once, you found something basic in that heap and chose that piece to get started on. So many would be overwhelmed to the point of immobility." She set her coffee on the end table. "I'll be right back."

She was gone several minutes, during which time a huge black cat with a white patch on its chest slunk into the room, eyed me up and down as if sizing me up, then silently slunk out again. It left me feeling a little unsettled. Do black cats normally have blazing blue eyes? I'd have to look that up online to find out.

Nan bounced back into the room with some clothes over one arm. "I picked these up at some end-of-the-summer sales after you were here last, figuring I'd send them out for your birthday. And, as usual, I got sidetracked and forgot, but it looks like that's actually a good thing for once!" she explained, plunking the armload of new clothes on the couch next to me before sitting back down, coffee mug in hand.

I picked up a deep blue, cap sleeved tee with the saying "yes I ride like a girl ... try to keep up" on it. I felt a big smile cross my face. "I love this!" My favorite thing to do was ride half-wild mustangs like a crazy woman. It was the one thing my mother had not tried to talk me out of, which suddenly struck me as strange ... Why, of all the nutty things she'd tried to protect me from had she not forbidden horses?

Putting that question aside for when I could talk to her again, I pawed through the pile of new clothes, exclaiming over the wonderful selection of fun T-shirts, embroidered jeans, black summer-weight riding tights, a dark gray hoody, turquoise wind breaker, six pairs of vibrantly colored Darn Tough socks, and even underwear (Jockey, natch!) and bras. All too large, sad to say. Which I did, mournfully.

"Put them on," Nan said with a secret smile.

Feeling more than a little silly, I did. Huge underwear! Enormous! But as I pulled them on, something very odd started to happen. They shrank, and then shrank some more until they were a perfect fit. OK, so this was freaky but darned exciting, too, as I was plenty sick of oversized T-shirts and nothing else. I dragged on a pair of oversized jeans. Same result. Next came the T-shirt (the "ride like a girl" one, of course) and the gray hoody. I finished off the ensemble with a pair of impossible to ignore, fuchsia pink with eggplant purple polka dotted socks. No need for a bra yet, which was rather nice for a change. Voila! I was clothed again! Lord, it felt good. So good, I did a silly, little victory dance.

I was singing the Lovin' Spoonful tune *Do You Believe In Magic* like I'd done a thousand times, somehow one of my all-time favorites despite it being straight out of the '60s. Magic. MAGIC! I stopped mid-phrase and stared at Nan, who had a huge smile on her face.

"Magic!" I breathed. "It's real, isn't it?"

Nan wordlessly pointed to a pair of framed prints on the wall near the couch. I went over and read each aloud:

Any sufficiently advanced technology is indistinguishable from magic.
Arthur C. Clarke

Any sufficiently rigorously defined magic is indistinguishable from technology.

Larry Niven

"That rules," I declared. "And so do these clothes! Where did you get them?"

"Here and there," Nan said. "Old Navy, Gap, EMS."

"So, you did something to them, then."

She shook her head. "Nope."

I gave her a blank look. "Then how …?"

"You did that."

I blinked and shook my head. "Um, no … how could I?"

"You believed it was possible, so you did it." I must have looked completely bewildered because she chuckled. "It's the first step in any real magic: *Belief.* You were hoping that I'd done something to the clothes to make them fit you; but, notice, nothing happened until you started putting the clothing on. Your belief that I had the power to give you clothes that would magically fit made it happen. Now, lunar power helped, but you harnessed it with your belief. You made those clothes fit, Raven. It was you. All you."

Elias stuck his head around the living room entrance. "Amaris, a word with you, if I may." He's always sounded a bit like a holdout from another century. He caught sight of me in my new finery. "Raven! You look phenomenal! I love the new look."

May I mention that he is also super sweet?

Nan hopped up from the couch. "Yes, doesn't she?!" She went over to Elias. "Did you locate them?"

Elias shot me a quick glance then jerked his head away from the living room. Nan caught on immediately. "Who can stay with Raven?"

"Kellas can come."

Nan grimaced. "Kellas?"

"No one else is available."

Well! That's awfully encouraging, I thought.

"Kellas it is, then. I should have assigned him to Michael, instead of Erin. Hindsight is 20/20." She sighed and turned to me. "Other duties call, Raven. I'm sending in … um … company for you, his name is Kellas.

He's a bit different, but he's a good sort, really, once you get to know him. Hang in there. We'll get things working smoothly soon. In the meantime, make yourself at home. I'll be back as soon as I possibly can, and we'll keep working on things."

And with that, they were gone.

Geez. Now I'm being babysat. Yay.

Seven

I hate being treated like a little kid again! Nobody tells you anything; they act like you're too little to understand what is going on, even when it's as obvious as the nose on their face. Honestly! And to be assigned a babysitter is just, just ... ARGH!!!!!!!

Yeah, I'm mad. First, Nan was telling me how great I'm handling everything; that made me feel so fantastic ... and now she assigns me a flipping babysitter? Really? REALLY?!!!! I stomped out of the living room and up the stairs to my loft and slammed the door behind me hard enough that it made the house shudder. Literally shudder. Not just shake. Like it was a living thing I'd punched. That would register later, after I'd calmed down a little. Right then I was too furious to notice. I stomped over to the mirror and glared at my little kid self. "I am NOT a baby anymore!" I yelled at my reflection. "I'm NOT TWO, or three or even four. I'm 16, dammit, and you need to show me my real self RIGHT NOW."

It didn't work. I was still mini-me. It's so demeaning, being stuck in a baby's body! Snarling in frustration, I cast about for something to throw. Tidy rooms don't have a lot of suitable objects, unfortunately. I settled for punching my pillow repeatedly and yelling with every punch. "It's not fair!! It's not fair!!"

"Whoever said life was fair?" a voice drawled behind me.

I shrieked and whipped around, holding my pillow in front of me defensively. Nobody. The room was empty. Just me. "Who said that?" It came out as a squeak.

"I did." The huge black cat I'd seen earlier strolled out from behind the easy chair near the French doors. It leapt up onto the chair and sat down.

I admit—my first reaction was entirely knee-jerk. "I hate cats! What are you doing here? Get out of my room! Scat!"

"Fortunately for you, I'm not a cat," the cat purred.

"Yes, you are a cat. A cat that talks, and I can't stand cats, even the ones that don't talk. Get out! Get out now, or I'll ..." Again, I looked around for something to throw, and again found nothing useful for the purpose.

"Or you'll what, pillow-fight me?" The cat lazily licked one paw, and then extended its claws. "Fascinating. Feather pillows make the best mess, you know, and that is a feather pillow you're threatening me with. Delightful. Bring it on, Brannaugh."

"My name is Raven."

"Whatever makes you happy. Brannaugh."

Oooh, we're going to get along *great,* aren't we?! "Call me by my real name!"

"As you wish." The cat stretched and yawned, then curled up on the chair. "Really, I would have thought you to be more interesting, what with you being a moon child and all. Sad situation. Ho hum." He closed his eyes as though he meant to take a nap.

A low growl started somewhere in the vicinity of my belly, and I leapt off the bed and ran at the cat, swinging my pillow with all my might. "Get out of my room, you creep! Get out, get out!"

The first blow landed full on the cat, the second swing was abruptly terminated when the pillow was jerked out of my hands by a young man with a messy mop of black hair and gorgeous blue eyes, sitting where the cat had been, laughing in my face. "Nice try, little sister. You thought you could chase me off with this?" He tossed it behind the chair. "Unlikely."

OK. This is too ridiculous for words. First, troll people who nobody but us can see or hear, then enormous black dogs with glowing red eyes, horses that literally fly, and clothes that shrink to fit. Why not cats that are actually guys in disguise? Sure! I can handle it! Why not?

I sat down on the floor and bawled.

Cat man apparently had never dealt with childhood histrionics before. He was immediately clueless as to how he should handle the situation. Do any of these seem effective to you? "Hey kid, stop that! I didn't mean it. You're making me deaf, cut it out. Stop crying and I'll get you a toy. C'mon kid, we can play a game. Want to play checkers?" With every failed attempt, he got more and more frantic until he dashed headlong from the room.

I stopped crying (because the enemy had quit the field), retrieved my pillow from behind the chair, curled up on my bed, and promptly fell asleep. Meltdowns are quite exhausting!

I was standing on a stage, the curtain about to go up. I was completely unrehearsed, did not know a single line of my part ... and I was the lead actress in the play about to be performed. I was terrified. I could see all my fellow actors in their brilliant costumes, see the set in full color, feel the heat of the spotlights trained on me, hear the strains of the overture and knew it was nearing its end, although it was not one I'd ever heard. I hadn't a clue what I was doing there. There must be some sort of mistake.

The curtain went up. A huge auditorium full of people was on the other side. Mine was the first line.

"Um, hi?" I managed. I waved, a tiny wave. A murmur went thought the audience, as though they too had been caught off guard. "I ... don't actually know what I am doing here," I continued. "Sorry to be such a huge disappointment, as I know you must have come here specially. I ... don't belong here, really, so I'll just be going. See ya!" Louder murmurs started in the audience as I headed for the wings, only to be stopped by, you guessed it, the cat man.

"You can't go," he sneered. "You're the star of the show. If you go, it all goes up in flames."

"But I don't know my lines!" I protested.

"So? Nobody here does. We're all just making it up as we go along. Get out there and do your thing. Whatever that is," he added with a smirk. "Bawling, maybe?"

He really is the worst! Even in my dreams! "You know what, cat man? You're a jerk, and I don't have to do anything I don't want to do."

"Oh yeah?" he snarled right back. "You wanna know something, smartie pants? Go ahead and leave the stage. Enjoy those trolls out there all waiting for you, see how you like facing them by yourself."

"Trolls?"

"Millions of them. Just waiting to "grind your bones to make their bread." If you don't want to die anytime soon, you better get back out there and start making things up, because ..." He swung an arm wide to indicate all the other actors on the stage ... Nan, Dad, Mom, Iku, Elias, and many more I did not know. "They're all gonna die because you're a coward."

"Why should I believe you?"

He stepped back out of my way and bowed, gesturing toward the wings. "You don't have to," he said. "Go on ahead. But I warned you."

I glanced at all my loved ones standing there looking at me, then back at the darkness in the wings, where I could now see many eyes glowing in the dark. I turned and walked back into the middle of the stage.

"OK, then, it's show time!" I glared at the cat man, then called down into the pit. "Play "I Was Born This Way."

And dang me if a teleprompter screen didn't light up over the audience's heads, and the orchestra struck up my song.

I belted out the lyrics of the Lady Gaga song all the while glaring at the cat man in the wings. Didn't need the prompt screen because I knew the lyrics by heart. I wasn't going to let anyone make me feel small ...

But something changed as I sang. The theater faded away; the defiant words turned into shimmering shards of light in the air around me. A silver sword formed in my hands; blue energy crackled along the blade. I felt myself growing until I was 10 feet tall, armor formed along my limbs, a helmet on my head. I was standing on a barren, blackened landscape, surrounded by ugly, misshapen ghouls. The song continued, even though I no longer felt myself singing, the shards of light that it formed striking the ghouls like arrows, cutting a swath through their ranks. They fell back, slowly at first, then it became a rout, those left alive fleeing the field.

I lowered my sword, immensely weary. A beautiful dark-colored horse came up beside me and bowed. "You have won your first battle, Raven Light Bringer, but there will be many more. Come, let us return to the other world now. I will take you there." He knelt so I could easily step up onto his back. Once I was in the saddle, he leapt into the air ...

Eight

I awoke with a jolt. The light in the room was already fading into early winter darkness. Somehow, I had slept most of the day. I scrambled off the bed and galloped downstairs, looking for my family, hoping I wasn't alone.

They were in the living room, my Dad in his favorite chair, Nan and Elias sitting on the couch. They'd been talking but stopped immediately as I entered the room.

"Hello there, sleepyhead!" Dad greeted me. "We were beginning to think you were never going to wake up."

For some reason, that made me feel faintly queasy. Like he had come closer to the truth than he knew. I shuddered a little; like someone was walking over your grave, as my Iku would say.

I stomped over to the one empty chair and plopped down. "I'll have you know I've been fighting demons. I won. Now you better tell me what's going on, because you aren't fooling me and I want to know, NOW." I glared at Nan. "And you can take that stupid cat man babysitter and kick him out the door, because if he shows his face around me again, I will stomp all over him!"

Elias snorted. I thought he *might* be sympathetic to me, given his expression, but I wasn't certain. "Kellas made quite the first impression I see."

"What do you mean, babysitter?" Nan asked, puzzled. "You mean, Kellas?"

"If that's his name, yes, Kellas. He's a prize jerk." I grumbled.

"But he wasn't babysitting you, Raven. He was supposed to be guarding you."

"Well, he stinks at that too."

"Says you," the cat man said, stalking into the living room. I whipped around to glare at him. He slouched against the wall next to the fireplace, arms crossed. He was scowling. "I was there the whole time, only she couldn't see me. She went and slept all day like some pampered little princess."

"Easy duties, then," Dad said.

"Not exactly," Kellas retorted. "She went haring off on a lucid dream, and I had to go in after her. She damn near didn't make it out. She got lucky this time, but she's clueless as to what is at stake."

Dad looked grim. Elias merely closed his eyes and shook his head. Nan went even paler than normal, if that were possible. "The night mares were warned to stay away," she said softly. I blinked at her, because that almost sounded like there should be capital letters there— like it was a Thing and not a creation of the mind.

Kellas grunted. "T'wasn't the night mares. It was that damned dark horse colt of Moon's, Knight. He took Raven in." He sneered at Nan. "You don't have him under your power, milady. He does what he wants to do, and to hell with the rest of us. You'd do well to be rid of him."

They all started talking at once then, and the resulting babble was unintelligible. It was some manner of fierce argument: Dad taking exception with Kellas's tone, and Nan and Elias speaking more or less at once. It was a solid wall of noise I couldn't comprehend.

I briefly tried to sort it all out, failed, and abruptly gave up. "Shut it, all of you!" I yelled. Amazingly, it worked. "I can't make sense of any of this. One of you had better start explaining, because apparently even taking a nap is not safe for me now? News flash! I really need to know these things, people!"

"Perhaps you should tell us your dream first, Raven," Dad said quietly.

He looked so somber; I got even more squirrelly in my stomach. I told them about my dream, what I could remember of it. Dreams do that; they start fraying at the edges after you wake up and are soon forgotten, and all but the way they made you feel remains. "I didn't know what else to do," I finished. "Karaoke is the only thing remotely like performing that I've ever done. I didn't know the words would form light arrows and kill the ugly things. They just did."

"Words have the power to heal and to kill," Nan said softly. "The greater your belief, the more focused your intent, the more powerful they become. This time it was a favorite song, and the focus was your anger toward Kellas. You had no idea of the danger your dream put you in, the risk that you took. The Knight horse did, and he must answer for that."

Yes, but who *is* the Night Horse, I wondered. Or is that Knight, with a K? And why would he intentionally put me in danger; what did I ever do to him?

Nan continued. "Your dream took you into a parallel world, Raven. What happens there affects here and vice versa. It's part of quantum physics known as the multiverse, or Many-Worlds theory. You and I can access these worlds with our moon magic, with the help of our night mares and the Knight horse. It's incredibly dangerous, however, and you need to learn how to protect yourself before you go."

"I just fell asleep. I have to sleep!" It came out as a wail.

"Oh, you can sleep alright," Kellas grumbled, "Just cut out the lucid dreaming for now."

"Stop talking like I did it on purpose! I didn't!" I snarled at him. "What's this 'lucid dreaming' you keep talking about, anyways?"

"It's when you take control and actively change the course of a dream," Dad explained. "Not a lot of people can do it. Apparently, *you* can."

"Really?" I had a hard time believing it, because I could not remember ever NOT being able to do just that.

Elias rubbed his forehead wearily with one hand then dropped his arm over Nan's shoulder. "We need a plan," he declared. "We can't keep on simply reacting to disasters after the fact. We need to have some idea of what we are doing, where we're going, and how it's all going to happen."

"I second that," Dad said.

"Especially if it keeps my tail out of harm's way," growled Kellas. "Otherwise, you're going to have to find a different cait sidhe to be that maniac's bodyguard. Even I'm not crazy enough for that duty."

"Maybe I don't want you for a bodyguard," I retorted. If I had been a cat, I'd probably be bristling from head to toe.

"Maybe you don't have a say in that, kid," he snapped back.

"Maybe you both need to take a deep breath and give each other a second chance at a first impression," Nan said crossly. "Squabbling gets us nowhere."

"Priority one," Dad said, obviously steering the direction our group chat was going. "Raven's safety. Which will make the rest of us safer as well. What needs doing first? Next?"

"Raven needs a crash course in what moon magic entails," Nan said firmly. "That'll be my job. Michael, you need to be our relay between the outside world and us. Anything remotely odd happens, we need to know about it right away."

"If I were to let you know of every little thing, I'd be on the phone with you all the time," Dad grumped. "From Washington on down, everything is in turmoil."

"The mess in Washington is troll mischief as well?" I asked. I was answered with a combination of eye rolls and somber nods. Apparently so. That did not increase my feeling of well-being whatsoever.

"I'll organize the fey," Elias said. "I've already started there anyway."

I sent him a sideways glance. Fey? As in *fairies*? Curiouser and curiouser. But, hey, we have trolls, a hell hound, a couple flying horses, and a cat man—why not fairies, too? I was getting downright blasé about nonconforming life forms. Just open any book of fairy tales, and the creatures within stepped off the pages and walked into my life. Yay.

Which is perhaps why I didn't quite pass out when a large white hawk flew into the room, straight through the closed glass as if it did not exist, settled onto the floor, and transformed into a tall pale lady in a long silver dress that shimmered with tiny points of light.

Nan, Elias, and Kellas all immediately jumped forward and dropped to a knee, bowing. Dad hastened up from his seat and bowed. I sat there like a dimwit with my mouth hanging open until Dad pulled me out of my chair. "Manners!" he hissed through clenched teeth.

I managed to duck my head, never taking my eyes off the lady. In these odd times I'd learned not to. Too many strange things happening. "Hi," I managed, then demanded "Who are you, anyways?"

Yes, I know. Rude of me. It's been a very long couple of days, okay?

There were audible gasps from everyone else in the room. However, there are times when looking like a little kid will save your hide. This was one of them.

Initially the lady stiffened as if offended, then relaxed very slightly and smiled. "Ah, this is our new moon child, Raven," she said in the tone reserved for offending toddlers. "I am so pleased to meet you, finally." Her smile was the sort that made you wonder if it prefaced a punishing left hook. "I am Cerridwen, Goddess of the Moon. I am the source of your magical powers."

Nine

I am not sure why this instantly put me in a nasty mood, but it did. "Oh, great," I snapped. "Now I have a Fairy Godmother, too?"

Cerridwen's smile froze on her lips. She turned to Nan. "I will take the child and attempt to teach her what she needs to know," she said in tones as cold as the dark side of the moon. "If that is at all possible," she added, sending me a glare that sent chills down my spine. She turned back to Nan. "You would do well to enlist Edona's help with the Dark Horse, the one you call Knight. And you," she looked at Kellas "will accompany us to act as this upstart's bodyguard in the meantime, because I cannot be watching her every move while we are among the Tuatha Dé Danann."

"Take Raven to Tír na nÓg? Milady, she's just changed. She's had so much thrown at her these past two days. Please let her stay with us, those she knows, at least for a little while longer. A month or two," Nan pleaded.

"Because you all are doing such a wonderful job, I suppose?" Cerridwen said nastily. "I'm afraid not. She'd be dead before a fortnight was over. Not that it is entirely your fault," she added, relenting a little at the distress on my family's faces. "The offensive taken to procure this child has been well planned and forcefully executed. You were ill prepared to handle their strike."

"I'm here, aren't I?" I demanded, stung that she was being so nasty to my Dad and Nan. Who did this lady think she was, anyways? "I'm alive and ..."

"Silence." The goddess of the moon made a small gesture with one hand, and I was instantly unable to speak. I clutched at my father's leg, pulling at him, terrified. Tears poured down my face.

Dad knelt next to me and pulled me close. "It will be all fine, kiddo," he said soothingly, not understanding. I patted his face to get his eyes on me, then clutched my throat and tried to speak. I could only form words with my lips. No sound came out. "What's wrong?" he asked.

"She has been struck dumb," Cerridwen sounded smug. "For now, until she learns to be properly respectful."

Nan stepped forward in distress. "Milady! Words are her power! You must not ..."

"Must not?" It sounded like a threat. "I will do as I see fit. I am tiring of this chitchat, as they say these days. You will spend the time I have afforded you to properly prepare for Raven's return. I will do what I can to tutor her in her new role. An interesting challenge," she mused, the hardness receding from her face, replaced with a thoughtful gaze as she considered my tear-streaked baby face. "It should relieve the boredom of the Otherworld for a while, I think. Come," she beckoned to my father, indicating he should give me to her.

Had I voice to speak, I would have shrieked; as it was, all I could do was cling to my father's neck with all my strength. Dad gently tried to get me to let go, tried to reassure me that all would be alright, but I was having none of it.

I heard the goddess laughing softly behind me. "Ah, she has so much to learn," I heard her say. There was a soft touch on my back ... and I instantly fell asleep.

~

When I woke up, I was in bed. A very nice bed: firm yet cushy. The pillow just the right firmness, the crisp sheets smelling of sunshine and clean breezes. I was aware of sunlight shining on me, could feel the warmth on my face and hands, but I refused to open my eyes. Too much was wrong with my life for me to want to face it, so why bother.

"You might as well wake up, Brannaugh. There's no hiding to be done around here."

That insufferable cat again! So, I'm taken away from Dad and Nan and I'm stuck with him?! Not funny!

"Besides," he went on, "it's a beautiful day and I want to go outside."

"What's stopping you?" I muttered, keeping my eyes firmly shut. *"Go outside. I'm tired. I'm sleeping."*

"No can do, not while you're in here. Orders."

"Go. Away!" I burrowed deeper under the covers, hiding from the sun. I did not want to deal with anything that had just happened. It was too much.

WHUMP! A heavy body on four small feet landed on top of me, catching me completely by surprise. Yelling angrily, I threw off the covers, the cat with them, and sat bolt upright. *"You jerk!"* I snarled at the cat, who was extricating himself from the bedclothes. *"Get out! I hate you!"*

Instead, Kellas jumped back up on the end of the bed and settled himself, fixed his startling blue gaze on me.

"Notice anything important?" he demanded.

I was too incensed to answer so I just glared at him, teeth bared, breathing like an angry bull through my nose. Why did this infuriating cat man refuse to get out of my bubble?!

"Look around," he invited. "Take your time. There's a mirror over yonder if you need it." He dropped his gaze, lifted one front paw and gave it a few lazy licks. As if he had all the time in the world.

Unable to resist, I looked down at myself. My grownup self! Jumping from the bed I ran over to the mirror—a huge oval thing framed in carved wood and suspended in a clawfoot stand— and saw my figure reflected back at me. Still wearing my "ride like a girl" T-shirt and the embroidered jeans, but I was a full 5'6", my long black hair wild around my shoulders and cascading down to my rear. Words could not describe my joy and relief.

"I'm back!" I whispered, then as another realization hit me, *"and I'm talking again!"* I whirled toward Kellas. *"I have my voice back!"*

"Not so fast," the cat responded. His face was grim. "Actually, you don't."

"What do you mean, I don't. I'm talking, aren't I?!"

"You don't have your voice back," he said. If I didn't know him better, I would have thought I heard a touch of regret in his voice.

"But ... we're talking. You and me. We're having this conversation."

"We're not actually talking. We're communicating." His tone was so infuriatingly even, part of me wanted to hit him.

Honestly? Cats! I flapped a hand from him to myself. *"Talking!"*

"You're thinking," he replied. "I'm thinking back." He jumped to the floor. "Try talking to me now." His cat body stretched upward, morphing into his human form, and he looked at me, both hands beckoning.

I tried, I truly did, but no sound came out of my mouth. Angry tears welled up in my eyes. Kellas immediately turned back into a cat.

"Why?" I demanded through a tight throat.

He shrugged. "Beats me. Apparently, you and I can communicate telepathically as long I am in cat form. Just not in human form. The *geis* Cerridwen put on you does not forbid that, at least. Fortunately."

"Geis?" There I go, parroting words I don't understand again.

"Curse," he supplied. He stalked over to a tall door and looked back over his shoulder at me. "C'mon. I'll show you around milady's castle."

Castle. Huh. I looked around briefly at the room we were in. It was round, the walls were all stone, floor-to-ceiling diamond-paned windows to one side where the sun shone in through. A large oak mantled fireplace, no fire. A couple huge tapestries on either side of the fireplace. The room was furnished with the aforementioned mirror, a ridiculously ornate four-poster canopy bed with deep red coverlet (now halfway onto the floor), an antique washstand with a basin and pitcher, a small writing desk and chair, and a wardrobe of unusual size. An old-fashioned settee upholstered in deep red velvet with a white shawl tossed artfully across the back was positioned near the windows. The floor was wide oak boards burnished to a shine; a bear skin rug was on the floor at the foot of the bed. That was it.

Kellas waited in silence as I got my bearings. I stared for a long minute before taking in a deep breath and letting it out.

"Right, then." I went over to the door and was mildly surprised to find it unlocked. Opening it, I followed the cat out into a long hallway, also with stone walls and wide-plank oak floors. The ceiling was so high it was in shadows, but I sensed big, dark beams, with more wood planks overlaying them. More of the tall, diamond-paned windows punctuated the walls at regular intervals and the sun poured in through them, laying bars of lights across the floor and up the walls. Kellas trotted on ahead, but I went over to one window and looked out. Summer was in full swing outside, the grass an emerald green, massive beds of flowers in full bloom, trees covered with leaves that danced in the breeze. Apparently, I was not only in a different place but also in a very different season.

"Done gawking yet?" Kellas had come back. I swear, had he been in human form, he'd have been tapping a foot in impatience. He stalked off again. I took a final look out the window and hurried after him.

"It's summer," I said, catching up and slowing to a walk next to him.

"No kidding," was the retort. "We're in the Summer Lands."

"Excuse me?"

"The Summer Lands," he repeated with perhaps a bit less impatience. "Otherwise known as the Otherworld, the Underworld, or if you want to get fancy, Tír na nÓg. One of the perks is that here it is always summer, with a bit of late spring and early fall thrown in for variety. Beats the nasty cold and wet of your world." He shuddered as though repelled by the memory of the wet November we'd left behind.

I was confused about one of those titles. The Underworld? As in … the afterlife? Wait, how could I be in the afterlife if I wasn't dead? … I'm not dead, right?

Somehow, I didn't think Kellas would respond to the question with any sympathy, so I held on to the hope that I would at least have noticed had I died.

At the end of the hallway, we came to a flight of stairs. We started down. I nearly fell before getting more than a few steps, catching myself just in time and gasping a swear word that my Mom would not have approved of.

Kellas turned. "Oh, forgot to tell you. The stairs are all different heights. Watch your step."

"Really, Sherlock? I hadn't noticed." I snapped at him. He only gave me that snarky cat grin and started down the stairs again. I kept a strong grip on the handrail, and even so nearly fell a couple times. *"Who builds stairs like this?"* I grouched after one particularly close call.

"It's meant to slow down invaders and give the rightful occupants an advantage because they are familiar with the mixed-up heights," Kellas supplied.

Oh! OK, I guess that makes sense, in a warped and twisted sort of way!

We continued down a long spiral that I guessed followed the inside of yet another tower, its outside walls punctuated by windows, the inside by doors along long landings. We bypassed these and continued down three or four flights ... it was a bit hard to say, as the floors seemed at odd intervals, some came sooner than others ... but perhaps I was not paying adequate attention because I was so focused on not falling gracelessly down the stairs. We came out into a massive, vaulted space where my footfalls echoed as we passed though.

I slowed down and stared around me, but Kellas continued like a cat on a mission toward a set of enormous double doors of dark wood massively armored with strips of black iron reinforcements, hung on elaborate strap hinges that must have been four feet long each. On either side of the doors stood two guards, clad head to foot in armor of silver metal and leather, their faces hidden by their helms. They held pikes upright at their sides.

Kellas stopped by the doors and glanced back to where I was goggling like a tourist at my surroundings. "Will you kindly hurry up?" he demanded. "You've been asleep for bloody ever, and I need to get outside and ... stretch my legs."

I hesitated, eying the guards nervously. When so much had happened in such a short space of time, I could only wonder what was going to happen next.

"Come on." Kellas's tail was twitching with impatience. I started toward the doors again, but slowly. "They won't hurt you," he snapped. "You're allowed anywhere you like, as long as I'm with you."

"Your sympathy is overwhelming, Cat," I retorted, keeping a wary eye on the guards as I caught hold of the huge handle to open one door. To my surprise, it opened easily without a single squeak. I hurried through before the guards could change their minds and stop me, even though neither moved a muscle nor even seemed to acknowledge my presence.

We emerged onto an enormous courtyard ringed with waist-high stone walls. Everything around was incredibly green, summer in full swing. Two raised flower beds, also of stone, one to the left, the other to the right, were filled with a single flowering tree each, the ground covered with a tumbling carpet of white flowering petunias. The center of the courtyard was dominated by a fountain ringed by a low stone wall. The water danced and sparkled 20 feet into the air, splashing down into a pale blue basin before draining away. It looked like something out of a fairy-tale film.

The sky was a clear azure; beyond the castle walls, a forest beckoned with deep and verdant greens. Birds sang all around. Breezes ruffled the leaves and flowers and teased water droplets from the fountain to spray beyond its basin onto the stone floor of the courtyard.

But the truly wonderous part was that all this beauty combined to create a magnificent combination of sound like something Beethoven would have composed. The sound hit my ears as soon as I stepped outside, like I'd walked in on a symphony orchestra.

I stood awestruck, not even realizing Kellas had left my side until he reappeared suddenly. I would not have noticed his return either, except that now he, too, made music. His instrument was an oboe, expertly played.

It startled me so much I shied like a startled horse.

"Boo!" was his irrepressible response to my fright. I shot him a stern look, and he laughed. He was lucky I had strong feelings about anyone who dared to kick animals. "Sorry, not sorry. Shall we go for a stroll, or are you going to stand here and gawk all day?"

I remained rooted to the spot, instead making a small gesture to indicate our surroundings. *"It's singing,"* I whispered.

Kellas shot me a sideways quizzical look. "Birds do that," he said.

"It's not just the birds," I countered. *"It's everything. Everything here is making music. Even you. You're an oboe."* I was not about to tell him that an oboe properly played was one of my absolute favorites.

"An oboe?"

"Yeah. Like Peter and the Wolf.*"* I sang a few bars of the cat's song to him.

If a cat's face could show wonder, Kellas's would have. As it was, I knew how he felt because his song rose in pitch and tempo until it ended mid-note with the sort of hideous squawk only a reed instrument can accomplish. "You must not tell anyone else." He spoke urgently, in a whisper. "No one, not even those you love and trust. *Please!"* he added. "No one other than we two must know you can hear nature sing."

"But what harm could come of it?" I was baffled by the intensity of his belief.

"Because of ..." he hesitated.

"'Because of' is a preposition, not a reason," I parroted a favorite line of my Mom's. Great. Yet another thing not being explained to me.

"Because it would put you in even greater danger than you already are," he amended. "You've got to trust me on this one." Odd as it might seem, the clear strains of his oboe reassured me that he was sincere in his concern. That reminded me that as frustrating as he could be, he *was* supposed to protect me. I had to trust him, if only because my Nan said I could. He hesitated, then continued. "You said I sound like an oboe. Think: How might this prove useful?"

I puzzled about this for several seconds, staring at the fountain without really seeing it. The fountain at play sounded like harp music. *"Everything has its own voice,"* I said slowly.

The cat nodded. "And?"

I tried but could not follow what he was trying to get at. Trees, rivers, flowers, animals and people: What am I missing?

"What about trolls?" he asked, a touch impatiently.

"Oh." I thought about that. I made a sheepish noise; yeah, that was obvious in hindsight. *"I don't hear anything right now that might be a nasty thing."*

"And that might prove useful how?" Kellas prodded.

"I don't need to see them to know they are there." I realized. The

thought gave me a flood of relief. After being yanked every which way since I woke up as a two-year-old, even the thought of just having a warning was incredibly comforting.

"Or even if they are disguised somehow. Exactly. Forewarned is forearmed. Pretty powerful magic, Brannaugh."

A solo violin voice approached us from the castle. I turned with Kellas to see the goddess Cerridwen approaching. My reaction was somewhere between alarm and anxiety—she hadn't made a good first impression, but I knew now she was far more powerful than I could imagine. Whatever she wanted, I was better off giving it to her. Maybe then she'd let me go home!

"How lovely the two of you are up so early," she spoke smoothly, with warmth in her voice. Her violin was pleasant, lilting, happy, upbeat. She was in a good mood. She looked beautiful ... the way tigers and lions looked beautiful, when there was a nice heavy glass window between you and them.

Forgetting my voice problem, terrified of displeasing her somehow, I responded as I thought she would appreciate. *"Yes, Milady."*

I was startled to see her frown, but it was quickly replaced with understanding as she remembered the result of our last encounter. "Oh. That!" She made the curious gesture she'd done at Nan's house. "Speak!"

A warm flush spread across my neck, and I involuntarily raised a hand to my throat. My muscles contracted to form words, but nothing came out. I couldn't figure out what it meant. Was I just frozen in fear? But no, I could still think.

"Well? What do you have to say for yourself?" she demanded.

Are all goddesses so short-tempered? I wondered. I briefly feared that she could read my mind, but she didn't react to that thought, so ... *"Thank you,"* I said. Or thought I did.

Her scowl deepened and the violin music took on a dark and ominous tone quality. My heart immediately started hammering in panic; oh, bloody skies, please, say something, Raven! "You have your voice back, human. Use it!"

"I did!" I protested, and looked at Kellas, alarmed. *"Didn't I?"*

"It didn't work." Kellas sounded concerned. "The *geis* remains, Milady. She still cannot speak."

Alarm flashed across Cerridwen's face and was as quickly hidden. I could still hear it, however, quivering in her music. So even she doesn't know what's happening? Gah! "Well, this is convenient," she stated flatly. "You must be holding back on me, out of spite. I have done my part. I have removed the *geis* from you. You have permission to speak and apparently chose not to. I command you: speak!"

Her order hit me like a punch to the throat. I tried, again and again, only to produce breathy noises that needed no larynx to produce. The harder I tried, the angrier she grew, until her music sounded nothing so much as the Devil's violin in *The Devil went to Georgia*: dark, discordant, and vicious. I wish I could say I wasn't shaking in my boots, but that would be a lie. A goddess could probably do much worse than just muting me. Had probably done worse over situations just like this. Cerridwen in a foul mood was seriously bad news.

"Enough!" Cerridwen was red in the face, glaring at me as though this was all my fault. And maybe it was, as I still barely understood any of this. What was I supposed to do? "Go! Begone from here. Until you recover your voice, wherever it went, you are not welcome in my domain." She glared haughtily down at Kellas. "Nor you, cait sidhe. I bind your fate to the human's until she regains her voice. Leave now, before I set the guards upon you both."

Ten

We left quickly, not that I had wanted to be there in the first place. But now I was set loose in an unfamiliar world where the rules of nature were dramatically different from what I knew, with nothing but the clothes on my back. Without any food, either, not even breakfast in my belly. It's a good thing I couldn't talk, because I'd probably be screaming.

We didn't run, nor did we waste any time exiting the castle grounds and descending a long set of stairs into a small town huddled around the base of the castle walls. I hardly noticed the townspeople and animals, the shops, and the bustling activity. Kellas led me through all of it to the outer fortifications, though a massive set of doors, across a drawbridge over a moat to the land beyond. A narrow dirt road led off into the distance, disappearing on the far side of farm fields into the forest I had seen from the castle's courtyard.

At no point did the music stop, but it now played in a mournful minor key as if all nature empathized with my plight. Sad to say, it didn't give me much comfort.

For lack of a better idea, we remained on the road, following it past the fields until it reached the woods, where I finally plopped down in despair, my back braced up against an oak tree. I felt like I couldn't get up even if I wanted to; my stomach was burning from hunger, I was trembling from being in Cerridwen's presence, and I still couldn't speak. This was turning into the single worst day of my life, and that's saying something, considering the last few. Kellas settled down to wait.

"I tried!" My thought voice cracked. I was nearly in tears.

"I know. I heard." The end of his tail twitched, and the oboe deepened with an indecipherable emotion. Sympathy? Disgust? I was too wrapped up in my own pain to bother sorting it out. At my back, the oak tree sighed as though a single breath of air had stirred its branches.

"What are we to do?" I asked after a bit. I was approaching the end of my rope. *"I don't know this place. I've nowhere to go, I know nobody, except you, of course. And I'm hungry."*

"Problematic," the cat agreed. I wish he'd sounded a bit more concerned. I wish he would give me a little bit of sympathy, even a kind look in my direction. I waited a bit, hoping he'd make some suggestions about what we should do, beyond endlessly trudging down this road going who knows where. He remained silent.

Finally, giving up on him volunteering anything useful, I asked *"Do you have any ideas? Because I'm fresh out."*

"I think we need to go find your voice," he answered.

"Well, DUH!" I snorted. *"And food, and shelter, and dumb stuff like that!"*

"You can continue sitting here like a bump on a log, or we can continue looking," he retorted calmly.

I fought the increasingly strong desire to throttle him. *"Sure! But where?"*

"I see only one road to follow here, Brannaugh."

"Raven," I corrected him automatically, and heaved myself to my feet. *"OK, one road going who the heck knows where. Hopefully to some place with food I can eat. Lead on, cat. I'm Raven-ous."*

"Oh, yuk yuk," he groaned. "Save the jokes, kid. Not your forte."

I snorted, pleased I'd finally managed to bug him even a tiny bit. The music surrounding us transitioned back to a major key, still guarded, still quiet, but more hopeful, too. Action, no matter how small, was apparently far more useful that sitting around feeling sorry for myself.

~

By noontime, however, nature's orchestra was seriously messed up. Somehow, that was the thing getting to me the most now—not having a goddess mad at me, not being lost only the gods knew where and separated from my family, not even being stuck as a mute. No, it was bad music that was going to end me—like it was the one Jenga block you pulled out to make the whole stupid tower collapse. If the instruments weren't off key, they were playing wrong notes or mangling their parts. When the aspens (as flutes) came in at the wrong time, I'd finally had it. *"Stop it! You're killing me!"* I cried in agony, startling Kellas as well as a flock of chickadees that flew away in a fright. I slumped to the ground groaning loudly, hiding behind a curtain of hair. I wanted the world to go away and just leave me alone.

Kellas came over and sat nearby, waiting patiently as I wallowed in my own misery. "Want to tell me what that was all about?" he prompted finally.

"It's the music," I moaned. I clawed at my head. It sounded so stupid put into words, but it was grating on every nerve that Cerridwen hadn't already fried. *"It's all wrong, and it's driving me crazy!"* To add insult to injury, a ruffed grouse chose that moment to interrupt the aspen flutes with an ill-timed drum roll. *"Oh, lord, they can't play anything straight!"*

"Perhaps it means something?" he mused.

"Easy for you to say; you can't hear how awful it sounds!" I whined. His calm was really infuriating right now. *"We're hungry, we're lost, I'm getting really worried, I want my family back, and I really, really HATE that I'm stuck here and don't know the way home!"*

"It could be that your attitude is all wrong," Kellas concluded.

Oh, *my* attitude was wrong?! Gods forbid I be upset or put off or unhappy about being stranded in whatever this place is with no way back, at the mercy of a powerful woman who lost her temper at the drop of a hat and gave me a job I didn't know how to complete?! *"Attitude, schmattitude. It doesn't change the facts! And as if this whole mess weren't enough, these trees can't count their rests properly and come in at the right time! Gar!!"*

"Right on the hungry part," he agreed. "But we're not lost. I'm pretty sure I know where we are and where this road is probably going. But we can't find that out if you continue to sit there carrying on like a spoiled brat. C'mon, up. On your feet." He grabbed me by the hand and hauled me to my feet, just as something cut loose with a series of symbol crashes, overpowering the cacophony of sound around me and rendering the orchestra instantly silent.

Kellas's warning hiss had me instantly on guard. He'd jumped between me and a large raven that had appeared out of nowhere and perched in an aspen tree nearly. As I watched, the leaves withered on the branch the raven sat on and fell to the ground. They just ... died. Right in front of me, at high speed. Seconds after the ... Oh. Yikes. Not your average bird, that one. I took on the best defensive stance I could manage. Right behind Kellas. Yeah, that was brave of me, right?

Kellas was growing larger by the moment until he was puma sized, ears flattened to his skull, crouched as though to spring, tail lashing violently.

"What a lovely greeting for an old friend, cait sidhe," the raven remarked. "Do relax, Kellas. I'm not about to hurt the human."

"I'm not reassured, Morrigan." If anything, Kellas was becoming more agitated.

I blinked, confused. Who is Morrigan? Wasn't that a name from *King Arthur* folklore?

"Of course, you aren't," was the raven's mocking rejoinder. "I prefer to have you a bundle of feline nerves. It's ever so much more amusing." At that, the bird hopped to the ground and transformed into a petite woman dressed in black and crimson, with black hair floating around her artistically. Of course. I should have guessed: another goddess. Apparently not a nice one, given Kellas's behavior.

Now what? How are we supposed to get around *this* goddess?

He was now pressing against my legs, forcing me farther away from the woman, a menacing growl rising in volume by the moment.

The goddess followed as we backed away. "How touching," she cooed. "Kellas the free agent has been forced into the role of knight errant." Her laugh was like breaking glass. "Stand down, fair knight. Your lady is in no danger from me. At least not today. I merely stopped by to observe Cerridwen's latest massive screwup for myself."

"What is she talking about?" I whisper-thought at Kellas. I think I sounded admirably calm, all things considered.

"Shh!" he thought back. "I'll explain later."

Amusement flitted across the Morrigan's face. "It would appear the cat has got your tongue, pretty girl." She ceased to pursue us, settling herself on a convenient rock instead. "Perhaps that explains the unusual energy I see bonding the two of you together, then. Amusing! And how perfectly appropriate a punishment for an avowed bachelor." By the end of this, her voice had become hard, mean.

"There'll be none of that, Morrigan!" he warned.

"Oh, I can let bygones be bygones, cat," she sneered. "Your loss, not mine." She stood up with a haughty toss of her floating mane. "I know when I'm not wanted ... far be it from me to delay you on your journey. I daresay you seek Taliesin. It would seem a reasonable first step." The sneer deepened. "Or would be, if you had enough sense to figure that out." She transformed back into the raven. "Have fun, children." Cymbals clashed violently, nearly sending me to my knees from the pain of it, and as suddenly as she had appeared, she was gone.

With her disappearance, the music started up again, but so softly the discord was almost bearable. Kellas remained panther sized, still wary. His ears flattened slightly as I touched his shoulder. *"Who was that, anyways?"*

He started off down the road again. "The Morrigan. The Death Goddess."

My knees went so weak, I wobbled. *"Death?"* He stalked onward and I had to hurry to keep up. A horrible chill rolled down my spine as I ran that word over in my head a few times, trying to process it. *"Why? What did she mean by all that? Kellas, please, just stop a moment."* My head was starting to throb again as the discordant music, emboldened by the Morrigan's departure, began again, growing steadily louder by the moment. *"Ow!"* I clapped a hand over one eye as a trumpet blare sent a stab of pain through it so sharp, I thought it would pop out of my head. *"Wait!"* Not thinking, I grabbed Kellas by his tail.

He whipped around and knocked me flat on my back with a single swat of one huge panther paw.

I lay on the ground gasping for air, tears squeezing past tightly shut eyelids as I struggled to breathe. And that ... was just it. Something inside me snapped so hard it was almost a physical *twang* in my chest. I'd been threatened, I'd had my voice ripped away by someone who then couldn't even give it back. I'd been taken away from my family, and now my so-called protector had just hit me hard enough to send me sprawling.

"Brannaugh?" I heard him come near. My fingers dug into the earth to keep my reaction at bay. Good people don't kick cats, no matter how awful this one was.

"Go away," I whispered.

He completely ignored me because that's what he does best. "Hey, I'm sorry. You can't go grabbing me like that. I reacted, I ... geez ..." He actually sounded sorry. Like he'd just realized how much I was hurting. A lot of good that did me now.

"Go away," I repeated a little more forcefully, opening my eyes to see him practically nose to nose with me. The pupils of his eyes were thin slits in the startling blue of his irises.

"Raven ..."

Great! Now he finally calls me by my actual name? *"Go AWAY!"* I thought-screamed at him and sobbed in silence as my ribs protested with a knifelike thrust.

He recoiled as if I'd punched him, retreating well out of reach before sitting down, clearly insulted. It was hard to read his expression. I couldn't see much through the haze in my eyes. I rolled over very gingerly and got painfully to my feet. My ribs ached horribly where he'd swatted me. Even now it was hard to catch my breath.

"I'm going back," was all I said, then turned my back on him and walked away, back down the road we'd come on. He didn't follow. I knew without even looking. His oboe faded slowly until I could no longer hear it.

Eleven

I was a mess and knew it. My head hurt. My ribs hurt. My belly ached with emptiness, and now I'd alienated the only companion I knew and could sort of trust. It did not improve my mood one little bit. But what else was new? I still barely understood the situation I was in, and no one had seemed interested in explaining it to me. At least if I were alone, I didn't have to endure constant insults, right? The only thing I could figure to do was continue walking.

Which I did ... for about 10 minutes, whereupon I plopped down in a heap under a small hemlock/alto recorder that was singing softly but sadly out of tune. I tried to ignore it, but finally could not any longer. I tossed my head back, glaring up at its branches. *"You're flat!!!"* I snarled at the tree.

To my surprise, its voice stopped abruptly, and the tree trembled. It caught me by surprise: a tree had feelings? It could hear me?? I honestly hadn't expected any kind of response. I figured it would just ignore me.

Mostly, I felt horribly guilty. *"Listen, hey, I'm sorry I yelled,"* I apologized, reaching up and awkwardly patting the rough bark. *"That was mean. You really are flat, though, and it's making my head hurt really bad. Please, go back to playing, but tune it up a little bit first, okay? Your voice is lovely, it really is. Just flat."*

A soft sigh whispered through the little hemlock's branches, then the recorder voice started to play again, a bit more softly, timidly, but incredibly, it was now in tune.

"That's so much better. Thank you!" I reached out gratefully and stroked one spray of its needles. To my astonishment, another branch brushed against my cheek as if moved by the wind. But there was no wind. It brought a smile to my face, the first I'd felt in a long time. It lifted my spirits.

That was when I noticed the music around me had become somewhat more muted than it was before. There were fewer wrong notes, more cohesiveness, less discord. It made my head hurt less dreadfully, made it easier to think, and the more I thought, the more worried I got about being away from Kellas.

He had protected me from the Morrigan. Or he'd been ready to. Had been ready to fight an actual death goddess to protect me. Mm, maybe I'd read him wrong. Maybe he did care about me ... and I had left him behind.

I got to my feet and headed back the way I'd just come. Maybe he'd still be there.

Only, I discovered that the farther I went down the road in that direction, the worse the music got, louder and more discordant by the moment. It stopped me in my tracks, threatening to bring my headache back full force, which caused a sudden epiphany. Could it be that the music was trying to tell me something? Slowly, I turned around and walked back as though I was returning to Cerridwen's castle. More melodic. Turned, headed back toward where I'd left Kellas. Discord. Again: one way, harmony; the other, discord.

"Geez what an idiot I've been," I whispered. *"The music has been trying to guide me all along."*

Wishing now that I had not been quite so hard on Kellas, I set off to follow the music. It was slow going at first, as I tried to interpret every little sound. I gave that up after a while. It just wasn't possible. Perhaps it was like the noise of a city street: not every sound you hear is important. I gradually narrowed my focus to the melodic line, with some attention given to the harmony. Occasionally another instrument would add helpful hints such as "Watch your head! Low branch!" That sort of thing. Being able to read the music gave me a little more confidence. Like I wasn't in so deep over my head in a world I didn't understand, as I'd initially feared.

After an hour or so of proceeding this way, there was a change in the music. I had reached a big bend in the road where it swung south and went downhill. I remembered the hill, as it had seemed to go upward forever after we'd left Cerridwen's. It was also where the music had initially started to go sour.

I hesitated. Should I go downhill? There was no other path I could follow ...

Shrugging, I started down the hill and was immediately scolded by a squirrel who dashed to the center of the road and sounded off with a series of harsh scratching noises on violin strings. Think new Suzuki player: *Er e er e er r er er.* Holy crap, it was like someone was shoving needles in my ears!

"OK! Got it!" I clapped both hands over my ears and hastily backed up. Right move: the squirrel immediately stopped scolding. I took the hint: NOT down the hill!

But where to? I turned around slowly, peering off into the woods, looking for anything that might resemble a path I'd overlooked somehow. Nope, no path, but a doe stood at the edge of the woods, looking at me expectantly. As I spotted her, she dropped her head almost as though she were nodding, then backed up one step. I took a step toward her and she backed up one more. Perhaps I was supposed to follow her? Cautiously, I walked closer. She turned and moved away, then stopped and looked over her shoulder.

Yeah. Pretty clear I was supposed to follow her. Fervently wishing a second time that I had not banished the cait sidhe, I left the road behind and struck off through the woods in pursuit of the deer.

She stayed about 50 feet ahead of me, leading me along a long spur of wide-open forest until it started dropping gradually down to where two streams joined forces into one. We forded at the junction and angled up through the forest beyond. The trees were getting closer together and there was more deadfall through here, plus the ground was littered with jumbled rock. It made the going infinitely more difficult and my progress slowed to a crawl as I scrambled over fallen trees and made my way around rocky areas too rough to cross. My deer guide, nimbler than I, had to wait for me to catch up on more than a few occasions.

"Isn't there an easier way?" I panted to her, after a particularly difficult scramble. She merely looked at me with her soft eyes, waggled her tail, and wandered on through the woods.

There was no way I'd find my way out of these woods on my own, so I hurried to keep up with her. For a third time I wished I'd not sent the cat packing. At least my misery would have company.

"That sure took you long enough!" Kellas's familiar drawl brought me up short, as he appeared out of nowhere. It startled me (of course) and I stumbled, cracking my shins on a jagged rock. I choked on a couple bad words and whirled toward him, eyes wide as plates.

"Drat you, anyway, Cat!" I snapped, but there really wasn't much oomph behind it. I was far too glad to him. *"Where have you been all this time?"*

"Watching you struggle," he retorted. His tail wasn't thrashing, though, and he sounded less aggressive than I remembered. More like ... worried annoyance? "And waiting for you to wish me back three times. Do you want to continue to beat yourself up following that deer, or might you care to take the path that is maybe 15 feet uphill of where you are?"

"She's showing me to some place," I pointed at the deer. *"The music says she's going in the right direction."*

"The music?" Obvious that he was waiting for clarification.

"Yeah. The music." I didn't elaborate. I was still cross with him.

Apparently, he was not to be baited by my stubbornness. "Suit yourself." He bounded up the hill a little way, then sat down.

I looked at the deer, who also had stopped as Kellas and I talked. Once she saw she had my attention, she started off again. I struggled after her. Above me, on the trail, Kellas strolled along as though he had all the time in the world.

I had to take another tumble over some loose rocks before I gave in and climbed up to the trail where Kellas was. The deer bounded uphill as well and fell in ahead of us before setting off again, Kellas and me in tow.

"Was this ruddy trail here the whole time?" I grouched.

"Nearly," He bounded lightly over a fallen branch.

Why'd she drag me through all that crap then?"

"It made no difference to her, and apparently you are determined to do everything the hard way, so she was trying to accommodate you."

"I am not," I protested. I mean … I wasn't doing it on purpose!

"Could've fooled me," he said. "Don't yell at me," he added. "Perhaps the original way you took was a self-fulfilling prophecy. You figured it was going to be difficult, so it became that way."

I thought about that for a bit, remembering Iku as she'd shown me better ways to do some things. "There's a hard way and an easy way to do most anything," she'd told me more times than I could count. "Sometimes the hard way is better, but often as not; easy does it is just as good and has the advantage of being easier."

Apparently, traversing these woods fell into the latter category, because now that we were on the path, faint as it appeared in the underbrush, the going got a whole lot easier and we were making better progress. The deer continued ahead of us. The path continued to climb gradually for a while before turning sharply due east and leveling off. Now a larger trail, it led along the top of a huge cliff face that afforded a spectacular view of a wide valley far below. We stopped to gawk and for me to catch my breath. My ribs were still sore from Kellas's love tap earlier. It didn't hurt as much now, but there was a dull ache there that got worse after hurrying.

"There's Cerridwen's castle," Kellas pointed. "You can just make it out on that far hill yonder."

I could see it, or I thought I did: a small structure on a hill at the very farthest side of the valley. *"That's a long way away."*

"Not as the crow flies," he replied as we set off again, for the deer had become impatient with our sightseeing and stomped her feet at us as though to say, "Hurry up! I haven't got all day."

We were making even better time now, following along the edge of the cliff. We'd gone perhaps another half hour due east when the woods abruptly ended on a windswept promontory overlooking both the valley to our right and another one on our left. Ahead was a small stone cabin perched overlooking both valleys and the scenery beyond. From there, you would be able to see both the rising and setting sun.

The deer stopped at the edge of the clearing, looking at us expectantly. She pawed the ground and bobbed her head up and down.

"This is it? Here?" I asked her. She bobbed her head again, then turned tail, bounded away into the woods and was gone. *"Thank you,"* I called after her. *"I guess this is where she was leading us,"* I said.

"That would appear to be the case," the cat agreed. "Shall we?"

Twelve

As we walked toward the stone cabin, I screwed up my nerve and asked *"I told you to leave, but you didn't. Why?"*

He briefly glanced at me but didn't hold my gaze. "Cerridwin has our fates magicked together. I couldn't leave you even if I'd I wanted to. Even though you banished me thrice."

Hmm! He hadn't wanted to leave? Curious ...! *"How was it that you were there all along and I couldn't hear you?"* His oboe certainly was purring along with me now.

"I disappeared myself," he said. At my quizzical look, he clarified. "I can make myself invisible. All cait sidhe can. Kinda like the cat in *Alice in Wonderland*. Rather like any cat. You're not going to see a cat who doesn't want to be seen."

"And when you are invisible, I can't hear you." I reasoned. That made a strange amount of sense, with him being a cat.

"I was counting on it, actually. "

"So, can others go stealth on me like that?" I was suddenly worried. It had been rather reassuring thinking no one could sneak up on me anymore. Especially in this crazy place. But now there's a stealth element.

There was a pause as he considered the question. Thankfully, after a second, he shook his head. "As far as I know, only another cait sidhe."

"Should I be worried?"

"There are only about a hundred of us left worldwide," he said, and I felt his pain in a brief minor key. I resisted the urge to offer some sort of comfort, as I didn't know how he'd take it. "I shouldn't think it would prove a huge issue."

"Let's hope," I said.

"Indeed."

We could hear lute music coming from inside the cabin as we approached the front door. It started and stopped in brief phrases, often repeating, as though the someone was practicing or perhaps composing, alternating playing with writing down the notes. A man's voice, heard in short bursts like the music, but no reply. I could not help but feel a little apprehensive, wondering what kind of person was waiting for us inside.

Kellas changed into his man form and stepped in front of me before knocking on the door.

The lute music abruptly stopped, and we could hear footsteps approaching on the other side of the door. An elderly man's face appeared briefly at the sidelight, then the door was thrown wide open. His smile was warm and open, eyes sparkling with good humor. "Good morning! Or afternoon, rather. What a pleasant surprise! Guests are always welcome, unexpected or not. Do come in!' He started to step backward out of the doorway.

Before Kellas could move, I caught him by the sleeve and tugged. I pointed to us, then to the open door, and held my hands at shoulder height, palms up, my face as wrinkled up in puzzlement as best I could manage.

Kellas looked confused for a moment, then hesitantly said, "Excuse me, sir, we're not sure if we've come to the right place?" He gave me a quizzical look. "Is that it?"

I nodded, rather embarrassed. What a nuisance not having a voice was. Funny how you think you know these things, but it isn't until you suddenly lack access to them that you truly understand. Made worse by having Kellas not being able to hear my thoughts while he was in human form.

The elderly man watched intently as Kellas and I interacted. "I see," he mused. "How unusual! Perhaps I could offer you a bite of supper while we puzzle that out together?" He backed up into the room beyond and waved us in. This time I did not stop Kellas but clung to his sleeve for reassurance.

The man ushered us to a couple chairs at a small round table near the hearth fire over which a black pot hung. Something cooking in it smelled so wonderful my mouth instantly watered.

He dragged a third chair over from a desk by the front window, then busied himself setting the table with three bowls, tableware, and three white napkins. "I was about to eat, anyways," he informed us. "How lovely you showed up when you did! Eating by oneself is rather lonely, truth be told." Grabbing a glove, he lifted the pot from its hook over the fire and brought it to the table where he ladled generous portions of a meaty stew into our bowls. "Don't stand on ceremony for me," he instructed. "Eat, eat!" he returned the pot to its hook, but swung the whole contraption away from the fire. "I'll be back with some bread and ale." He shot me a kind but teasing look. "Water for *you*, however, young lady!"

Aww, darn ... I've never drank any sort of alcohol before, but I felt like could have used some after everything that had happened to me recently.

That accomplished, he settled down across from me. "Do dig in, I can see how hungry you are!" He followed his own advice with enthusiasm.

Reassured that the stew was probably harmless if he was also eating it, I followed suit. We ate in silence for several minutes, long enough for me to have put a serious dent in my portion. I was starving! After all, my last meal had been breakfast at Nan's a day and a half ago. It didn't hurt that the stew was truly delicious.

I looked up to see Kellas sending me a "really, girl?" quirk of an eyebrow, and a smile on the old man's face. I blushed. I had just been eating like a total pig, hadn't I? *"Sorry,"* I mumbled, not that he could hear me.

"I knew you were beyond hungry!" he was positively beaming. "Let me get you some more." He bounced up with the energy of a much younger man and soon had my bowl refilled. "Eat as much as you like, dear girl. I have plenty more."

I ended up eating three bowls full to Kellas's two and the old man's one before I finally felt sated, pushing my empty bowl away and wiping my mouth on the cloth napkin. Having a full belly made such a difference … like I could handle whatever came at me next. The situation didn't quite feel like an unending nightmare anymore. I reached over and touched his hand to get his attention, then when he looked up, looked straight at him, and mouthed "thank you."

"The pleasure is all mine," he responded, his face lit up with happiness. "What a joy to see someone enjoy my poor cooking so much." His expression was so warm and genuine I could not help but smile in return.

He jumped to his feet and began clearing the dishes. "No, no, young man, keep the weight off," he urged as Kellas rose to assist. "You've both come a long way today, I'll be bound. I'm not exactly on the beaten path, after all!" He chuckled at his own wit. He disappeared through a doorway in the back, but quickly returned, dusting his hands briskly. "The pixies will have that shipshape in no time," he said, settling into his chair and leaning back, his long fingers steepled in front of his chest. "Pixies?" part of me wanted to ask, but the other part decided to just roll with it. I'm in the fae realm; of course there's pixies. "Now, where were we?" He looked expectantly from Kellas to me and back again. "There's a story in this if you care to share it with an old man. I'm all ears and have all the time in the world."

Kellas looked at me askance, and I nodded. What harm could there be in singing for our supper?

Leaving out all details of my lunar tendencies, Kellas relayed how Cerridwen had kidnapped me from my Nan's house, placed a *geis* on my voice, and then, when she had not been able to undo her handiwork, had banished to the two of us with orders to find my voice. The gentleman listened intently, interrupting only once, when Kellas mentioned the Morrigan's strange visit when she had told us, in a roundabout sort of way, that we should be seeking someone named Taliesin.

"Did she now?" was his comment. If he were fazed at all by any of this, I couldn't tell. "How curious!"

Outside the world grew dark as Kellas relayed our adventures. "... and the doe led us here," he finished.

The old man nodded thoughtfully, then rose from his chair and walked to the front door, where he took a large key down from a nail by the door and locked it. "Pesky wood sprites have been coming in after dark and making a mess," he told us by way of explanation. "I hang the key here," he made a show of hanging up the key on its nail again "if you need to get out anytime." Making it clear we were not being locked in, but that the rest of the world was locked out. I couldn't help but glance warily at the wooden door, wondering what exactly constituted a "mess" and "pesky wood sprites."

He rejoined us at the table. "So, you are seeking Taliesin?" he prompted.

"I'm not sure we know what we are doing." Kellas shot me a quizzical sideways glance.

Honestly, what was that supposed to mean? Miffed, I stuck my tongue out at him before looking square at the man so he could lip read. *"I was following the music."*

His bushy eyebrows shot straight up, and Kellas kicked me under the table. "You dope!" he hissed, but the man did not give any indication that he'd heard.

"The music, you say! And it brought you here."

"The deer did, but the music let me know we were to follow her," I explained.

Kellas kicked me under the table again. I shot him an ugly look and moved my smarting ankles out of his reach. I thought we were over this!

"Well, well, well. This is quite curious! But how wonderful, too. Under the circumstances, perhaps I should not delay any further to introduce myself. I am Taliesin."

Thirteen

"**I** should have said something sooner, I suppose," Taliesin continued, chuckling a little at the flabbergasted expressions on our faces. I'm just glad I didn't gracelessly choke on my water. "Perhaps being a hermit for so long has caused me to forget my manners. I have so few visitors these days."

He smiled sympathetically at me. "I have small reason to love Cerridwen myself, young lady. However, there are blessings that arise from catastrophe as well as hardship and lessons learned. I think we can safely assume you will regain your voice at some point."

We can? I still don't understand the rules of these things.

"We simply need to discover why it did not come back immediately upon the goddess undoing her thoughtless *geis*," he continued. "Far more interesting is that you hear the music. Hmm ...!" His forehead wrinkled even deeper with concentration. "Might the two be connected somehow? Hmm ..." Jumping up, he strode over to his desk by the front window and brought back a pencil and paper, shoving them across the table toward me. "Here. These might make communicating a little easier."

"When did you first hear the music?" he asked.

"When I came out of her castle," I scribbled and turned the paper so Taliesin could read it. Kellas moved closer so he could read as I wrote.

"Not beforehand?"

I shook my head no. This seemed significant somehow now that I was pondering it in those terms.

"Perhaps the stone walls muffled it?" Kellas suggested.

Taliesin's face lit up. "Of course, they would. It's one reason this cabin is made of stone. Otherwise, I would go quite mad."

"You hear it too?" I scribbled.

He nodded before I could turn the paper around, having read my hen scratching upside down. "All bards can."

I drew "???"

"A bard is a person with musical or storytelling talent. Usually with a great deal of training, too. People like Beethoven, Mozart, Copeland, Shakespeare, Wordsworth, and many more. They are tuned into the universe at a level most are not, which inspires their creative expression. Do you play an instrument? Write? Compose?"

I hesitated. Technically, I'd had a child's desire to write my own music, but ... let's be charitable and call them *attempts* at scribing something. My own efforts weren't exactly fit for public consumption. *"I like to sing karaoke."*

He looked puzzled. "What's that?"

"I sing other people's songs. With musical accompaniment, usually."

"A troubadour, then," he concluded. "Do you play a lute or a theorbo?"

I shook my head no. I had no idea what a theorbo even was. *"I make up silly rhymes, sometimes I sing them,"* I wrote. But not for some time, I thought with a pang. That was something Dad and I had done together before he'd moved out. He'd play his guitar and sing a line, and I'd have to make up the next line and sing it back. When Dad had been in the house, there had always been music playing. All kinds of music, from madrigals to Mozart, Copeland to Three Dog Night. jazz, soul, silly kid songs ... I blinked back tears. Dad had promised to teach me how to play his guitar once my hands got big enough. He'd left before they had. Now I wondered if we'd ever get the chance to do so again.

I'm pretty sure Taliesin noticed my wet eyes, but he was too much of a gentleman to comment. "So! Talented but untrained," he said briskly. "That's entirely fixable."

That might be the nicest thing anyone has said to me in days.

He looked at Kellas. "Do you also hear the music, young man? Play an instrument?"

"Don't hear any music, but I play drums."

Taliesin nodded. "Ah! Very well, then. Fortunately, we have the Goddess to thank that she had enough sense to render you duty bound to this young lady as her guardian. This bouncing back and forth between parallel realities can be a bit, shall we say, disconcerting."

I gathered from his prevarication that he was censoring himself a bit. *"Dangerous, you mean,"* I wrote. *"And what do you mean duty bound? How do you know?"* The Morrigan had alluded to much the same thing. As had Kellas.

"So many excellent questions! Sadly, not all can be answered at once," Taliesin countered calmly. "However, you could not ask for a better guardian than a cait sidhe ..."

Kellas's breath left him in a sibilant hiss.

"Yes, young man, I knew you were one of that exalted clan the moment I saw you. It's in the eyes, you see, and I have been around quite a long time—millennia, really. Your people were far more numerous in times past." He shook his head sadly. "A terrible loss, very unfortunate."

I looked between them, my heart twisting in my chest. What had happened to the others like Kellas? He gave me a warning look when I lifted my pencil to ask, so I let the question die.

Taliesin brightened quickly. "But here we are in the present! Perhaps you would honor me with a first name, just so I could address the two of you properly? Just the one name," he looked sternly at me. "Only ever the one name in this dimension, young lady. Remember that. Names have power. Give away your full name, and you relinquish your power."

"Call her Brannaugh," Kellas supplied before I could even set pencil to paper. I was sorely tempted to give him the stink eye. What's wrong with Raven? Raven is a perfectly nice name! "I am Kellas."

Taliesin's expressive eyebrows waggled up and down. "Very clever, young man. Kellas. The Scottish Wild Cat. Entirely wise. And so shall I call you." He smiled at my dark scowl at the cait sidhe. "Although it might not be the name you are accustomed to hearing, my dear, nevertheless it honors you, for Brannaugh means 'beauty with hair black as a raven.' Entirely fitting!"

At least I had the pleasure of seeing Kellas's obvious discomfiture. The cat thought I was beautiful, eh? Very interesting! Particularly because I had never thought of myself as other than perfectly ordinary. My heart jumped a little; it was surprising, but nice to be called pretty by someone outside of my family.

I shot a sideways glance at the cat. He was doing his level best to avoid looking at me. Was he a little flustered? HA! I gave him my best sweet innocent smile. I might be temporarily stuck with a name he'd given me, but now he was stuck with me knowing what it meant. Never let anyone tell you that knowledge isn't power.

Despite my best efforts, my smile morphed into a barely suppressed yawn.

"My dreadful manners!" Taliesin jumped to his feet. As if he'd done something rude, somehow! "You must both be exhausted. I shall show you to your beds; you will need sleep after your adventures. We can continue in the morning. No! No!" he interrupted Kellas's protests. "I will not hear any of that. Death herself sent you to my door. I most certainly will not countenance your leaving before we get to the bottom of this mystery. Besides, it's far too fascinating, and a lovely change of pace for me. Come, let us get Brannaugh to her cot before she passes out."

Although he disparaged his guest room ... a low attic under the steep pitched angles of his cabin's roof ... the narrow cot I curled up on shortly afterward was as comfortable as my bed at home and infinitely more appreciated. I lost no time falling asleep, never once aware that Kellas, back in cat form, had curled up on the end of my bed and kept watch over me all night.

<h1 style="text-align:center">Fourteen</h1>

I awoke to the smell of coffee brewing and bacon cooking. My stomach growled, craving some breakfast and a warm drink. I hurriedly descended the steep stairs to the cabin's main room, where Taliesin was cooking breakfast over the fire. Kellas came in from outside, booting the door closed with a thump and a clatter, his arms loaded with firewood. From the heaping pile in the wood box, I surmised that he had made several trips already.

"Morning, sleepyhead," he said, dumping the armload of wood onto the pile and brushing off the bits of bark and dirt that clung to his black shirt. I merely wrinkled my nose at him, still too sleepy to make a clever response.

"A hearty good morning to you, Brannaugh," Taliesin had pulled the bacon out of the frying pan and was cracking eggs into the hot fat left behind. He was humming as he worked, finding joy in the simple task.

I waved and smiled, the best I could do, considering.

"Coffee's here," he pointed to a pot hanging near the fire. "Cream and sugar on the table, I suspect you take both? Mugs over there too. And tell me, how do you like your eggs cooked?"

I was somewhat more circumspect about the sheer volume of food I ate at breakfast, but still managed to eat more than either of the men despite a valiant attempt not to. Taliesin just gave me a beaming smile when I glanced sideways at him.

"Have you always eaten so much or are you going through a growth spurt?" Kellas teased.

I felt my cheeks go warm and shook my head no. I was just hungry. Odd, for me. Usually, I wasn't such a hog.

Taliesin slid the paper and pencil my way. "In case you need it."

Smiling at him thankfully, I promptly snatched up the pencil up and started writing. *"I just haven't had much to eat lately,"* I scribbled. *"Other than last night and breakfast 48 hours ago."*

"That would tend to do it," Taliesin said comfortingly, and the look he shot Kellas was enough to stop the cat man from teasing me further.

After the dishes were cleared and the fire banked to hold it until a later meal, the bard suggested a post-breakfast stroll around his property. "So you can get your bearings," he said. I had to admit I was a little curious about what his place was like, so I nodded without hesitation.

Once outside, Kellas changed into his cat form. "I'll be nearby," he told me before disappearing into the underbrush nearby.

Taliesin offered me his arm in a completely anachronistic gesture. I'd seen enough old movies to know it would be rude to refuse, so I took it, although hesitantly. He patted my hand reassuringly and proceeded to show me around his place.

Beyond the cabin—which was quite small, consisting of the two rooms and loft under the roof—there was an outhouse and an open-sided shelter near the back porch to kept firewood off the ground and protected from rain. Farther away was a chicken coop with an enclosed yard for a dozen hens and one large red and gold rooster. I was surprised by how ... well ... *normal* they were. I was half expecting him to have unicorns and phoenixes on retainer, after everything that I'd seen in this place so far.

A large, sturdily fenced paddock had a small lean-to shelter for a family of pigs. Yet another even larger pasture divided down the middle sported a two-sided shelter, one side for a small brown cow and her calf, the other for my own favorite sort of animal—a horse. Taliesin's gelding was a big, amiable chestnut with a small white star and a bit of gray showing around his muzzle. He snorted and ambled over when he saw us approaching, accepting Taliesin's offer of an apple, then brushing the old man face with a slobbery muzzle to show his appreciation.

Taliesin's smile was fond as he ran his fingers through his partner's mane. "We used to ride all over, Eachann and I," he told me a bit wistfully. "We're both a little too old for that now."

"Do you still ride?" I thought, then remembering he couldn't hear me, I pointed at him, then his horse and pantomimed riding a horse.

"Oh, yes!" he replied. "Just not for days on end to all corners of the country. There's enough here to keep me quite busy as it is."

I could see how that would be: milking the cow, slopping the pigs, brushing the horse ... I wasn't a farm girl by any means, but I'd heard enough about subsistence agriculture from Iku's stories to have an idea of how much work it entailed. People really should have more respect for farmers.

We ended the tour in Taliesin's vegetable garden. Although small, it was jam-packed with a variety of vegetables, and not a weed was to be seen anywhere. I could see tomatoes and corn and pumpkins and squash and various kinds of beans. Those were just the ones I recognized on sight. There were a lot of plants here. "The pixies help me with that too," he admitted. "I've gotten a bit too stiff and sore to be bending down all the while to pull the wretched weeds out. I would be in a peck of trouble if it weren't for the pixies."

We returned to the cabin, where we sat in a couple rocking chairs on the back porch and could see the twin valleys and the scenery beyond. It was like a painting come to life, reminding me of the various museums my Mom had taken me to when I was younger. The colors and the sky were like something out of a dream ... sometimes it was hard for me to remember that this was the realm of the Celtic gods, a world beyond anything I'd ever known. For all its hostility, I couldn't deny how lovely it was.

We admired the view in silence for a while before Taliesin dug a pad of paper and a pencil from a shirt pocket and handed it to me. "Time to go to work," he said with a smile.

I'm not sure I'd have called it work what we did next, it was so much fun. He had me single out individual things nearby and describe the "voice" each one had, and its song within the orchestral music that soared endlessly around us. Having someone else who could hear what I was hearing was considerably motivating, and soon we were debating musical intricacies, concepts of intonation, tone, and rhythm that I had no idea how I'd come to grasp so easily. I'd never been much for the technical part of music before, but all at once, it just seemed easy to grasp. I wondered if I was missing something before deciding to just ask.

"I never learned this at home!" I exclaimed on paper. *"How is it I just seem to understand it now?"*

"Magic," Taliesin said, using his fingers to sketch quotation marks in the air. "Or maybe it's by osmosis from a musically enriched environment. Talent such as yours certainly helps."

Kellas returned from his explorations at some point while we were working and curled his cat body on the porch railing. *"Don't let all that goody-goody praise go to your head, Brannaugh,"* he drawled in thought form.

"Punk!" I retorted.

He merely did that smug cat smile of his and seemingly settled himself into a nap.

"Are you able to communicate with Kellas by thought?" Taliesin asked, having watched our short but silent spat with shrewd interest.

I nodded. *"He can be a bit of a jerk,"* I scribbled.

"Careful, girl, I can hear you thinking," Kellas thought at me.

I blew a raspberry at him. You don't need vocal cords for that.

"Cats can seem that way," Taliesin countered. "But they make fierce allies and excellent companions."

Smugness practically emanated from Kellas's body. I resisted the urge to roll my eyes at him.

"Is it possible you can communicate with other animals? Those without speech of their own, I mean." Taliesin wondered aloud. "Perhaps with Molly, my cow? She's been a little off lately and I'm not sure what's ailing her. Would you be willing to try?"

I tuned into Molly's music—hers was a lovely bass trombone voice. I'd noticed before it was a touch mournful in tone but had not really focused on that. *"I think maybe she's sad,"* I wrote.

"But you can surmise that from her song," he urged. "Keep trying."

I closed my eyes, trying to reduce the sheer amount of information pummeling me for attention. Slowly I separated out the various tunes until the bass trombone alone filled my ears, trying to narrow my search to just the one consciousness of many around me. *"Molly? It's me, er, Brannaugh. Can you hear me?"*

The trombone voice lifted in a questioning note. Then, oddly, a picture of me and Taliesin standing by her fence line drifted into my mind's eye, with the same questioning tone. I blinked rapidly, taken by surprise for a moment.

"Yes, that's me," I answered quickly. *"Would you tell me what's bothering you, please?"*

A wistful note entered her music, and a picture of her all alone in her pasture floated though my inner eye, followed soon afterward by an image of her in the company of a lovely white goat. The two of them were practically nose to nose eating grass together.

"She's lonely," I wrote Taliesin. *"She's dreaming of having a friend, a companion. A white goat."*

Taliesin looked stunned, the way people do when they realize they missed something that seems terribly obvious in retrospect. "She was pastured at her last home with a white goat," he told me. "I never would have thought she would miss her. Please tell Molly I will do my best to find her friend and bring her here."

I did so with alacrity, and Molly's music soared with joy. I cautioned her that it might prove hard to find her friend, but she wasn't concerned at all. Just knowing Taliesin was going to make the attempt was reassurance enough. She moved away down her pasture, her music indicating her far happier state of mind.

That night I dreamed of Iku, in full color (as my dreams always seemed to be), in a location I did not recognize. She was overjoyed to see me and returned the crushing hug I gave her the moment we got close. We wandered hand in hand along a mountain stream that tumbled pure and clean from the mountains that soared high above us.

"How have you been, Raven?" Iku asked me, her face wreathed in smiles. She gently ruffled my hair. "We've missed you!"

"I've only been gone two days!" I couldn't help sounding a little plaintive when I said so; her incredible happiness and relief was a little startling.

"Perhaps where you are, my love, but where we are, it has been months since the goddess spirited you away."

"Months!" The revelation floored me. It took me a few seconds to collect my thoughts enough to come up with an intelligent response. "How can that be?"

"Time moves differently in different realms, dear." My Iku's voice was soothing, helping me come to grips with this newest revelation. "But let's talk about you. What have you been doing?"

I told her about my adventures, about the music, finding Taliesin and his kindness, and about Molly the cow. "Why is that, Iku? How is it that I can do this?"

Iku's eyes had about disappeared behind smile wrinkles. "It is a gift, Raven. To speak the language of the animals, to hear the music of the universe, those are special gifts you must cherish and hone to their highest potential."

"But, why me? Why now?"

"Why not you, why not now?" she countered. "My guess is your Native heritage helps put you on a level playing field with the Great Spirit, so that you can hear and see all of creation as your brothers and sisters, even those things some would say are inanimate, or have no feelings, like the mountains or the trees. Because you regard them as equals, they are free to speak to you as an equal. Be sure to honor their trust in you, Raven. You will learn much from their wisdom. It is far greater than any human you will ever meet."

I told her I would do my best and asked her to take my love to my parents and Nan. "I don't want them to worry."

"Oh, they worry, dear. But knowing you are safe will ease their minds a great deal." She gestured at the scenery around us. "We can meet here in your dreams safely. It is a world before time, so there is no danger here. Be well, Raven Light Bringer." She was starting to fade away.

"Wait! I still have questions!" I wanted her to stay a little longer, but I felt myself lifting away as well ...

I awoke to rain pattering on the roof above, hearing that name echoing through my head. *Light Bringer* ... It sounded significant, like the titles given to the Pevensie siblings in the *Chronicles of Narnia*.

It was still dark out. I could hear Kellas's rumbling purr coming from the foot of my cot, sensed his cat weight taking up an inordinate amount of room there. I held still, not wanting to wake him.

Light Bringer ...

Somehow, those words brought a flush of warmth through my body, of power, hope, strength. Taliesin's caution echoed in memory: *"Never tell anyone your true name"* he'd said. *"To do so is to relinquish your power."* Was this my true name? And why, in my dreams had I been called it twice, by two separate souls?

Sleep was overtaking me again and I left that puzzle to work out another day. If tomorrow was anything like yesterday, I would have my work cut out for me. I fell asleep and dreamed no more.

In another time, another world, my Iku relayed her dream to my family. I was safe, I was studying with a master. I would return when the time was right. My mother did not believe it. My father hoped it was true. Only my Nan knew what Iku said was real, because she knew the night mare who had taken her there.

Fifteen

Despite my lovely dream—or perhaps because of it—I awoke the next morning in as ugly a mood as I could ever remember being in. My dream reminded me of how violently I missed my family, how I'd been ripped away from them and dumped here by a goddess who threw fits at the drop of a hat. I *still* had no idea how I could get back home, or how to get my voice back. The weather seemed an echo of my mood, with heavy low clouds scudding across the sky and rain lashing at the windows in sheets. Sighing sourly, I pushed myself to my feet and got dressed.

Kellas, the coward, took one look at me when I descended the stairs, straightaway borrowed rain slickers from Taliesin and headed out the door, saying he'd tackle the morning chores.

I glowered after his departing back, then plopped down on a chair by the table and rested my forehead on the tabletop.

"'Tis a darkish sort of day," Taliesin remarked mildly, loading up a plate with breakfast and setting it by my elbow before returning to finish his own breakfast. If he was perturbed by my mood, he politely declined to comment on it.

I picked up my fork and ate, hungrily, but not especially enjoying myself, unlike yesterday. My family was all I could think about now.

That and solving the problem of how to get back home, voice restored.

Taliesin said nothing more, merely finishing his meal and clearing his plate to the back room. When he came back, he was carrying his lute. "It's a good sort of day for a story," he announced, made himself comfortable on his chair, and tuned his instrument. Kellas came in from caring for the animals at this point, and after shedding the rain gear, plopped down in another chair near the fire and changed back into cat form.

Taliesin played a chord and smiled at me. "This, my dear, is the 'Ballad of Cerridwen and Gwion Bach.'"

"Once there was a Goddess fair
Who lived by Tegid Loch
Her daughter fair beyond compare,
Her husband brave and tough.

But the goddess grieved
    For all could see
    Her son was truly not.

Poor Morphran was ugly
    As ugly as could be
    That did not sit well with Mother Dear
    For her this could not be!

Cerridwen, Cerridwen
    Call on your power, do!
    Enlist the wisdom of the world,
    In Awen's cauldron brew.

Young Gwion Bach would stir the soup,
    Old Murda fed the fire

For one whole year the two would toil,
Despite that they did tire.

Cerridwen also worked posthaste
    Adding to the pot,
    The ingredients that would produce
    A one-time wisdom draught.

Three precious drops would give
    The wisdom of all time
    The rest of it pure poison be
    Should anyone imbibe.

Cerridwen, Cerridwen
    Call on your power, do!
    Enlist the wisdom of the world,
    In Awen's cauldron brew.

Alas, three boiling drops by chance
    On Gwion's thumb did fall,
    Reflex took it to his mouth,
    And lo, he knew it all.

The wisdom of the age was his
    From Morphran was it lost,
    Once Cerridwen found out
    Gwion's life would be the cost.

Alas, poor Gwion! Though he fled
    Changing forms, o'er land and sea

The goddess pursued apace
More skilled even than he.

Alas, he fell exhausted to the ground,
    Changed to a grain of wheat
    Amongst millions more grains was he
    Her vengeance he might cheat.

As a hen Cerridwen did seek,
    Scratching through the pile
    At length she found poor Gwion Bach
    And ate the hapless child.

Cerridwen, Cerridwen
    Call on your power, do!
    Enlist the wisdom of the world,
    In Awen's cauldron brew.

Have faith good fellows, be not sad!
    For Gwion Bach lived on
    In 9 short months he was reborn
    As Cerridwen's own child.

She knew him, but could not kill
    One so fair and weak
    He in leather bag she sewed, tossed in the sea
    his fate she cared for not.

The sea placed him on Gwyddno's weir
    ill lucked Elphin, rex, did find

Caught up the babe, then straight home
to his wife he did ride.

Oh, lovely babe how fair thy brow
How fortunate, reborn!
Bringing Elphin good fortune and bright song
As Taliesin, the bard.

There was a long moment of silence as I processed all of that and understood the weight of what he'd just told me. It was a little overwhelming, and I spent a moment searching for words. *"So that's what you meant when you said you had little reason to love Cerridwen yourself,"* I wrote, then added. *"She's your mother?"*

He smiled and nodded. "Families can be complicated."

I just stared at him for a few seconds. *"How does that work for you?"*

"Much as you might expect. Cerridwen is by turns repelled and yet proud of her handiwork, as well she might be. My older sister is cool and cautious, but quite fortunately, Morphran and I are close."

"He doesn't resent that you were gifted with wisdom and not he?"

"Quite the contrary. He is enormously relieved. It has allowed him to lead a quiet and retiring life, to spend as he chooses. He is a master smith. His metal work is stunning; you should see it sometime."

"Cerridwen's husband?" The goddess had been alone when I met her. I suppose he could have been off doing something else.

"Tegan sees it as a huge joke. Periodically, he takes it upon himself to tease Cerridwen about it. It would be better if he would just let it be. Cerridwen has suffered enough."

I shot him a "you must be kidding" look. Cerridwen, suffered enough? That woman? *"She ATE you, then threw you in the sea to drown!"*

He shrugged. "It all turned out well enough in the end, didn't it? Life is too short to be holding on to grudges."

Maybe it was the work of the wisdom brew, I decided. Being so smart must have made him super Zen or something. I'd have been ready to rip her guts out. *"One of Cerridwen's massive screwups,"* I mused on paper.

He shot me a quizzical look.

"Something the Morrigan said," I explained. *"Seemed like she was gloating."*

"There is no love lost between the two of them, certainly," he nodded.

"Do they hate each other?"

"More like a professional rivalry. Jockeying for power, although why they bother any longer is beyond my ken."

I jotted down *"???"*

"Do you know anyone who worships the Celtic pantheon any longer?" he asked.

"Umm ..." My brain briefly went blank. I had a sneaky feeling I was treading into sensitive territory here. *"My Nan, maybe?"*

"And how old is your grandmother?" he asked quietly, his eyes narrowing a bit.

I should have known he'd been angling to get me to this point. Taliesin knew a lot more than he let on. Now, though, I was clueless. I shrugged. *"Sixties, maybe? It's kinda hard to tell."*

He chuckled at that. "Moon magic does make age seem somewhat immaterial, doesn't it?"

It took me a second to catch what he was implying; you'd think I'd be getting better at this by now. Shock rippled through me. Wait one stinkin' minute. Did he just say "moon magic?"

I shot Taliesin a hard look. *"YOU know my Nan?"* I scribbled the words out and very deliberately underlined them twice for emphasis.

He smiled as if at a distant memory. "Amaris, daughter of the Moon. Of course, I do. She's a legend in her own right, and legends are my specialty."

I sat there, stunned. It was all a bit beyond comprehension. If Nan was a legend—that Taliesin KNEW—and he was *here*, in the Summer Lands, and she was *there* in my world, dimension, reality, *whatever!* ... what the ...?!

"I don't get it," I wrote finally. I thought that was an admirably calm response, as opposed to the key smashing I might have done had I access to a computer.

Kellas snorted. In his cat form, it was more like a sneeze, but he was still clearly laughing at me. I stuck my tongue out at him.

Taliesin smiled at our interchange. "Let me tell you another story. Perhaps things will become clearer then."

"Back when the world was a little younger, when the Celts practiced their own religion before Christianity came to the lands, a baby girl was born to two druids of the highest order. She was their only child, born well after the normal childbearing years of those times. They knew her as a miracle and gave thanks to Cerridwen, the goddess of motherhood, naming her Amaris, Daughter of the Moon. Their child enjoyed all the advantages of her parents' rank and privilege, learning from babyhood her parents' craft, as she was expected to assume leadership after they died."

"Was she a princess?" I wrote, puzzled. I thought that back then, only boys were able to inherit leadership positions, except for certain circumstances.

"More powerful yet: a priestess," he responded. "Amaris was by all accounts a gifted child, learning quickly and far earlier in life all the intricacies of Druidry. First the Bardic traditions, then the skills of the Ovate."

"Ovate?" I scribbled.

"What amounted to medicine in those days," he supplied. "Among other things, but more on that another time.

"Unfortunately, as is often the case in matters of power and leadership, another druid saw Amaris's parents as rivals rather than colleagues and sought to undermine their influence so that he could ascend his own. He managed that by spreading rumors about Dunstan, Amaris's father, saying that Dunstan was plotting to overthrow the baron using magic."

I nodded in understanding. That was a standard part of most fairy tales, as well as real-life history at that ... Although it was still strange to associate this story with my Nan!

"The baron, being a gullible sort, believed the rumors and sent his guards to arrest Dunstan. News of their coming was quickly relayed to Dunstan and his wife Olivia. Although they had ample time to flee,

Dunstan sent his wife and child to safety while he stayed behind to confront the guards and plead his innocence.

"Sadly, the baron, being vindictive as well as a fool, chose to kill Dunstan rather than seek the truth in the matter. Hearing of his death, Amaris and her mother went into hiding in the deep woods. They were right to be afraid, as the baron's men rode frequently through the woods seeking them."

My heart squeezed at that. So ... Nan's dad had been murdered? She'd never said anything that even suggested something so awful had happened to her ... but then again, she'd never talked to me about her parents at all. I wonder if my Dad knew. Or how much he knew.

"Knowing it would be only a matter of time before they were discovered, Olivia prepared a ritual sacrifice to Cerridwen, appealing to the Goddess for assistance. Cerridwen appeared to her, telling Olivia that only the ultimate sacrifice could save Amaris's life. Whereupon Olivia, understanding what the Goddess was demanding, committed suicide just as the baron's men came on the scene. They returned to the baron with only Olivia's body. Amaris herself was never found."

"What happened to her?" I scribbled, horrified.

"Upon the death of her mother, Amaris was given the power of moon magic, and she then disappeared for some years."

"Where was she?" I wrote.

"Only she knows," Taliesin replied, "but she returned to avenge her parents against the dark druid and the baron both, fulfilling the dark druid's lying prophecy with a somewhat different version, becoming herself the baroness of the fiefdom. She ruled with kindness for many years, until she appointed a successor worthy of the role."

I sat in silence for a while, trying to square the grandmother I knew —quirky, fun-loving, and intense—with the horrific story I had just heard.

"When was this, roughly?" I finally wrote down.

"The early 400s AD," he said, the hint of a smile playing around his eyes.

I did some quick math. I was very glad I wasn't drinking anything because I might have choked on it. *"So you're telling me my grandmother is over 1,600 years old,"* I wrote, incredulous.

He smiled and nodded.

"Not possible." The words were shaky as I wrote them. It was just—how? How could Nan be that old? What did that make my Dad? What did that make *me*?

"Anything is possible. Improbable, certainly. But not impossible."

"You are saying that my Nan is basically immortal."

"It would take an event of cosmic proportions to kill her, yes. But cosmic events happen all the time. She's not immortal." He must have read the dubious expression on my face because he made a pointed "teacher" gesture. "Remember your science. Energy can neither be created nor destroyed. It can only change form. Think about my first legend today. Gwion Bach did not die but was reborn as Taliesin. Myself. That is less an unlikely miracle than pure science."

I shook my head in dismay. How much of this was this alternate reality? How much was truth as I knew it in my world?

"Listen, Brannaugh! Do not take legends literally. Look instead for what they tell you about the bigger picture." Taliesin urged me. "Stories can have different meanings when they aren't taken at face value."

I thought about that for a bit, then scrawled a line from the movie, *Brave. "Legends are lessons; they ring with truths."*

"Exactly," he agreed.

I sat a bit longer, then scrawled *"So … are you dead?"*

He threw his head back and laughed out loud as if I had said the funniest thing ever. "I am very much alive, in this dimension. In your *usual* dimension, I died a long time ago. In 596 AD, to be precise. I could reincarnate if I so chose, but so far, I prefer to remain here."

I paused and did my best to absorb this. Then I hesitated for a second before writing out my next question. *"Is this Heaven?"*

"As the ancient Celts envisioned it, yes."

I couldn't help myself now; I just had to know. *"And the Christian Heaven?"*

I half expected Taliesin to get angry or go on a rant or something. Instead, he just smiled easily, untroubled by the invocation of the religion that had overtaken that of the old Celtic gods. "Yes, it exists, as they envision it."

"Hell?" The question was asked before I managed to ask myself if I *wanted* to know.

The smile dropped off his face. "Unfortunately, yes. And it taints your dimension with its negativity, anger, and raw hate. To be fair, our Summer Lands remain tainted with the divides of rank and power, so who am I to criticize?"

"How do you know all this stuff?" I scrawled down.

He chuckled. It was a question of the ages, after all. What child hasn't demanded this of a parent?

"Remember the potion from the cauldron of Awen, Brannaugh. The wisdom I inadvertently stole from Morphran. The knowledge of the universe distilled into three priceless drops." He saw the look on my face and added soberly "Don't wish for it. It is as much a curse as it is a blessing."

However, it might be useful for filling in some of the blanks I was dealing with. OK, more like huge gaping wounds bleeding profusely than blanks. Whatever!

"I have questions," I scribbled.

He bowed his head gracefully, as though he had anticipated this. "If it is within my power to answer them, ask away."

"Why is my voice gone? How do I get it back? Why didn't it come back after Cerridwen lifted her curse? Why am I here? I don't belong here. How do I get home? I don't even fit in at home ... it's like I'm not really white OR Native American. Who am I, really? Why is this even happening to me???" It came pouring out like a scream set to paper. I hadn't even realized how much my emotions had been pent up inside and was heartily embarrassed when I could not stop the tears from sliding down my face.

Taliesin reached into a pocket and wordlessly handed me a clean handkerchief. There was a thoughtful expression on his face. He didn't answer any of my questions for so long, I was beginning the think he never would. Finally, he spoke. "Those are all questions that are beyond my ability to answer."

My heart sank to my toes, and I started to pick up my pencil. He held a hand up, stopping me.

"What you have so succinctly put into words is what some call 'the hero's journey,' my dear, and you are most definitely on your way. No one, not even I, can help you find those answers. You must find out for yourself."

"HOW?" I demanded on paper. *"Why did the Morrigan think we should seek you out if you can't help me after all?"*

To which the wisest man in the universe merely shrugged his shoulders. Gah! What good is all-knowing wisdom if it doesn't have answers?

As if he could read my mind, Taliesin just smiled. "However, there is one thing I can help you with, and you may find it a useful tool to assist you with your journey of self-discovery," he added briskly, changing the subject entirely before I had the chance to react. "It's time to get you started on an instrument." He picked up his lute and plucked each string in turn, tuned one that had gone a bit flat, then handed the precious thing to me.

Sixteen

I held it as gingerly as someone handed a baby who had never held one before. I sent him a look of dismay, my forehead a washboard of wrinkles. I'd never held an instrument like this before, much less played it.

"It's not going to break," he urged me. "Here. Tuck it under your arm like so, your hands here and here." He moved my hands to the proper positions on the lute. "Now, play. Play the first thing that comes to your mind. Trust your instincts. I think you will find they are quite good."

I sent him a look that communicated more clearly than words that I thought he'd lost his mind.

"Go on!" he urged again, the ghost of a smile playing across his face.

I touched one string timidly. A soft note responded. In my mind, another note called. My hand moved as though guided, fingers pressed on the string. Plucked it. Another note, the right one, the same that had called me in my mind. How I had done this, I had no idea, but more notes followed the first one, my fingers moving instinctively. A lullaby began to hum from the instrument, one drawn from deep memory, perhaps one that had been sung to me many times as a baby, I don't know. I simply remembered it. I was caught up in the music, I became the music, my hands a little stiff and clumsy, but gradually gaining dexterity and precision. I starting adding chords, arpeggios, grace notes, and then variations on the original theme, my fingers flying across the strings as if magicked until the final chord sounded and faded into memory, the lute once again silent beneath my hands.

There was complete silence for a long breath, then Taliesin slowly started to clap. Emanating from Kellas, I felt something akin to wonder —not words—just a strong feeling. I was stunned. How had I done that?

"She says your lute is magic." Kellas passed my thought on to Taliesin.

"You yourself are magic, Brannaugh," he responded. People had said this to me before, but now—after everything I'd been through—I finally started to believe maybe there was something to it. "Or maybe it's just good old osmosis again. At any rate, you have the makings of a master, although you are in need of a bit of practice. As any child prodigy, you have much to recapture from your previous lives, so let us waste no more time and get you going on that."

This was the first time in my life that I wasn't upset at all at the thought of spending a whole day learning. I was excited, wanted to fill the whole house with music. My music.

The rest of the day disappeared in a blur as Taliesin instructed me on the lute, then the guitar, and finally the banjo. "Now you have a few to draw from," he explained. "Each has a different language, a different repertoire that they are connected to."

Whenever my fingertips became sore, he would smear a smelly salve across them, and the pain subsided immediately.

The rain passed. We settled on the back porch that evening after supper, our bellies full. The animals had been cared for, and joyful duet music emanated from the cow paddock as Molly the cow and Celeste the goat got caught up with each other.

"Thank you for letting me know what the problem was," Taliesin said, as we enjoyed listening to Molly's bass trombone and Celeste's tingling silver bells interact. "I hadn't a clue."

They are an odd couple, I jotted down.

He nodded. "But refreshingly different. A surprisingly effective juxtaposition of instruments. Shall we make a little music ourselves?" he asked and produced two banjos from behind his chair. We checked the tuning on our instruments while Kellas, in cat form on the porch railing, sat up in anticipation.

Eyes twinkling, Taliesin sent me a sly look and plucked out five notes, ones that were wildly familiar and clearly a dare: "Dueling Banjos." Back and forth we played as the song settled into its joyful toe-tapping glory.

The music flowed through every cell of my body, filling me with joy. I became the music, and the music became me ... no longer a separate entity but One with the Universe. I never wanted to leave.

However, all songs end, and this one was no exception. I slowly came back to myself as the final chords faded into the ether. No one moved, even the voices of the animals in the forest had hushed. Finally, a long sigh emanated from Taliesin. "Now that was some serious fun," he said softly. I could feel the joy he was feeling like the warm glow of a campfire.

"It has been far too long since I've done this," he added. "I'd forgotten how much fun it can be. Here," he handed me a guitar (Where did he get all these instruments? It was as if he pulled them from thin air!) "Let's try something a little more lyrical now." He started in on a melody I'd never heard before, vaguely Spanish sounding.

I must have looked worried because he smiled. "Just let your fingers find their way," he urged me. "Don't think it, just be it."

The guitar in my hands was practically humming its impatience, so I followed his instructions, closed my eyes, shut down conscious thought, and let my fingers find their way across the strings.

We spent the evening like that, playing one song after another, periodically switching instruments. We finished up with the Irish lullaby I knew from childhood. This time Taliesin sang the words softly in a language I did not recognize but which stirred a long-forgotten memory. It was too dim to pull into consciousness, but there was a familiarity that tugged at the heart strings. I felt tears well in my eyes, and I ducked my head to hide them.

As the final notes faded away, a full moon mounted over the horizon, pouring bars of light and shadow across the landscape. We sat in silence, soaking up the beauty of it all until finally a huge yawn forced its way out of my throat.

Taliesin chuckled. "I feel the same way," he admitted. "I'm ready for bed. Tomorrow is another day. Thank you, my dear, for what has been a most enjoyable evening of music and companionship."

He stood up and set his lute aside. I rose as well and held the lute I had been playing out to him. He shook his head and refused to take it. "No, Brannaugh, that one is clearly yours. You've earned it. Please accept it with my utmost appreciation and gratitude."

Mine! I held the precious instrument close, could almost feel the wood vibrate with the promise of music. I teared up again, hiding my tears with a deep bow. I felt a happiness I couldn't possibly put into words.

"The Morrigan brought that to me many years ago," he said. "It once belonged to a famous troubadour who died in battle. She told me that one day I would give it away, that I would know in my heart to whom it truly belonged. She was right. Here," he added. "Sling it over your shoulder like this," he did it for me, and suddenly the lute was no longer there.

Panic must have shown on my face because his lips broke into a small smile. "It's not gone, Brannaugh. It's safe in another dimension where only you can pull it forth. That way, you may always keep it with you without it getting in your way. If you wish to play, simply reach over your shoulder. Left hand."

At his suggestion, I reached back with my left hand over my shoulder, and felt it bump into the neck of the lute. I pulled it back in front of me in amazement. It hummed under my hands like a happy cat. I looked at Taliesin in wonder.

He smiled and shrugged. "Magic. What can I say?"

Seventeen

❧

I awoke before dawn the next morning and slid out of bed carefully, so as not to wake the sleeping cat on the end of my bed. I checked to make sure my lute was still in its hiding place behind my back, then made my way downstairs and out the back door to the edge of the cliff overlooking the twin valleys. I dangled my legs over the edge of the cliff, despite it dropping hundreds of feet down to the treetops below. Heights had never bothered me much. The full moon still hung low in the western sky: the sun was still a faint glow on the eastern horizon.

I drew my lute (mine! the wonder of it!) across my body and cradled it close, checking its tuning before waiting for the music to come. When it did, it was soft, lyrical, gentle. I bent over my instrument, became as one with it and the music that poured from its generous wooden heart. I was unaware we were attracting an audience of woodland creatures until they added their voices to that of the lute's, gradually swelling into a symphony as the trees and grasses joined in with the others.

When the field mice abruptly abandoned the song and ran away, I looked around to see Kellas in cat form approaching. He sent a grumpy *I haven't had my coffee yet, what in the world were you thinking?* thought my way before settling down next to me. I laughed at him and kept playing.

My mind wandered to our situation, stuck in an "away" place with no answers, no idea why I had lost my voice, no idea how to find our way back, and my mood darkened. My anger at Cerridwen and her blundering interference in my life burned in my chest like a hot coal. Unbidden, the lute echoed my anger, the music that my fingers called forth grew dark, harsh, swirling with all the unvoiced frustration and fury I had kept inside. I wanted to punish Cerridwen as she had punished me, make her pay for her arrogance and interfering busy body-ness. Who demanded suicide as a condition of saving the life of a child, anyway? Ugly creature! I wished she were dead. Yeah. Not cool of me, right? But it was how I felt, here on the edge of her perfect little world, away from my loved ones and everything I had ever known ...

Kellas clawed my arm. "Brannaugh. Stop. Listen!"

Annoyed, I shook his paw off my arm, still caught up in my anger, but then noticed that all the animals had ceased singing with me. I was confused. I let my music falter and the lute fell silent under my hands. Then I could hear it faintly: a terrible dissonance gradually growing louder. It wedged its way under my skin like a colony of ants and scraped against my brain like nails being dragged against a chalkboard. I leapt to my feet as all around me my small friends fled as though for their lives.

"What's wrong?" Kellas's alarmed thought came through.

"Something wicked this way comes," I quoted. My heart hammering in my chest, I clutched the lute tightly and looked around for the source of the sound.

"What is it?"

I shook my head. No idea. I pointed toward the cabin. *"Here comes Taliesin."*

The bard was running toward us as fast as he could, yelling. "Get away from the edge!" He sounded afraid.

We ran toward Taliesin, Kellas swiftly transforming into his puma avatar.

Taliesin reached us. "Something is terribly wrong," he panted, voice thick with concern. I nodded and cupped one ear, letting him know I heard it too. It was coming closer rapidly if the sheer volume of the chaos approaching was any indication. Then, as if on cue, over the edge of the cliff it came, many "its"—twisted humanoid figures covered with lank hair, faces deformed into caricatures of wolves.

"Werewolves!" I thought at Kellas.

Taliesin reached over his right shoulder and pulled a broadsword out of thin air. "Stay back, Brannaugh!" he warned, then spat a single word command and flung his free hand open at me. Instantly the air crystallized into a bell-shaped dome around me, trapping me inside. I threw myself at the crystal walls, clawing at them in silent protest as Kellas flung himself at the nearest wolf man and tore out its throat. Taliesin roared a challenge and cut down the next one with his sword.

The next few minutes were a blur as more wolf men surged forward, surrounding Taliesin and Kellas, who were barely able to hold them at bay with flashing sword and ripping teeth and claws.

Others paced around my icy prison, attacking its walls with nails and teeth that barely scratched the surface, although they continued attempting to break through, teeth bared, red eyes filled with the fever of hate. I was terrified. I could barely breathe; this was too much. Too much. Why? Why was this happening?

It was not going well for my team. Taliesin lost the use of his left arm from a severe bite. Kellas's sleek black hide was streaming blood from multiple wounds. Then Taliesin was driven to his knees by a concerted attack by two werewolves, and when Kellas went to his aid, he was driven to the ground by several others who jumped on him from behind.

They were dying in front of my eyes ...

Eighteen

"NO!!" The cry ripped up from my very core, tearing through my frozen vocal cords and filling my mouth with blood. I felt rage course through my body as never before, dashing away the fear as if it had never existed. My body grew violently upward and outward, and I smashed through my icy prison as I reached over my right shoulder in a move that was completely reflexive ... drawing forth a long sword, light energy crackling a blue electricity along its wicked double-edged blade. The werewolves had fallen back at my sudden appearance, but ringed around me now, abandoning their attack on my companions. One, braver than the others, surged forward. I spat blood in its face and kicked it violently in the chest, sending it reeling backward.

"'No one puts Baby in a corner!'" I screamed at them and cut the nearest one in half with a single slice of the murderous blade. Perhaps it was odd to quote a romance movie as a battle cry, but I wasn't thinking too hard at the moment.

The weres grew more cautious after that, pacing around me in a wary circle, rabid foam drooling from their gaping jaws, teeth like white knives bared, growling a menace that would have turned my blood to ice if I had still been myself, but I wasn't. I was a giant with a magical sword. I was focused, intent on finishing off every one of them, the bloodlust in my heart demanding kill, kill, kill ... waiting for one of them to make the next move. Then two did, and my sword leapt in savage joy, biting through both in a vicious swing left and right ... Dimly, I heard myself roaring in defiance, matching their menace, and raising it tenfold. I had become a killing machine, and ... I LOVED IT.

Loved it ... Gods ... Somewhere deep inside my crazed avatar, my Raven-self shrunk back in horror at the destruction I was wreaking.

When the sun rose over the battlefield, I was the only one left standing. The sun's rays set the bodies of the dead and dying werewolves on fire, clearing them away as though they had never been there, the only proof remaining was charred patches of grass. Taliesin and Kellas lay among the smoking ruins, broken and still.

I sheathed my sword over my right shoulder and kneeled next to Kellas. He had reverted to his human form and was breathing in faint shallow gasps through his mouth. He was completely covered in blood that continued to well from every cut. I swiftly checked Taliesin. He was breathing too, but he was unconscious and badly wounded.

A thought picture/feeling pushed its way into my mind: distress, concern, a desire to help. I turned my head and saw for the first time Taliesin's pixie friends hovering nearby. There were three of them, barely two feet tall, reed thin, and clad in greens and browns. *"Can you help?"* I thought at them, and was rewarded with feelings of surprise, then a vigorous nodding of heads.

I almost broke down crying in relief. I didn't know how to patch up injuries except for the most basic of basics, and that wasn't enough here. Not for these wounds.

They rushed to Taliesin and after a bit of high-pitched quarreling among themselves, lifted him between the three of them and bore him off toward the cabin. My avatar's strength fading fast, I lifted Kellas in my arms and followed.

By the time I struggled into the cabin, the pixies already had laid Taliesin on blankets by the fire and were cutting his torn and bloodied clothing off his body. They had laid out a blanket for Kellas as well. I put him down on it as gently as I could with my remaining strength, then wearily dropped to my knees beside him. I stayed there until pulled away and guided to a corner nearby by two of the pixies, who immediately returned to minister to Kellas's wounds. It was way too quiet. The desperation with which the pixies worked and my own feeling of uselessness was overpowering.

I slowly collapsed into my corner, exhausted beyond words. My lute bumped against the wall behind me, its strings sounding a soft protest. Without giving it thought, I drew it around and cradled it in my lap, wrapping my arms around it protectively. It hummed at me as though it were alive. A lute that incredibly had changed when I had, metamorphosizing into a sword as I became an armor-clad warrior. Wonders never ceased in this world, I thought hazily.

A pixie hurried by with a bucket of clean water, saw the lute and her face lit up. A thought picture formed in my mind: me playing the lute. She nodded encouragingly and made a small pushing motion with her free hand. *"You want me to play?"* I thought at her. Her vigorous nodding confirmed it. Another picture formed, one of Kellas and Taliesin whole and hearty again.

I stared for a second before Nan's words came back to me: words have the power to kill and to heal. Well, the lute as a sword had certainly killed; maybe as a lute it could heal. In a world of magic, why shouldn't that be possible? But what sort of music could heal the terrible wounds that had torn their bodies to shreds?

Tentatively I touched the lute's strings, asking for guidance. It responded freely, sounding arpeggios that repeated, changed, and repeated: an accompaniment of sorts. I cleared my throat, still raw, my tongue still tasting the bitter iron of my own blood. Foreign words formed in my mind, moved to my lips.

The lute hummed urgently under my hands. Hesitantly, I whispered them aloud. The lute sang with me, encouraging me.

I could not sing, could barely make a sound because my throat was so sore, but I whispered the words as best I could, my hands playing the melody and chords. Imperfect as it was, the pixies were elated by my efforts and returned to their nursing even more diligently than before.

The air in the room slowly gained a silvery sparkling quality, forming swirls that danced across the room where they disappeared into the prone bodies of my injured companions. One swirl wrapped itself around a pixie's arm as she watched in wonder. Soon she shook the arm with great delight, a wide smile on her face. She chirped at me, sending me a feeling of gratitude, then went back to her work.

The magic was working on me as well. I could feel warmth in my throat and coursing through muscles sore from swinging the great sword. The longer I played, the stronger I felt, until I was singing softly instead of whispering. I could see the wounds on Kellas's and Taliesin's bodies knitting closed and healing before my eyes.

I must have sung for hours until first Taliesin, then Kellas sat up. They moved their limbs gingerly, testing them. I could see the new scars on their torsos, crisscrossing their skin in bright red lines.

Under my hands the lute fell silent at last. I felt like I could just lie there and pass right out, and the darkness of unconsciousness was sorely tempting.

Kellas gave me a look that could have meant anything. "That was quite the battle cry, Brannaugh."

I gave him a puzzled look.

"'Nobody puts Baby in a corner?' Come on, really?"

I laughed out loud. How wonderful to laugh and hear that sound come out of my mouth. "You heard me?"

"The whole world must have heard you; you weren't exactly using your indoor voice. But, really, a line from a movie and not even that good a movie? Couldn't you have used something from *The Terminator*, at least? Would have been a bit more befitting of the persona you took on."

I snickered, could not help myself. "Romance isn't silly," I said with as much sternness as I could manage. "Honestly ..." Well, romance movies tended to be silly, ridiculously so, but what the hey, I rather liked chick flicks.

"Perhaps you could fill me in on the movie thing?" Taliesin rose from his blanket on the floor and gingerly made his way to a chair nearby. One of the pixies brought him a pile of fresh clothing, and he slowly started to put on his shirt, wincing as he slid his left arm into a sleeve. "It's a bit out of my realm of experience."

"She broke out of that dome you shut her in, yelling a line from a dumb old movie." Kellas started, then seeing Taliesin's furrowed brows added "Oh, right, you don't know movies. A movie is sort of like a picture book where the pictures move about. Thank you," he added, as another pixie brought him clothing as well.

Taliesin's eyebrows rose in surprise. "And you think my world is magicked." He looked at me. "You have your voice back." It was a statement of the obvious, meant to encourage explanation.

"It took nearly losing the two of you for me to break it loose," I told them. The nearness of our miss still made me shaky, and I lowered my head in shame. "I'm so sorry."

"All part of the hero's journey," Taliesin said comfortingly.

"We're missing part of the action, Bran. Care to fill in the missing bits?" Kellas asked. "Things went dark after you went full-on raging Amazon."

Taliesin eyebrows went north again, questioning.

I explained that when they had nearly died at the hands of the werewolves, I had somehow changed into an avatar warrior 10 feet tall and my lute had become a magical sword.

"Typical teenager," Kellas drawled.

I smacked a fist into my other hand, sending him a dark look, and he rolled his eyes at me. It felt good to be back to squabbling over silly stuff instead of fighting for our lives.

"Ten feet tall and bulletproof too, no doubt. It's not the first time she's done that," he told Taliesin. "She pulled that one off in a dream dimension, too."

"How fortunate for us all," Taliesin said mildly.

"What was that dome you stuck me in?" I asked, curious.

"Ice," he supplied. "The moisture in the air froze around you. A temporary shield in the Summer Lands, I know, but one I hoped would last long enough to keep you safe. What were those ghastly things anyway?"

I was honestly surprised he didn't recognize them. "Werewolves; humans transformed into monsters by a curse." Kellas offered. "Boogeymen from Brannaugh's world."

"Are they still here?" Taliesin asked, alarmed.

"Burned to a crisp the moment the sun came up," I said. I briefly wondered if they had been actual transformed humans or just magical creations; I shied away from thinking too hard on that. If they were actual people ... no, no, no, not going there ...! "Legend has it they are a full-moon phenomenon."

"So that would suggest that a full moon brings them out, and the sun polishes them off. Full moon, however," he mused, a thoughtful expression on his face. "This is all a little too coincidental, my dear. You wouldn't have inherited some of Amaris's proclivities, would you?"

I looked at Kellas for guidance; he shook his head slightly.

"Perhaps it is better that I do not know any details." Taliesin, no dummy, had picked up on our silent exchange. "It would not do to trumpet such information far and wide." He continued to study me as if seeing me for the first time, then he frowned. "How did the wolf men come through in the first place?" Then understanding flooded him and he looked aghast. "You did it, Brannaugh. You called them through."

"No!" Like any kid, my first instinct was to deny. But there was that guilty feeling, like somehow, yes, it was my fault, even though I had no idea why, or how.

You could almost see the gears turning in the old bard's brain. "You were playing that lute," he said. "What were you thinking as you played? What was happening?"

I looked at Kellas in despair. "I don't know. I was playing. I was happy, everything was singing with me."

"But then something changed." Taliesin pressed me.

A flush of shame spread through me as I realized what had changed. "I started thinking ... about Cerridwen and my voice and being stuck here with no way to get home. I ..." I hung my head. "I got angry."

"And your music reflected that. There, on the edge of the cliffs, where magic is concentrated. Gods above, Brannaugh." He turned away, the fingers of both hands scraping through his hair. He stood that way for a moment then swung back to glare at me, a wild look on his face. "That was reckless. Foolish. Selfish."

I glanced at Kellas for support, but the cait sidhe's expression was closed, eyes slitted, unreadable. "I d-didn't know," I stammered. "I ..."

Taliesin glared at me for what seemed like forever but was likely just a few seconds. "You didn't know," he repeated then, some of the anger draining from his voice. "Of course not. How would you know? My fault, then. I gave you a magical artifact and failed to warn you." He drew a deep breath and blew it out through his teeth. "Brannaugh, that is no ordinary lute. It once belonged to Uiscias, the warrior bard. One of the most powerful Druids of his day. It is imbued with magic that ordinary mortals can only guess at. And that sword … that's got to be Fraegarthach …" A look of horror crossed his face. "My gods, I should have realized …" He stood with his head bowed for a long moment then looked up at me, stern, but no longer angry. Deep wrinkles of concern lined his face. "Besides the wolf men, did anything else come through?"

I shrugged, feeling awful.

He looked at Kellas. The cait sidhe hesitated.

"Possibly," Kellas said at last. "There was enough going on with just the werewolves approaching, I could not say for sure."

"But it's certainly possible. Likely, in fact. You do not rip a gap in the veil between worlds without attracting a whole lot of hurt. We need to go out there NOW." He was dragging on his pants as he spoke, and Kellas followed suit.

As Kellas and Taliesin were still very fragile from their wounds, our haste was necessarily slower than any of us would have liked, but when we got to the cliff edge where I had sat and played that morning, there was nothing to be seen. Everything seemed normal. Well, almost normal. To the naked eye, all was as it should be. No obvious gaps in the fabric of the world. However, the music was 'off.' No longer like a Beethoven symphony, but a more modern composer with odd chords and rhythms, notes that jarred the ear and unsettled the stomach.

Taliesin and I exchanged looks. "We've got a problem," the old bard said.

Nineteen

Faintly, in the distance, a trumpet fanfare cut into the music, oddly out of place in the disjointed mash-up of notes we were surrounded with now. I sent Taliesin a questioning look.

"Epona, the goddess of horses, is headed our way," he said. There was a relaxed quality in the way he said it that suggested he felt at ease with this goddess. That was a little comforting.

We hurried around the house, looking toward the edge of the woods where Kellas and I had emerged a few days ago. We didn't wait long.

A huge black horse burst out from the woods, galloping flat out across the clearing, and sliding to a halt a few feet from where we stood. A young woman leapt lightly from his back and gave the horse a quick pat on his sweaty neck. She had long and wild black hair, unbound and flying freely around her shoulders; her green eyes blazed with energy. "Whee! That was fun!" she exclaimed. The horse shook his head and snorted; he too had enjoyed the gallop.

"Greetings, fair Epona, equestrienne without equal," Taliesin said, bowing low. "You honor us with your presence."

"Ah, noble Taliesin, you've grown no less flowery with your flattery over the years," she retorted, but there was a smile on her face as she said it. "Alas, this is no social visit, but rather a summons. You and your companions are ordered to report to Cerridwen's court. Immediately would not be nearly soon enough to suit her. The goddess has her panties in a twist ... something about a breach in the curtain between worlds. Apparently, she thinks you have something to do with it."

Ah, dang ... Ms. High and Mighty already knew about my mess? That figured! I wanted to complain that it wasn't my fault, that I hadn't asked for a single thing that had happened to me since I turned 16, and wasn't it the *goddess's* job to make sure her precious magic realm was safe? But I suspected she would be less than sympathetic to my teenage frustration, so I held my tongue.

Taliesin bowed again. "We will come as quickly as we can, but given our shortage of horses, it will not be soon."

"Actually," the horse goddess started, then looked around as if to see if there was anyone nearby to overhear what she had to say next. She leaned closer and spoke in an undertone. "My suggestion would be to disappear yourselves. Otherwise, answering Cerridwen's summons would be like taking yourselves to your deaths. Let's just say she's ... not in a good mood."

Aw, geez ... just what I needed on top of everything!

"You can't blame her entirely," Epona added. "She currently has her hands full dealing with a flying worm that is making a hash of the outlying villages, burning them down and eating everything in sight."

"A dragon?" I asked, my stomach sinking.

Epona shook her head. "Not like any dragon we have ever seen. This is more like a snake with a giant head, long whiskers, and no wings. How it flies is beyond me."

Kellas and I exchanged looks. "That's a Chinese dragon," Kellas said.

"What is ... Chinese? I am not familiar with this." A confused look crossed her face. "Whatever it is, it's bad news," she declared. She turned her gaze on me. "I'm guessing you're Amaris's granddaughter." I nodded, startled that she somehow knew who I was. "If, in fact, it is your fault it's here, you need to get gone as soon as humanly possible because Cerridwen will not be understanding, nor kind." She laid a hand on the big black's neck. "Your grandmother is a close friend of mine. She tells me you are a capable horsewoman. You must take this horse and ride him home to your own world."

Kellas leaned close so he could whisper in my ear. "Say no thanks."

I gave him an odd look. "Why?"

"That's Moon's colt. The dark horse. Knight."

Really?? I swung around and looked hard at the big black. He was exactly the sort of horse that took your breath away: beautiful conformation, nicely proportioned, well-muscled and high-spirited, with a glossy black hide and long mane that glistened in the sunlight. He captured my heart instantly. "I'd love to," I told Epona, and grinned wickedly at Kellas's deep groan.

She grinned back, for she'd heard Kellas's warning too. "Dark horses have an ill-deserved reputation for being unpredictable," she said. "You just need to be smarter than the horse! A rare trait these days. Have you ever used a neck rope before?"

I shook my head no.

"It's pretty simple, actually," she said. "Just like with a bridle, it is always your last resort. Signal your intentions with your seat first, then feet, then hands."

I nodded in comprehension, though I couldn't ignore a niggling feeling of worry. That neck rope was not much of an emergency brake, but maybe Epona was used to riding better trained horses than I was. All my most recent riding had been on mustangs just started in their training. Wild and wooly and full of fleas ... not exactly ready for finesse work, which a neck rope most certainly was more in tune with. I explained as much to the goddess.

She smiled. "Just tone down your cues," she instructed. "A tiny shift of weight instead of an exaggerated one. Even your thought 'we're going this way' can cause you to shift enough that this horse will feel it. If you are clear with what you want, all will be well."

I wasn't so sure about that, and it must have shown on my face because she grinned. "You'll figure it out." She turned to Taliesin. "How quickly will you be ready to leave?" she asked.

"I won't be leaving," he said quietly. I swung around and stared at him. "You and Kellas must, of course, Brannaugh," he continued. "The dark horse will be able to take you both to safety. I have nothing to fear from Cerridwen. She might fuss and fume, but she will not harm me. She knows better than to try. Besides, I am past the time of life when I care to go dashing about on adventures."

Epona gave him a stern look. "Only by choice, Taliesin. You can be any age you care to be here in the Summer Lands."

He merely smiled. "This age suits me," he said. "It's far more peaceful, and peace is what I crave most. However," he added looking somberly at Kellas and me "you two must leave immediately."

Twenty

Epona must have agreed with that assessment because she stepped closer to Knight, laced her hands together, and nodded at me. "I'll give you a lift up."

Swallowing my anxiety, I went over, gathered the neck rope in my left hand and grabbed a handful of mane as well, put my left foot into her hands, and jumped up. She pulled up as well, nearly tossing me over the horse, but I caught the saddle and righted myself in time.

Epona looked questioningly at Kellas. "Pass," he said grimly. "I can get myself there without the horse's help."

She nodded. Apparently she knew about Kellas's abilities, maybe because she was friends with my Nan. She looked at me. "Think clearly about where you want to go, and ride forward at a gallop. It will help him get the necessary momentum for the leap. Hold tight to the pommel; you'll need that help when he starts."

I gave her a tight nod and took the front of the saddle in a death grip.

"Breathe!" she ordered sternly. "You're too tense." Then her face relaxed the tiniest bit. "You can do this."

Yeah, right. And I had all my flight certifications successfully completed and filed away with the FAA ... Not! But there was no time for practice runs, so ... here we go! I pictured my Nan's house as clearly as I could, a nice open section of lawn near the front door where we should be able to land safely and urged Knight into a gallop. He lunged forward like a racehorse out of the gate, and I was grateful for my grip on the saddle as we were at full speed in just a few strides. I felt him gather himself and leap into the air ...

$\sim$

I awakened slowly, dimly aware of the hard ground underneath me, voices murmuring nearby. Was I home? Gads, that was a hard landing. Oh man, I hurt. Oh, my head! I groaned and attempted to sit up, only to be stopped by someone's hand on my shoulder.

"Stay still, Brannaugh." It was Kellas, the bossy Bert. Figured he'd still be ordering me around.

"Are we home? What happened?" I asked. Other faces crowded around. Taliesin. Epona. The pixies. *"Why are they still here? Did they get dragged along?"*

There was a dismayed look on Kellas's face, which he quickly smoothed away. "Hang in there a moment." A moment later he was back in cat form. "Try that again."

Wasn't this hard enough the first time? Dang, cat! *"I said, are we home? Why are they here, shouldn't they be in Tír na nÓg?"*

"They are in Tír na nÓg. And so are we. You crashed. Something stopped you. We're still trying to figure out why."

"What about Knight? Is he okay?" I tried to sit up again; same result.

"Will you stay put? You bashed your head when you fell. You're concussed. Just hang out there a bit until we figure out what to do about it!" There was a combination of frustration and fear in Kellas's voice that effectively stopped me from attempting to move again.

Taliesin leaned in closer. "It appears you have lost your voice again as well. The head injury we can manage. Your voice?" He looked concerned. "Not a clue." He looked over his shoulder and made some scratching squeaking noises that sounded a good bit like what I'd heard the pixies make after the attack of the werewolves.

Dismay flooded through me. I'd lost my voice again? How? WHY?

One of the pixies pushed her way up by my shoulder and laid a hand on my forehead. More scratchy squeaky noises, then she leaned closer, smiling and nodding, and patted my cheek. Squeaky scratching voice. NO idea what she just said.

"She says your concussion is mild. Just needs a day or two of rest." Taliesin translated.

"They don't have a day or two," Epona said in a grim tone. "Cerridwen ..."

"They need to hide, then," Taliesin said, unfazed. "I know of a place. It's not too far." He turned to the pixies again, and there was that rapid-fire squeaky scratching language again. The pixies responded in kind and scattered. "Perhaps you would be so kind as to assist Brannaugh to the house for a minute?" he asked Kellas. "We need to wrap her head with some herbs I have for this purpose. Then you must go quickly." He turned to Epona. "Is the Knight horse able to carry her? Is he injured at all?"

"He's fine. Landed on his feet like a cat," she supplied.

Kellas's irritation was palpable. *"Like a cat, my ass,"* he thought at me. *"The big lummox smashed into some invisible barrier and dropped you like a stone before floating himself back to the ground. Jackass!"*

A wave of fury not my own washed over me, and a moment later the Knight horse and Kellas were nose to nose over top of me, glaring at each other, trading some not-so-choice mind-to-mind insults.

Epona stepped in and shoved the two of them apart. "We're wasting time. You two can carry on whatever your disagreement is some other time, although you might better kiss and make up if you are to survive. Help me here, cait sidhe." She leaned down and lifted me gently to a sitting position.

Kellas shifted back into man form, sent the dark horse a parting glare, then bent down, scooped me up in his arms like I weighed nothing at all, and carried me to the cabin.

Oh, gods above. Maybe it was the head injury, but my stomach was doing fish-out-of-water flip-flops and my heart was pounding so hard in my chest I could hear it in my ears. It was a good thing the cabin was only a few yards away, because I probably would have passed out from the hormones surging through my bloodstream. Down girl! Sit! Stay!! ...

OMG, can he hear my thoughts? Yes, he can hear my thoughts. No, wait, he had to be in cat form to do that …

Kellas deposited me on one of the chairs in front of the fire, and Taliesin, aided by two of the pixies, set to work patching up my noggin. The herbs they used smelled a bit like rosemary and ginger, but I couldn't be sure. The third pixie sidled up close and handed me a leather bag with something in it. A thought picture came into my head. Food for our journey, teas to drink to heal my head. A bottle of water. Medicine for pain. She patted my arm and made a reassuring sound in her squeaky language. I managed a weak smile in return. Man, my head ached. I was so darn dizzy; my stomach was turning sour.

Taliesin finished tying a knot in the fabric he'd wrapped my head in and stepped back. "That's all we can do for now," he said. His face was lined with concern. There was a moment of hesitation, then he apparently came to a decision. "Here." He reached under his shirt, pulled a medallion on a leather thong from around his neck and handed it to me. "Wear this always. It will bring you good fortune."

I took it and was immediately aware of its weight. Was it gold? Had to be. About 2 inches in diameter, a perfect circle, a pattern of three connected swirls. Beautiful! "This is too valuable," I protested, started to hand it back.

He pushed my hand back. "Keep it, I insist. Now you must go. Kellas, a moment, please."

The two left the room. Epona laid a hand on my shoulder. "I will take my leave as well."

I looked up, wanting to thank her, but a weak smile was all I could manage. Voiceless again. Unfair!

She smiled back. "You'll figure it out," she said, and left.

Just like that. No instructions, no great insights. Nothing. Thanks a bunch.

Looping the medallion around my neck, I grabbed the bag of food and wobbled my way to the open front door. I saw the goddess swing up on another horse. (Where had that one come from? But of course she'd have a spare. Horse goddesses don't walk around on their own two feet like ordinary mortals, do they? That would be too mundane.) She waved at me, then turned her horse's head, cantered away into the woods and was gone.

"C'mon." Kellas came up behind me and grabbed my arm, hustling me outside and toward Knight. "As little as I like you getting back on that idiot, it's the only way we have a shouting chance of living to see the sun rise tomorrow." He lifted me onto the saddle like I weighed nothing, then grabbed the horse's neck loop and urged him forward. I could feel the horse's dislike of being bossed about by the cat man, but he went along quietly. I clung to the saddle, the swaying motion of the horse's walk making me feel even woozier. Glancing back at the cabin, I saw Taliesin watching from the door. I raised a hand, all I could do, not able to call goodbye. I saw him raise one hand briefly, then let it fall.

It was a lousy way to say goodbye.

Twenty-One

Here we go again. On our own, no idea what we need to do or how to get it done. At least I have a horse to ride and a bag of food the pixie gave me. Couldn't even have a conversation with Kellas, because he had to stay in man form to lead the horse. Apparently, Taliesin had given him some specific instructions of where to go, because he didn't hesitate as we crossed the clearing in the direction opposite of where Epona had left, a gap in the trees becoming apparent as we approached. We entered the woods and followed a narrow, rutted dirt road leading downhill along the cliff's edge. The road didn't get much use, apparently, because we had to skirt around fallen trees and duck low branches, slowing our progress. The ambient music wasn't much help guiding us, as it was so messed up to begin with. Ugly music. How I hated that I'd been the one who'd made it so, and there was no way to turn it off, like you could with a radio.

But maybe I could drown it out! Annoyed I hadn't thought of that to begin with, I pulled my lute out of its hiding place and settled it as best as I could on the high pommel in front of me. I closed my eyes and tried to hear the music I needed to pull from its strings. I waited. And waited. Nothing.

"Won't it play?" Kellas's voice was so unexpected my eyes flew open in shock. He'd turned his head to look up at me.

"No. No, it won't," I said, then realized I hadn't spoken that aloud, and substituted a small shake of my head.

He tripped on a fallen branch, caught himself before he fell, and went back to paying attention where he was going. "Keep trying," he ordered, and fell silent again.

I stuck my tongue out at him, not that he saw me. What did he think I was trying to do, anyways?

We followed the road as it left the woods and gradually shrank down to a path that worked its way steeply downhill where it ended near the bottom of the cliff. We were now in a broad valley with rolling hills, broken up by miles of stone walls that wandered hither and yon over an emerald landscape. A dirt road ran past the cliff face, leading deeper into the valley.

"Which way?" Kellas asked, and grimaced when all I could do was shrug. "Point!" he suggested.

Apparently, Taliesin's hiding place was not a specific place, then, if Kellas was asking me for input. OK! I pointed left, where the road led deeper into the valley. I was tired of cliffs and woods. I craved open spaces again. At least we might be able to see Cerridwen coming when she got done dealing with the dragon I'd somehow unleashed into her world.

The landscape was as green as I had ever set my eyes upon. North Dakota was beautiful, but nothing like this ... well, the Black Hills in South Dakota came close, but Tír na nÓg was poetry incarnate. Above us was a combination of deep blue sky and snowy-colored clouds that clustered high into the heavens, their bases a dark gray that looked foreboding yet beautiful at the same time. Dark streaks of rain falling from the clouds suggested we might be getting wet in the not-too-distant future. Sheep wandered the pastures in fluffy groups, calling to one another every so often. An old gray cart horse raised its head from where it grazed. He whickered at Knight and managed to trot a few stiff steps in our direction before stopping. He watched as we rode past, then went back to eating. A European robin, a bit like our American robin, but smaller and cuter, perched on the rock wall we were passing and burst into song. A flock of starlings wheeling in their crazy winged dance across one of the meadows.

Kellas noted it too. "There's a merlin going after them, see it?"

I didn't see the merlin, but I knew the intricate aerial acrobatics were meant to confuse predators. What it must be like to be able to fly like that, as if of one mind. How I envied their ability.

"We'll stop in the next village for the night," Kellas said. "I don't want to be caught out after dark, not knowing what might be prowling then."

He'd get no argument from me, even if I'd still had a voice to say so. Not that he even looked back at me to see if I agreed or not! Like it or not, I was tiring fast. From the fight with the werewolves in the morning to the fall from the Knight horse in the afternoon, I'd been crazy busy. Just another day in paradise ...

And just like that, my lute, which I had never put away, hoping that inspiration would hit it or me somehow, started to ring under my fingers.

I was singing out loud, full-throated and clear, my lute accompanying me as we belted out the Phil Vassar song. I felt the Knight horse shudder in surprise under me and Kellas nearly fell on his arse as he whirled in midstride to look back at me. I laughed as I sang and, weirdly enough, tears welled in my eyes and spilled down my face at the same time. But I didn't stop singing, because thank the gods I was able to sing. Like the robin on the wall, like the starlings whirling above us, I could sing.

I COULD SING.

The final chord died away and there we stood, in the middle of the narrow dirt road in the middle of an unfamiliar land with an unknown number of boogeymen to deal with ... and I was at peace, with myself, with the situation, with whatever what might come next. Maybe. Well, for the moment at least!

"That was fantastic." Kellas said quietly. The Knight horse gave a little snort indicating he might have agreed.

"I don't usually sing Country Western songs," I said, then frowned. Voiceless! Again! Still?

Kellas looked puzzled, then thoughtful. "Try singing that."

Huh. OK! Worth a try at least. "I don't usually sing Country Western songs," I sang, playing a couple accompanying chords on the lute and feeling more than a bit self-conscious. But, hey, it worked. Weird, but helpful. I was no longer rendered voiceless. OK, so I had to sing everything. There were worse things than that! I shrugged and grinned at Kellas.

He shot me a lopsided grin in return. "Whatever works, right?" He gave Knight's neck loop a small tug, "C'mon, we need to find shelter before it gets dark."

Twenty-Two

The darkness and the rain had reached us by the time we stumbled into a tiny group of thatched houses clustered around a crossroads. There was an inn at the crossroads itself, or maybe it was what the Irish called a pub. I slid off Knight's back and led him under a lean-to roof where, oddly, there was a hayrack full of hay waiting. How providential! But I did not question it, I merely untacked the dark horse and rubbed him down as best I could with a handful of hay while he tore into his meal.

"Don't you be going off somewhere without me!" I thought at him and was rewarded with a chiding sideways glance and a snort of disgust. Reassured, I patted him gently and thanked him for the lift today. Then I followed Kellas into the pub.

We stopped just inside the door to let our eyes adjust to the darkness inside. As it was lit by only candles, the lighting was extremely poor. I was dimly aware of a long narrow space, a few windows along the front wall atop a hip high wall of stone, a long, dark wooden bar on the opposite wall, shelves full of bottles behind the bar. A few mirrors for the barman to keep an eye on the customers while his back was turned to them. Small round tables lined up along the front wall, together with an odd assortment of wooden chairs. High stools by the bar. The place was primarily occupied by roughly clothed men. A few had clothing that suggested they were a bit better off than the rest. A quick impression was that there wasn't a single woman in the place. Oh, gods above. I was going to stick out like a sore thumb in this bunch.

It didn't seem to faze Kellas in the least. He led me to an unoccupied table nearby and pulled out a chair for me. "You wait here, I'll be right back with something to drink."

I settled into the chair, clutching my lute to my chest like a security blanket, aware that nearly every eye was on me. I tried to play it cool, nodding at the two men at the next table over. The patrons of the pub were all ages, all looked like they earned a living with the strength of their bodies. They smelled like it too ... the body odor was overwhelming. I tried not to breathe too deeply. Didn't these guys ever bathe?

"You know how to play that thing, lass?" a man at the next table asked me. He was tall, I thought briefly. Why hadn't he taken off his long raincoat? Odd ... But to be polite, I nodded.

"You any good?"

I shrugged. What could I say? Voiceless, remember?

"Cat's got her tongue," his companion said. "Guess that rules out any singing from her."

Kellas returned, thank gods, ending the stares and questions for the time being. "I've ordered some food. It'll be coming shortly. There are rooms upstairs where we can stay the night."

When the food came, it was a lamb stew: carrots, onions, and potatoes in a thick gravy. The mutton must have been from an old sheep, because the meat was gamey and on the tough side, but I ate like I hadn't had anything all day ... which I hadn't, actually. Kellas ate more slowly, but he was also drinking from an enormous mug of dark beer. I gave him a questioning look.

He smiled slightly. "It's Guinness," he told me. "Want a taste?"

Why not? All I had was water. I nodded and held out my hand.

He passed the mug over. "Careful. It's heavy."

It was. I used both hands to steady it, took a small sip. Ugh, it was nasty! Kellas only laughed at the look of disgust on my face. I passed the mug back quickly and tried to wash the taste out of my mouth with some water. It lingered. Bleah. If that was what beer was like, I wouldn't be drinking much of it!

"Just don't be insulting their beer to the gentlemen in this establishment," he warned. "They won't take kindly to it."

And how would I be managing that now? Me without a voice and all? I gave him an eye roll. He just laughed.

Nearby, the man who'd asked me if I knew how to play the lute picked up one of his own and began tuning it up. He sent me a sideways glance and raised his eyebrows, as if inviting me to join him. I shook my head and held up my spoonful of stew, letting him know I was still eating. He nodded and started playing a bouncy little tune that soon had me tapping a foot and nodding along. A couple men jumped up and started dancing along, the boot stomping and rough laughter completely comical.

We'd just finished our meal when a man at the bar seemed to reach a decision, twisted around on his stool to face me, and leered openly. "Ain't you the quiet one, lassie," he drawled, his words slurred just the tiniest amount.

Kellas stiffened and a dangerous look came over his face. He half turned his head. "Not your type, man. Leave it be. You're half cut as it is."

It didn't dissuade the drunk. He slid off his stool and stood up, swaying slightly. Booted feet planted well apart as though the floor was rolling under him.

Kellas saw that and his lip curled. "Make that totally bolloxed," he muttered and turned his back to the guy.

"Leave the kids be, Finn. They ain't bothering nobody," one of the drunk's companions said.

"I ain't bothering nobody. Just looking for a bit of fun with the lassie, here. Wanna dance?" he asked me, lurching closer.

I shook my head vehemently. Kellas growled low in his chest. Pushing back his chair, he got to his feet deliberately and turned to face the drunkard. "Stand down, man. You're asking for a fight and in no shape to start one. The young lady doesn't want to dance with you."

"How would you know, jackeen? Let the little lady speak for herself! Or are you afraid she'd like me over you?"

Pretty clear there was going to be a fight if things continued in this fashion. I jumped to my feet, slung my lute over my left shoulder, and, dodging around the table, grabbed Kellas's arm, tugging him in the direction of the door.

He shook me off, ignoring me, (what else is new, right?) and glared over the drunk's shoulder at his buddies. "Maybe one of you wants to do this man's thinking for him, seeing as how he's not doing so well for himself?"

From where I stood, it didn't look as though there was much chance for that. They just gave him the blank look I'd seen in the eyes of the boys at my high school who followed the bullies around. The "like I give a crap about what you think" look. No empathy, no feeling of maybe this wasn't the right way to treat others. And this was the Celtic idea of Heaven?

The drunk threw the first punch. It was also his last. Kellas moved so fast I was unable to follow the action with any clarity. All I knew was the drunk was on his way to the floor, out cold inside of a second. Kellas stood over the man's prone body, a spine-chilling snarl curling his lips back from long, sharp incisors. I won't call them canine teeth because he was at the moment pure feline fury. Yup, definitely cat teeth, those ones.

"Cait sidhe! It's a cursed soul stealer!" I heard one man exclaim, and it was like the temperature in the pub dropped 50 degrees in a second. The hostility was palpable. I grabbed Kellas's arm again and tugged. We had to get out of there, dark or no dark. We were not about to stay here any longer than necessary. Kellas was resisting me ... and then he wasn't. A large man had gripped Kellas's other arm and was shoving him toward the door as well. I was dimly aware it was the lute player.

"Move your cussed tail, cat man, there's no point in dying here tonight," he growled, his size and strength not brooking argument.

Kellas must have come to his senses also because we were suddenly moving fast, out the door, and into the dark.

"*Feistigh!*" the man exclaimed, and threw a hand out at the door as the men in the bar charged after us. The door slammed closed by itself, remained fast shut despite the howls of anger and furious pounding from those trapped behind it.

"This way," the man ordered, and broke into a run. Kellas caught my hand and pulled me along after our rescuer.

"*Knight!*" We were leaving the dark horse behind, not that Kellas could hear me, or would care, even if he could hear me, but as I cried out, there was a swirl of dark energy next to me and suddenly Knight was there anyway, fully saddled. (Really? How could that be? Would I ever get used to magic?) I shook Kellas's hand off me, grabbed a handful of mane, and launched myself into the saddle. So glad I had practiced that move back in North Dakota!

The lute player led us out of town, through a gate in a stone wall and into the field beyond. We could hear shouts in the distance behind us and now there were lights bobbing about in the street. The door must have given way, and we were being pursued. Panic rose bitter in my throat. On Knight, I could outrun them, but what about Kellas?

The man stopped so suddenly we nearly ran into him "*Oscail!*" he commanded, and a door rose out of the green hill in front of us, shining with an otherworldly luminosity. "In here, quickly," he ordered. "The horse, too," he added with a note of annoyance. We obeyed him with alacrity. The man followed us in, the door shut behind us ... and disappeared.

We were in a towering cavern; the smell of moist dirt permeating the air. Despite the men's loud breathing, I thought I could hear water trickling somewhere nearby. The entire space was illuminated with a glow that came from everywhere, as though from an unseen sun.

"Thank you," Kellas started.

"I'll have that lute now," the man said, walking toward me, holding out a beckoning hand.

Twenty-Three

Huh? What? Um ... no? I backed Knight up, shaking my head no as emphatically as I could manage.

Kellas leapt in between us and the man. "Hey, we appreciate your help and all, but this isn't *tá go breá*, my good man!"

"That's my lute, and I want it back. Why else would I save your worthless fae ass, cait sidhe?" he spat at Kellas and sent him sprawling with one violent sweep of his arm. "Give it to me, lass, and I won't hurt your wee kitten."

I stared at the man. Not a small guy at all, fully 6 feet, maybe bigger, definitely taller than Kellas, and a good 30 pounds heavier. Despite the long rain slicker disguising his figure, he gave every impression of being fit and in his prime. And ... there was that wee bit of what I could only figure was magic, with his shutting and opening of doors with just a single word uttered. His face was all angles, lips thin, eyes hard, dark hair to his shoulders. Not the sort that I'd want to tangle with, given my druthers. But why was he demanding that I give him my lute?

I hesitated. Kellas had pulled himself together and was getting to his feet, reaching for the small blade he carried at his hip. The man did not even look at Kellas, just gestured at him with one hand and spat a single word. "*Reo!*"

Kellas gasped as the spell hit him and he froze in place, eyes open and staring, completely unable to move.

OK, I had to do something. I pulled my lute from its hiding place behind my back.

A thin smile twisted the man's lips. "An excellent choice, child. I'll take that now."

I strummed a chord and sang "This lute is mine and you will not harm my friend."

"So you can talk."

I shook my head, strummed the lute again. "I can sing."

You could almost see the gears turning in the guy's head. "You have a *geis* on your voice," he said, stating the obvious. "Fascinating." He started toward me again, and Knight backed away on his own. Apparently, the dark horse didn't like this dude any better than I did. "The lute is mine," the man insisted, still pursuing us. "I knew it the moment you hid it over your back in the pub."

Knight kept right on backing up.

"Not anymore," I sang. "It was given to me by the bard Taliesin, who received it from the Morrigan herself. It's mine."

Mention of the Morrigan stopped the guy in his tracks. "She took it from me."

"Which, if the Death goddess took it, obviously means you died," I sang back. "Where I come from, they say 'you can't take it with you.'"

"MY lute!" he exclaimed, and I could almost see angry steam coming out of his ears. "You will return what is rightfully mine."

"And what guarantee do I have that you will not harm us if I do? Release Kellas, whoever you are. You have no right to bully us with your magic."

He lunged at us, snarling. Knight neatly dodged him, then reared and struck the guy square in the chest with both front feet, knocking him flying backward, where he collapsed on the ground, groaning.

"Well done, my friend!" I thought at Knight, who snorted with satisfaction.

Knight's strike also must have released Kellas from the man's spell, as Kellas abruptly unfroze, collapsing to hands and knees, gasping for air. He didn't stay down long. "Took you long enough," he managed, pushing himself to his feet. "We've got to get out of here."

"How? I sang. "There's no door."

"We go find one." Kellas staggered over to us and gave the dark horse a pat on the neck. "Thanks, big guy."

Knight merely blustered, a strong feeling of skepticism coming off him in a wave. Not best buddies yet by any means, those two.

We had started away when the man called after us in a pained voice. "There are no other doors. All the tunnels merely lead farther into the earth. I can guarantee you do not want to venture there."

"You give us no reason to trust you, nameless one," Kellas retorted, and kept on.

There was a brief silence, just the sound of Knight's steel shoes echoing on the stone floor, then:

"It's Uiscias," the man said. "My name is Uiscias."

That stopped Kellas in his tracks, and he turned around. I swung Knight around to face him. "Uiscias?" Kellas asked. "The warrior bard who wielded the sword of Nuada?"

"The same," Uiscias groaned. He was slowly pushing himself up to a sitting position, one hand holding his ribs. Probably a few of those had been broken by Knight's blow. I almost felt sorry for him, knowing how that felt after Kellas's love pat a few days ago. Breathing would be a challenge for a while. Briefly, I wondered about that. Didn't ribs take months to heal? Why didn't mine hurt anymore? Maybe they hadn't been broken in the first place? Or was it more sinister ... like how my Iku had warned me of the different way time moved in our dimension versus here in Tír na nÓg. A chill washed over me, leaving me shivering.

"Why didn't you say so in the first place?" Kellas demanded. "We could have avoided all this misunderstanding."

"And why would you care, cait sidhe?" the bard snapped. "Your kind has only ever looked out for themselves, and to hell with anyone else." Slowly, he made his way onto his feet, groaning a bit as he straightened up.

Kellas merely growled low in his throat, like a cat warning off a dog.

"Don't you be trying any more magic tricks on us, mister," I sang.

He sent me a glare that could have frozen hell over. "All I want is for you to give my lute back. Why is that such an issue? You can always get yourself another one."

Kellas inhaled sharply, catching my attention. There was a fierce look on the cat man's face. "Because it's not the lute you're wanting so badly, is it? It's the sword," he exclaimed. "This lute turns into a sword, and not just any sword, is it? It's Fraegarthach, Nuada's invincible sword. You want that back. Now I get it!"

Chagrin on the bard's face said louder than words that Kellas had figured it out correctly. "Yon wee lass isn't even a Celt, from the look of her. A foreign female is not suitable to carry that blade. If she could even lift it!" He sent me a disparaging glance.

"Oh, she can lift it alright," Kellas snarled. "Don't you be getting any funny ideas in that department."

It was likely not a good thing to have said to the bard. Especially one with magic at his command. Hadn't Taliesin told us he was a powerful Druid? Things would have gone downhill rapidly from there, if they hadn't gone rapidly downhill in a very different way just then.

Knight threw his head up, snorting in alarm. A shudder ran through his body. The men stopped squabbling and we turned as one toward the end of the cavern where dark maws of multiple tunnels started. Was it my imagination, or did the temperature in the cavern, never high, suddenly drop dramatically? And what was that horrible smell? Were-wolves? Ah, no, not again!

But it wasn't werewolves that came boiling up out of the dark, it was *mummies*, all groaning like in the movies, all lurching slowly toward us, the dark slits in their wrappings where their eyes should be (but weren't) all looking our way. Knight half reared, snorting in terror, which made it extra difficult to strum a hasty chord and sing/yell at Kellas. "Mummies! Change into cat form!" suddenly grateful for the wasted hours watching stupid mummy movies, where I had learned that mummies were afraid of cats and fire. Fortunately, I had a cat on retainer, but where could I find fire?

Uiscias! "Can you summon fire?" I sang at the bard. "Fire will kill those things!" Uiscias stood as if made of stone, a look of horror on his face. "Dear gods, man! We need fire now! Haven't you seen mummies before?" Of course, he hadn't, Raven! They were

EGYPTIAN scary dudes ... and it was probably my own fault they were here, too, but now was not the time to think about that. Right now, we had to get rid of them. Thank goodness Kellas was a bit quicker on the draw than the druid. He'd changed into his puma avatar and taken up a position between us and the creepies. Sure enough, they had lurched to a halt and were groaning among themselves.

But we still needed fire and there was nothing burnable in the cavern ... except the mummies themselves. All wrapped in cloth soaked with resins, they'd go up like tinder, if we could only set some sparks into them! But how?

"I can summon fire, but only with the sword in my hand," Uiscias had finally come out of his statue mode. "Give me the lute and I can destroy those things."

"Don't give it to him, Brannaugh!" Kellas thought screamed at me. "Bad idea!"

"But how long can we have this standoff?" I thought at him. *"You can't stand in between us forever!"*

"Long enough to give us a chance to figure this out," he thought back.

Meanwhile, Uiscias was still standing there, one hand outstretched.

The front line of mummies lurched forward as if pushed from behind. Some of them were falling and getting trampled by those in back. Maybe mummies feared cats, but the ones in back didn't know there was a cat, and they were pushing, pushing ... inexorably coming closer.

Oh, gods ... I thrust the lute at Uiscias, who leapt forward to take it. I heard Kellas's caterwaul of protest, and then the bard's fingertips hit the neck of the lute.

A shower of sparks flew in all directions, some landing on my clothing where they burned small holes before dying out. Knight shied violently as some of the sparks landed on him as well. Already unbalanced from holding the lute out, I lost my seat and fell gracelessly to the ground. Uiscias's scream of pain echoed in my ears, and I was dimly aware of his hand smoking as if exposed to flame.

I clambered painfully to my feet, checked the lute for damage ...

thank the gods it was unbroken! Okay, Raven, plan B! Whatever the heck that was. We needed fire, *now*! If only I could summon fire!

The song burst out of me before I consciously thought about it, and I was singing like my life depended on it: Alicia Keys's "Girl on Fire." And I was.

On fire, that is. Not that it was burning me, but it was like I had become Johnny Storm, the Human Torch. Unlike Johnny, however, my flames were not red, but blue, more akin to lightning. In fact, rather like the electricity that surrounded the sword's blade when I wielded it. And why not, the lute and the sword were one and the same, right? However, now was not the time to be reflecting on fictional superheroes, not while I had some mummies to dispatch.

I walked toward the mummies as quickly as I could manage while still playing the lute. The ones in front immediately recognized the peril they were in and tried to escape, but the ones in back, the ones who hadn't seen the cat earlier, kept pushing forward, preventing escape. I neared the front line and saw my flames light the first ones on fire. They were jumping about and screeching, the flames spreading rapidly to others until the entire mass was on fire, the heat from their immolation pushing me back.

I drew back further, letting the music die. The flames that surrounded me died as well and I sunk down on my knees, utterly exhausted.

Kellas, still in puma form, came up and leaned against me, his concern for me coming off him in waves of emotion. "Brannaugh?"

I took a deep breath and let it out slowly. "I'm okay. Don't worry. Really tired is all." I slung the lute over my back.

"Sorcery! You are a witch!!" Uiscias exclaimed from over near the cavern wall. A safe distance from the mummies and the bonfire they were making, I noted. Oh. My. Gods. This dude was seriously wearing on my nerves. Resentment boiled up inside me until I was no longer able to contain it.

"You are a jackass," I stated flatly. "A patriarchal white jerk of the first order. In case you didn't notice, I just saved your lily-white backside from being eaten by a bunch of dead guys in cloth bandages." I slowly rose to my feet, assisted by Kellas who had switched back into man form as I had started to speak. Yeah, that's right, I had my voice back again. For how long was anybody's guess, but right now I was on a tear, and everything I had held back for so long was coming out, so watch out, world.

"Sure, I don't have porcelain skin, green eyes and red hair, but I am still half Irish ..." I stalked toward the druid, my gaze locked on his.

"And you just got the Irish part all riled up," Kellas added, his eyes twinkling like he was on to some giant joke at Uiscias's expense.

I ignored him. "... and what's more, I don't work witchcraft or sorcery, but magic every bit as good as yours, and because I am female and not some high and mighty white man on his fancy horse, you cannot go about making me out to be evil, just so you can stay in control and have everyone else treat you like you are somehow special and better than everyone. Get that out of your head right now, druid, because I'm not gonna tolerate it for a New York minute, ya hear me?" I yelled all this, the anger burning through me like a white-hot flame of its own, punctuating the last bit with a finger poking at the man's chest. Never mind that he was head and shoulders taller than me, outweighed me by, gosh, probably a hundred pounds, and probably knew tons more magic than I ever would, but so help me, I was not thinking too clearly right now. All I knew was rage. Rage that I had tamped down over the years of being taunted for my darker skin, for my mixed heritage, for my very differentness from anyone else I knew. I was done with being treated as somehow not as good as anyone else. I glared up at Uiscias, daring him to retaliate, daring him to defend his indefensible behavior, daring him to ...

Instead, the big jerk began laughing. It was not necessarily a mean laugh, or the taunting sort I'd heard too many times from people who were trying to make me out as some stupid little kid who was out of line. It was, well, the sort that expressed surprise and maybe a grudging admiration, but there was an extra something else to it ... enough to give me pause. Not an ally, that one. Best kept at arm's length.

"I stand corrected," Uiscias said. "You are not a witch or a sorceress, but a fine musician with a special lute and you did save us all from those ... things, whatever they were, and for that I am grateful." He stepped back and bowed low. "Thank you, *bhean deas*."

"Don't think your flattery is going to get you off the hook, druid," Kellas told him. "Let's get out of here," he muttered in my ear.

I was still glaring at Uiscias. "Yes, let's," I agreed. "Knight?"

The dark horse responded immediately, appearing at my elbow with the now familiar swirl of darkness, blustering from flared nostrils. I got the sense that he was still pretty freaked out by the mummies and the fire. "Time to get a move on," I told him, and attempted to swing onto his back. I failed miserably. I was simply too tired. Kellas must have figured that out, because he was by my side offering a hand up immediately. Even so, it wasn't pretty. I had to pull myself up by the saddle, and once there, slumped over like a limp noodle. I could feel Knight's disapproval of my clumsiness, but what could I do? I felt like I had run a hundred miles, and my muscles were trashed.

Kellas switched back into cat form. "Where to?" he thought at me. You know, this telepathic communication was coming in handy!

"Out of here," I responded, and suppressed a chuckle at his exasperation. *"The same way we got in."* I urged Knight toward the cavern wall, threw up a hand like I'd seen Uiscias do, and commanded *"Oscail!"* Hey, it had worked for the druid, why not me?

And miracle of miracles, it did. The same shining gap in the wall, the world beyond still in darkness. Out we went, leaving Uiscias behind.

Or so we thought ...

Twenty-Four

Kellas led the way back out to the road; the rain having driven our pursuers back into the pub once they realized we had well and truly disappeared. I could feel Kellas's dislike for being wet. The dark horse wasn't overly pleased either, as he'd drawn his face back and felt all hunched up and unhappy under me. I was wet through and shivering inside of a few minutes, and the weariness I'd felt after burning up the mummies was overwhelming. Adrenaline would get you only so far, then you got to pay the piper afterward. *"We need to find shelter,"* I thought at Kellas.

His response was less than couth, along the lines of "No s^&* Sherlock." I might have laughed if I hadn't been quite so miserable. Kellas broke into a trot and Knight followed suit. The extra speed helped keep the cold at bay, but the effort it took to post the big horse's trot was wearing on me rapidly. Suddenly, Knight veered off the road and launched himself over a stone fence, nearly unseating me. I clawed my way back into the center of the saddle, stifling a rush of panic. *"A little advance warning would be nice!"* I scolded him. As usual, all I got was a disgusted snort in response. The horse didn't have much faith in my ability to ride, apparently. In fact, I got the distinct impression he thought I was about as good as a sack of potatoes.

Kellas caught up. "What was that all about?" he demanded.

"Knight has something in mind, apparently," I told him. He subsided, grumbling, and we continued for several minutes in silence until an old structure loomed close out of the dark and the rain. Knight slowed his pace and walked right in. I nearly bonked my head on the doorframe, just managing to avoid doing so at the last possible moment.

Knight halted. Apparently, we were where he'd figured we should stop for the night. Sighing heavily, I slid down and peered around in the dimness. I couldn't see much, just vague impressions of a rounded space, stone walls, and a low roof accompanied by the overwhelming smell of sheep manure. We were in an ancient sheep shelter of some sort. At least it was dry and currently without sheep. There was still some hay in the wooden hayracks that lined the walls, because Knight was already tearing into it, eating as though he'd not had anything for days. I untacked him again, setting his saddle and neck rope over the side of one of the racks before crawling up and over into another one and curling up on the hay. Kellas jumped up next to me and cuddled his cat form close against my back. The warmth and familiarity of it was comforting, even though I was still so cold I couldn't stop shivering. Outside, the rain continued to come down steadily, dripping off the edge of the roof and splashing in the puddles that formed around the building. I strained for sounds that our hiding place was being discovered but heard nothing other than the rain pattering down on the thatch above and dripping onto the puddles. Finally, unable to remain awake any longer, I fell into a deep sleep.

I dreamed someone was sticking needles into me as if I were nothing so much as a voodoo doll being used to curse some hapless soul. I tried to get away, but the needles persisted until I lurched awake to discover the needles were Kellas's claws, and he was getting insistent about sticking me with them.

"For the love of all that's holy, wake up, Brannaugh!" he thought at me, his agitation palpable. "Someone is coming!"

That got me up. Bleary-eyed, clumsy in my not-quite-all-there-yet mode, I managed to clamber out of the hayrack and stood stretching, peering out the sheep shed door at a sunlit meadow sparkling with raindrops. Someone was whistling, and the whistling was coming closer. We had to get gone, and now ... but where was Knight? For that matter, where was his saddle? Crap.

Kellas leapt out of the hayrack and beelined for a second door on the opposite side of the shelter from where the whistling was coming. For lack of a better idea, I followed. We ducked behind the stone side of the shelter out of sight of the whistler and hastened away as quickly as we could manage. A scramble up and over a stone wall put us back onto a dirt road. Somewhat safer territory, it seemed, as at least it gave us plausible deniability ... hey, we were just passing by! Not trespassing in your sheep shelter overnight! I chanced a look over at the shelter, now a good hundred yards away, and saw the stooped figure of an older person carrying a pitchfork full of hay making his way up to the shelter, followed by a dozen white sheep who were jostling each other for a chance at a nibble of hay. A couple of the younger lambs jumped about and ran circles around the person, just full of life and silliness. It brought a smile to my face. A bit of country normalcy instead of werewolves, mummies, and acquisitive druids.

As I had left our bag of food attached to Knight's saddle, we were without breakfast, never a wonderful situation. Breakfast was my favorite meal of the day, and I had the disturbing tendency to be a complete grouch if I did not get something in my stomach soon after waking up. Mom had called it being "hangry." All I know is an empty stomach did not set well.

"Where do you suppose Knight got off to?" I wondered.

Kellas's thought back was more of an "I could care less" shrug than an actual answer.

"He's got our food bag," I added. That got his attention. His irritation felt like a swarm of bees buzzing around in my brain.

"Ruddy equine," he grumbled.

I waved my hands around my head, trying to push the beelike sensation away. *"Do we know where we are going, and does that matter anyways?"* I asked him, thinking a change of subject might be helpful. That hauled him up short and I about stepped on him.

"Fair point." He was looking around, so I did too. It was still early morning. The road in front of and behind us was devoid of people. Stone walls lined both sides of the road, a long steep hill stretched behind us, and a wide valley crisscrossed by many more stone walls was below us. I didn't see any villages, but there was a scattering of thatched stone houses and barns here and there. There was enough up and down within the valley that a hill could be blocking the view, however. Lush grass grew everywhere, but few trees, just the occasional small cluster. The air was full of birdsong. Sheep bleated occasionally. A cow was mooing as if calling her calf, or perhaps the farmer was late for milking.

It was beautiful and peaceful, completely bucolic. However, something somewhere nearby was out to get me. What a horrible thought. How did I know? Well, remember the music that I can hear? It's a bit like background music in a restaurant ... you know it's playing, but you're not really focused on it. You don't really listen to it until something catches your attention. Like now. The music had shifted again, no longer the kind that had replaced the Beethoven-like symphony. Thank the gods it wasn't as discordant as the music I had heard previously. Perhaps our dispatching of mummies had helped restore some balance to Tír na nÓg, but now there was an underlaying minor key threat that was building through it. We weren't out of the figurative woods just yet, by any stretch.

I told Kellas as much, adding *"I don't know what it is or where it is, but I know that there is something close, and it's dangerous."*

I could tell that didn't make Kellas's day. "Suggestions?"

I shrugged and started walking downhill, because downhill is easier, and I hadn't had breakfast yet, remember? I was tuned into the music though, listening for any worsening of the melody, hoping it would give me some helpful tips. It didn't. No more or less discordant. Aw, heck. I turned around and marched up the hill. Abruptly the music got edgier, darker. Nope, not the right way. I turned around and headed back downhill again.

Kellas had observed my pacing back and forth with the stoic calm of a cat watching its nutty human dash madly about. Once I was headed downhill again, he fell in beside me without asking any questions. We walked in silence for a good hour, during which my stomach had gotten even emptier than before and had started to rumble its displeasure.

"Do you suppose Knight will show up soon?" I fretted.

"No great loss," was Kellas's reply.

"I gotta eat soon, and he's got our food bag."

"Why don't you call him, then? Maybe he'll come like a well-trained puppy." The disgust in his voice was readily apparent.

Somehow, I didn't think Knight would appreciate that analogy, but it was still worth a try. *"Knight? Can you hear me?"* No answer, not even a whisper. Great. *"We have to find food somewhere,"* I told Kellas. *"I'm not going to manage much longer without something."*

"I could catch you a mouse easily enough," he told me.

I sent him a disgruntled look. Ruddy cat!

Behind us, the rhythmic clip-clop of a horse's hooves on the gravel road caught our attention, and I moved over to the side to let them by, raising a hand to wave, and smiling as an old white horse pulling a high two-wheeled cart came up next to us and stopped.

"Up bright and early this morning, aren't ye, lassie?" An elderly farmer beamed down at me. "Might ye be headed to Derrylin, perhaps? Care for a lift?"

"Say yes," Kellas thought at me. "I'm sick of walking."

I smiled brightly at the farmer and hoisted Kellas up onto the cart seat, then clambered up myself.

"Never saw anyone walk their cat before." The farmer clucked at the cart horse, who moved off again.

I shrugged in reply, not that I could answer.

He sent me a curious glance out of the corner of his eye. "Hungry? The wife always packs more than I can eat, meself." I nodded enthusiastically and he smiled. "In the bag, there. Help yerself."

I obeyed with alacrity, pulling out a thick sandwich and biting into it like I hadn't eaten in ages. Kellas leaned on me, looking up with an expectant meow. What that must have cost him in dignity I cannot imagine. I tore off half the sandwich and held it for him so he could eat. The farmer watched us out of the corner of one eye, a friendly smile deepening the wrinkles carved in his face. I had already checked his music prior to climbing onto the cart: a pleasant baritone played competently and with restraint. I could trust this one.

"There's more in there if ye need it," he urged. "T'will make the little woman happy that it got all ate up. She's not a one to waste things!"

I hesitated a moment.

"Would you rather eat a mouse?" came Kellas's sardonic drawl. I gave him a snarky look and dug into the bag again, pulling out a hunk of soft yellow cheese and fresh scones. There were apples too, and I pulled one out for me, then hesitated and offered it to the farmer.

He shook his head. "Na, na, just had me breakfast. Told the wife I'd be grabbing a bite at the pub, later, but she wasn't hearing of me making the trip without something to sustain me. Can't convince her otherwise. That's just who she is. Eat all ye like, lass. Yer cat, too. Looks like it takes a bit to keep him fit, the size of him! A fine fellow, he is."

Trying not to giggle at Kellas's annoyed mental rumbling at the man's well-meant praise, I bit into the cheese ... and about died and went to heaven. It was tender and buttery and mild, and I loved it. Wished I could ask the farmer what it was. He must have read my expression because he chuckled. "That there's our secret family recipe, made from the milk of our very own Kerry cows. Only our cows make the milk just right for that cheese, and it's been our family's fame and fortune these many years. I'm pleased ye like it!"

I nodded vigorously and shared it with Kellas. I followed that up with the scone (also very tasty, although not as good as the cheese) and the apple, which Kellas declined. Once I was done with that, I held up the core and gave the farmer a questioning look and tipped my head at the horse.

"Whoa, Finnegan!" The farmer reined in the old mare. "Go ahead, she waiting for her share." Grinning, I hopped down and went up to feed the horse, who gently lipped the core from my palm and crunched it up, her eyelids closing, long white eyelashes fluttering in pleasure.

I climbed back into the cart, and we set off again, the rhythmic clip-clop of Finnegan's hooves on the dirt road and the beauty of our surroundings lulling me into a dreamy state of peacefulness. None of which was going to last for long, right? Because that's just another bit of Murphy's Law going on there: if anything can go wrong, it will, and in the most awful way possible.

<h1 style="text-align:center">Twenty-Five</h1>

In this case, it was fire. We first noticed a plume of dark-colored smoke rising from behind a hill in the distance. The old farmer straightened in his seat and sniffed noisily. "That's not good," he said quietly, then more urgently "Derrylin!" He chirped to his horse, urging her to pick up the pace. "Something must be on fire in the village," he muttered as we continued to watch the column of smoke grow thicker and darker. It felt like ages but was less than 10 minutes when we finally rounded a curve in the road and saw the village below us in the valley. It wasn't just one building on fire; it appeared that nearly half the place was burning up. The farmer groaned aloud and urged Finnegan into a canter. We bounced and jounced along over the ruts and potholes, every bone in my body getting jarred as I held on for dear life. Kellas scrammed off the cart at some point, not that I blamed him. I would have, too, except I didn't think I'd be able to stick the landing with any kind of grace.

We hauled up at the edge of town, unable to get any closer, as the heat of the fire was simply too great. There were townspeople standing around, many streaked with soot and with bits of their clothing burned and tattered, buckets in hand, emptied and useless at this point. There was no saving the village now. The fire had gotten a head start and was jumping from building to building like a living thing.

"What happened?" the farmer was asking one of the villagers. "What caused this?"

"There was a great snake in the sky," the other told him. "It frightened all the animals and they stampeded. Then the smithy caught on fire, no one knows for sure how, but we think the sky snake started it."

Sky snake? Oh gods ... the Chinese dragon I'd let in. This was my fault! Suddenly it was like I couldn't breathe. I'd done this. My anger, my stupid magic, had made all these people suffer. All. My. Fault.

I hid my face in my hands and sobbed silently, collapsing to my knees and rocking back and forth. Suddenly, it wasn't just the fire I was crying about, but the whole horrible situation, right down to my being here in Tír na nÓg in the first place. I was mourning the whole hideous mess of my life, and my inability to fix it, any of it.

"Hey there, Brannaugh, we'll have none of that now!" It was Kellas in man form, kneeling next to me. He snugged an arm around my shoulder, pulling my head to his chest, holding me as I cried my heart out. I turned and wrapped my arms around him, my face buried against his chest, my shoulders heaving with the intensity of my silent sobs.

I was barely aware of others crowding closer, and Kellas waving them off. "We're having a moment here. Give her some space, please. Thank you." The others must have agreed to let him deal with the emotional female, because they stepped away.

Gradually, things started calming down, or maybe I'd just worn myself out. At any rate, the crying slowed down and finally stopped, leaving me with an awful ache in my throat, a stuffed-up nose, and a blotchy face that would have scared away a saint. I drew back, a bit horrified I'd left such a large wet spot on the front of Kellas's black shirt. He handed me a handkerchief, and I blew my nose and scrubbed at my eyes, blinking blearily at him.

"*Sorry,*" I mouthed silently at him. He just shook his head and pulled me to my feet, leading me away from the villagers, who were still watching the conflagration, their livelihoods going up in flames.

He led me back up the main road and into a small group of trees out of sight of the others and switched back into cat form. "Talk to me."

I sank down onto the damp ground and balled his handkerchief up in my hands. *"They lost everything because of my mistake. It's my fault, and I have no way to fix it."*

"How is this your fault?"

I opened the veil between worlds. Because of me, the dragon came through."

"OK, true. But what can you tell me about Chinese dragons?"

I gave him a puzzled look.

"What are the powers of a Chinese dragon, Brannaugh? Can they breathe fire?"

I had to think about that. Chinese lore was not something I was all that familiar with, but ... *"I don't think so? Aren't they more water creatures? Something about overseeing the weather?"*

He nodded. "The dragon probably did not cause that fire. It was more likely an accident, precipitated by the dragon's appearance. People panicked and chaos followed. It's just an unhappy chain of events. Sadly, the dragon will be blamed for it and there will be a renewed effort to kill the thing. Not that I exactly blame the Celts for wanting the thing gone, but it is rather hard on the dragon."

"So it is my fault!" My eyes were leaking again, and I was unable to stop them.

He frowned. A frown on a cat face is not a lot different than a frown on a human face ... the eyebrows knit together. "That's not what I meant, girl! But what you did then, you can do now, too. Think!"

Thinking is challenging when your nose isn't working up to par and you're feeling all upset and unhappy, but I tried. This whole mess had started when I sat on the cliff edge at Taliesin's place. Playing and thinking dark thoughts. What had he called it? A place where magic was concentrated.

"I need a place where magic is concentrated," I told Kellas. *"Like the cliff's edge at dawn."*

"Easy enough," he responded. "Tír na nÓg had lots of magical places. What suits you? By the lake, by the sea? Maybe a fairy mound? A stone circle? Say the word and I'll take you there."

I shrugged, feeling totally defeated and uninspired. Kellas made an impatient huff through his nose and got to his feet. "When you decide you aren't helpless, let me know," he shot over his shoulder, and disappeared.

Like that was helpful! I started crying again, self-pity taking over. This was all so unfair! Kellas was such a meany. I had never asked for any of this to happen to me, it was just ... not fair. Other kids didn't have to deal with all this crazy stuff, why did I have to?

The mood lasted until I had to admit that, honestly, Kellas did have a point. Not that I wanted to admit it, but he really did. And, here all by myself, I was in a precarious enough situation. I probably didn't want to be all messed up and self-absorbed under the circumstances. Especially with what other craziness I might unknowingly have called in. That was a scary enough thought that I immediately drew a deep, shaky breath, swiped the snot off my nose and dried my eyes, and hastened up to my feet. Looked around, taking in my surroundings. Felt a quick sense of relief when I didn't see or hear anything terrifying nearby. Thank goodness.

Kellas had chosen here because it was close to the village and hid us from prying eyes, but honestly, I could not have asked for a handier place to work magic. Oak and ash trees formed the bulk of the small clump of trees, but thorn bushes crowded around the perimeter, creating a prickly barrier that would keep outsiders from pushing through. My Nan had told me that oak, ash, and thorn were three magical trees, and together they created the perfect place of power.

I reached over my shoulder and pulled out my lute, looked around for a convenient place to sit, and found a decent-sized boulder nearby. Plunking myself down there, I touched the lute's strings, tuned it a bit, strummed a chord, then another, looking for the right key. What song would call a dragon? And what could I possibly do to deal with it once it arrived? If it came, that is. Would my lute even know the five-note pentatonic scale on which traditional Chinese music was based? Wait, what? Where did that thought come from? What did I know of pentatonic scales? Listening carefully, I touched the strings again, asking the lute for the right notes ... and there they were. It was bouncy and happy and not at all what I had expected. My fingers flew over the strings, calling, calling. Come on, dragon, we need to get you home where you belong! My eyes closed; I was falling into the music now, hearing it, feeling it in my whole body, becoming the music ... somehow knowing the trees had joined in, filling in the harmony. Knowing that Kellas had rejoined me—even with my eyes shut I knew. Then, as I felt the song ending, another presence came into the circle of sound we had created. I played a final chord, let the sound die away, and opened my eyes.

Ten feet away stood a powerful looking Chinese man, dressed in a white shift heavily embroidered with a blue Chinese dragon down the front. I scrambled to my feet and bowed, thinking that was likely a good idea. He continued to stare at me silently. I noted a nasty long sword-like thing hanging from his waistband; a scimitar, maybe? But what did I know. Here was someone who had no business in Tír na nÓg, no more so than myself, and what was I supposed to do with him? It would have been a good idea to think this through before summoning him from who knows where. Not that this was going to help me now. I had to do something, but what?

Introductions. That might be a good place to start. I laid a hand on my chest and tried my unreliable voice, hoping the music magic I had just played might have translated again into a useable voice box, however transitory. "My name is Brannaugh." Yay! It worked!

His eyes narrowed, then he imitated me, laying a hand on his own chest. "Shen Long."

Kellas sidled nearer. "That's the azure dragon, dragon god of the east, rain, and new beginnings."

Oi. More gods. Just what I didn't need right now! "What do I do now?" I stage whispered.

"Maybe ask him?" Kellas sounded as uncertain as I felt myself.

Right. And did I know how to speak Mandarin? No. But I needed to communicate, so I just started babbling nervously.

"Shen Long, sir, I made a terrible mistake, and I am truly sorry, but it is my fault that you are here in this dimension. I want to help you return to your own place, but I am not sure how. Can you help?" My words tumbled over themselves in my haste to get them out. I could feel Kellas's astonishment and stole a quick glance at him from the corner of my eye.

"You're speaking Chinese," he said.

Really? Wonders never ceased. But we are talking magic, here! I shrugged and turned my full attention back on the dragon god. He'd not moved, nor did he even seem to acknowledge that I'd spoken to him. I wondered if I had somehow offended him ... gods being touchy creatures and all. In fact, other than introducing himself, he hadn't moved at all, like he was a statue or was frozen somehow. I watched him carefully for a full minute and he never even blinked. I started to raise one hand and he reacted, drawing his scimitar and bounding like an acrobat. In an instant the god's arm was clamped around my chest, his sword at my throat.

Twenty-Six

This was not going well.

"Stay where you are, or the girl dies." The dragon's voice was right in my ear. I could see Kellas, backing away, shaking his head slowly, and just at the edge of my peripheral vision: Cerridwen. Crap. Now things were really going south. She started forward, and the sword pressed harder on my throat.

"He says he'll kill me if you come closer," I squeaked out.

"It'll save me the trouble," she snarled.

Oh, lovely. "She says go ahead," I translated for the dragon god. "We're not besties," I added. "Please don't kill me though!"

I could feel his confusion, then a rush of anger. He released me with a violent shove that tossed me a good 10 feet to one side as he leapt into action, sword flashing, attacking Cerridwen. She immediately parried, energy crackling from her hands, blocking the dragon god's blows, and then counterattacking. Her magic came up against his sword like lightning, bursting apart like fireworks. The smell of sulfur and brimstone filled the air as the two struck, parried, and counterstruck, a blur of motion nearly impossible to follow.

I scrambled backward like a crab, then Kellas was beside me, yanking me to my feet. "We go now," he whispered, and ran, dragging me with him. We'd gotten less than a hundred yards before there was a swirl of dark energy and Knight appeared, blocking our path. Uiscias was riding him, holding the reins of a golden bridle that crackled with a sinister force. Knight's mouth gaped open as he did his best to avoid the cruel-looking wire bit that was savaging his tongue.

"Hello again," Uiscias drawled, a nasty smile twisting his face unpleasantly. "Going somewhere?"

Kellas hissed and shoved me behind him. It only made the druid's grimace wider. "It's not like you can escape me, or her ..." He nodded toward where Cerridwen was battling the dragon god. "Your days are numbered, earth girl. Then Fraegarthach will be mine again."

"I take it you two are working together on this?" Kellas spat angrily on the ground. "Coward."

A triumphant leer replaced the grimace. "One does as one must."

While the two were exchanging insults, I edged closer to Knight and tore the bridle off him in one swift motion. Knight reared with a triumphant scream and disappeared in a puff of dark energy, unceremoniously dropping the former wielder of Nuada's sword on his rear where he remained, temporarily stunned.

"How do you like them apples, horse thief?" I rapidly disassembled the bridle into its parts, stuffing the wire bit into my pocket and dropping the rest. I didn't want this obvious bit of magical artifice to get used against Knight ever again. My voice still worked, but for how long was anyone's guess. "C'mon Kellas, let's mosey."

On foot, we were unlikely to get very far once Cerridwen and the dragon god were done duking it out, and there was always Uiscias, but I'd rather walk away from a fight than engage, given a choice. Not that anybody else other than Kellas agreed.

Uiscias scrambled to his feet and ran after us, grabbing Kellas by one arm and slugging him in the face. The cat man collapsed in a heap. The druid grabbed me by my shirtfront, shoving his face close and breathing his nasty halitosis in my face. He drew a short dagger and held it up where I could see. "Say goodbye," he whispered.

I reached over my shoulder, pulled out my sword, transformed into my avatar, and threw the man backward like a toy. "Goodbye," I said gently, raising the sword high in an unmistakable threat. Uiscias took the hint, picking himself up and running away toward the burning town.

I sheathed the sword and helped a bloodied Kellas back to his feet. I offered him his handkerchief. "Lovely nosebleed."

"No kidding," he managed thickly, pressing the sodden cloth to his face. "Call that dark horse, and get us out of here, OK?"

Knight appeared immediately in his customary swirl of dark energy. I vaulted on, held an arm out for Kellas, who swung on behind me. "Let's go, big guy," I said to the horse. "Someplace safer than here." The dark horse obliged, breaking into an easy canter, taking us someplace safer. I hoped.

With Knight back, we once again had food and water readily available, so we steered clear of human habitation as best as we could for the remainder of the day. Not that we had any idea where we were going, or what we were supposed to be doing once we got there. Sound familiar? Let me assure you, it gets old quickly. We put as much terrain between us and the burning village as we thought reasonable, then holed up under what we hoped was an abandoned sheep shelter, not unlike the one where we'd slept the night before. Knight was off eating grass. Kellas and I had just finished supper and were sitting on the ground, our backs up against the stone wall of the shelter, watching the sun go down on yet another crazy day.

I'd lost the use of my vocal cords again, not a big surprise, given the vagaries of this dimension. We'd grown so accustomed to it that Kellas merely shifted back into cat form, and we continued our conversation telepathically, almost uninterrupted. Not that we talked much. Something was obviously bothering the cat man, and I realized he needed some quiet time to sort things out. It was pretty much my own way of handling crap as well, so we were both silent as the sun slipped behind the distant hills, lighting the sky up with a blaze of reds and oranges.

When it came, his thought was so unexpected that I startled. I could feel his amusement, but it was quickly gone. "There's something I need to tell you."

I sent him a sideways look that indicated I was listening.

"Before we left, Taliesin told me something."

"Um hmm?"

"The moon is waning. It's no longer full. You're getting younger again. We're running out of time, Brannaugh."

Oh, great. Oh, that's just ducky. Crap. *"How old do I look now?"* I asked.

"Twelve or 13. If we're lucky."

Oh, joy. I sat there motionless, feeling like the rug had been pulled out from under me ... again. This whole mess was so incredibly overwhelming.

"Brannaugh?"

I sighed gustily. *"Guess we need to figure this out, huh?"* Not that I had a clue what that might entail.

He grunted in agreement and we both fell silent again. Apparently, he didn't have any earth-shaking ideas either. It grew dark as we sat there, the stars winking into being one by one, until the sky was filled with a thousand brilliant points of light. No moon yet; it wouldn't be rising until later.

I'd always been a bit of a list maker. It helped me keep track of what needed doing. *"OK. Number one: How many critters do we have to find and send back where they belong or destroy before they destroy Tír na nÓg. Two: How exactly are we supposed to do that anyways? Three: Why can't I keep my voice going? And how is it I can speak Chinese now? Four: How do we get back home? Five: What happens if we can't do this fast enough and I de-age to a baby or even less than a baby ... what happens then?"*

Kellas grunted. Well, that was helpful!

"Got any ideas, cat man?" I nudged him with an elbow.

"Not many," he admitted. "One: we have no idea what you let in, or how many, or where they are. Two: Doesn't what we do depend on what we find? Three: your voice is the least of our worries right now. Four: I have no ruddy idea how. Five: I don't even want to consider that one. We need to fix this in the next few days, or we're toast, kiddo."

"Well, that was encouraging."

He grunted in agreement. "Just sayin'."

We sat in silence a short time longer. I was pondering the day's events, and something struck me. *"How do you suppose Cerridwen knew how to find us today?"*

"Maybe the fire? Maybe the dragon god? Maybe your music? Who the heck knows … but she's definitely out to get you. Uiscias, the giant jerk, is bound and determined to get that lute sword back, which means you need to be dead. From the looks of the fireworks when you tried to give it back before, it has decided you are its person and won't give you up unless you are dead. That's how Uiscias lost possession. He died on the battlefield. The Morrigan grabbed it and brought it to Taliesin."

"Why didn't it adopt Taliesin?"

"Unimportant. Let's stick to the immediate issues, OK?"

"'Let's stick to the immediate issues, OK?'" I parroted in disgust, making a disparaging expression, which he ignored. Of course.

We both fell silent again, deep in our own thoughts. Mine kept going around in circles, not coming up with any possible solutions. I was feeling more and more helpless about the whole thing. Sitting with my back up against stone wasn't exactly comfortable either. I shifted irritably and heard the lute chime softly. I pulled it out and settled it on my lap, hugging it close as if it were a cuddle bear. It chimed again, a bit louder this time, making me loosen my hug and draw back, puzzled. Another chime! Was the lute asking me to play it? Possibly. Shrugging, I positioned my hands and strummed a quiet chord. Felt my mood lift just the tiniest bit. OK. Music! What to play, I thought at my marvelous magical instrument. The notes came slowly at first, stringing together into a tune I didn't quite remember, if I had even known it in the first place. The lute boasted a much larger repertoire than I'd ever had. It still needed me to call it forth, though, so I listened hard, reaching out into the ether, listening for the notes as they formed a lilting melody.

I was singing full throated now, and the landscape around me joined in, yes, even the stones at my back.

The song ended, the final notes fading into the darkness, leaving only a sense of peacefulness behind.

"Sweet." Kellas had changed back into man form. "You might have attracted the crazies to us again by playing, but your music was nice while it lasted."

"I'll never get tired of it."

"The crazies?" he teased.

"The music, cat man." I sent him a snarky look. He just chuckled. We sat in a companionable silence for a while longer until he sighed, heaved himself to his feet, and extended a hand to help me up.

"You need to sleep. I'll take first watch. No," he cut my protest off even before I could get it out. "You need to be rested when we take on the rest of this mission. I can't play that lute, and that's the only way we're gonna fix this mess we're in."

'We.' Not just 'you.' That felt good.

I reluctantly agreed to his schedule, not that I had any say in the matter when his mind was made up. Incredibly, I fell asleep almost as soon as I lay down. He woke me up several hours later and we traded places. He curled up in cat form and was asleep immediately.

The moon had risen, no longer full, a big flat spot on its right side. Waning. Like me. How was I ever going to get used to this? What a price to pay for magic.

The landscape was shining with reflected silver light, quiet, its music peaceful. No scary things anywhere nearby. I could see Knight grazing nearby and walked over to join him. He lifted his head and looked at me as I approached.

"Hey there, big guy." I stroked his shoulder. *"How are you doing? Crazy days, eh?"*

He snorted softly and dropped his head for more grass. I got the impression that "crazy" was just a way of life for him.

"I've got to fix my muck up somehow." I was absentmindedly scratching his back. He leaned into it, liking it. *"I need to find the things that got in, but I have no idea how."*

He snorted again, and this time it sounded disgusted. Was he annoyed at me for messing things up? No ... it felt like maybe he knew something I didn't. *"Ideas?"* I stopped scratching him.

He raised his head again and gave me an impatient shove with his nose. Apparently, I was not to stop the scratching. I quickly resumed. *"Do you know where to find these things?"*

He huffed.

"So you can?"

Another huff, more impatient this time. OK! Apparently, he could.

"Alright, then, when the sun comes up, you take us where we need to go next." I stopped pestering him then and concentrated on giving him a nice scratchy scratching in all the usual itchy places.

Twenty-Seven

Kellas woke up as the eastern horizon was becoming lighter, full daylight a long way off still. We ate a breakfast of bread and cheese, then I saddled Knight, and we headed out, letting the dark horse decide what direction to head in. He was in a hurry, often pawing the ground impatiently whenever we had to wait for Kellas, who could not keep up with the horse despite being a strong runner. By noontime, the cat man was red-faced and streaming sweat, and in an ugly mood besides.

We'd stopped by a large lake where we could drink and refill our water containers. I'd pulled out our food bag and started to take lunch things out when Kellas surprised me by stripping down to his undershorts and wading into the water. Having just drunk from that water, I knew it was plenty cold … nothing I'd want to take a swim in. As he was in man form, I could not ask him if he'd lost his mind; I just watched as he waded in waist deep, then struck off in a smooth crawl farther from shore. Never a strong swimmer myself, it worried me, but it wasn't until the music around me changed that I got scared.

It wasn't much at first, just an ominous "bump, bump" under the background music. I stopped eating and listened. There it came again.

Closer this time: "bump-bump, bump-bump." Where had I heard that before, that ominous sound that meant something awful was about to happen? Then it struck me, and I was on my feet in one motion, jumping up and down, waving my arms wildly, trying to get Kellas's attention. He saw me and waved back before diving under the water and coming back up with a hearty splash.

Oh gods no. Not a good time to be voiceless! I grabbed my lute from its hiding place and jammed my hands over the strings in a horrible jangle of sound. "Shark!!!" I screamed. "*Jaws*! Get out of the water NOW!!!"

Fortunately, sound travels over water better than over land, so he heard me. Not that he immediately believed me, wasting precious time looking about as he treaded water. He glanced back at me, holding both hands up in an expression of "What do you mean?"

Then I saw a dorsal fin break the water surface and I pointed. "There! There!"

Kellas turned his head, saw the fin, and immediately started swimming for shore.

Not fast enough, though. The shark was gaining on him, catching up when Kellas had only gotten halfway to shore, ramming into him like a speeding car hitting a deer. Kellas was thrown into the air before falling back into the water and sinking out of sight. I ran into the shallows, screaming in horror. My friend was drowning, about to be eaten by a giant white shark, and I could do nothing. Nothing! I was not a strong enough swimmer, nowhere near as good as Kellas.

Knight had joined me in the shallows, trumpeting in alarm, but he didn't venture farther out either.

Something streaked by me and dove into the water, disappearing under the surface before I could get more than a glimpse. There was a moment of nothing, then a huge splash as the great white broke the surface and crashed over onto its back, something clinging to it, then nothing but waves until the shark broke the surface again, not as high, and fell over onto its side, sinking below the waves. The waves smoothed out, the water surface returning to a glassy stillness.

I turned and threw my arms around Knight's neck, sobbing. My friend was gone because I had brought monsters into this realm.

"A little help here, please?" Somehow, the voice pierced through my pity party, and a good thing it did. I whirled and saw a small woman struggling out of the water, dragging Kellas's limp body by one arm.

Kellas! I ran over and grabbed his other arm. Together we pulled him up on shore and laid him down on his back. The woman immediately started mouth-to-mouth resuscitation, while all I could do was stand by watching, unable to do anything at all to help. It felt like forever before Kellas started coughing and rolled over on his side, spitting out a ghastly amount of water.

I groaned and sank to my knees, overwhelmed by the sheer whiplash of this experience. Oh my gods, goddessess, whoever might be looking out for me (if any were, which was debatable)—this was too much. Kellas had almost died, and I'd been no help at all. I'd never felt so useless.

"There, there ..." the woman said sweetly, rubbing Kellas's back. "It's OK, just get it all out. Silly kitty ... I could have caught you some fish if you were hungry."

Kellas uttered a purring noise that made me do a double take. You know that happy sound that cats make when you give them food or scratch them in just the right place? It wasn't quite like that—there was a human edge to the pleased noise, dopey and bleary, that sounded like all his dreams had come true. It was so absurdly unlike him that the bit of hysteria I'd been working myself into dissipated instantly into stunned disbelief. I watched as the Kellas I thought I knew rolled over and sat up, a dopey, lovestruck expression on his face.

"You were very brave," The woman crooned, moving a bit of his wet hair away from his face. "Let's go back to my place and get you wrapped up in a warm blanket! The cold is hard on kitty cats. You deserve a nice, long rest."

"Ah ... thank you ...?" I mumbled, not quite sure I was excited about this prospect. Also, I was not sure she could hear me anyways.

The woman sent a brief glance my way, her expression hard. "Why are you still here?" Her voice was waspish and unkind, but then she went right back to cooing at Kellas as if I weren't there. I'd love to say that I got all indignant, but honestly, I was still processing the uncharacteristic purring sound Kellas was making.

"Issat you, Erin?" Kellas coughed. His voice was slurred like he'd drunk too much beer. He slung an arm around the woman's neck.

A brief scowl crossed his savior's face, then the icky sweet smile was immediately back in place. "Never mind Erin, whoever she is. I'm your sweetheart now. Come now, let's go home." She heaved him onto his feet, staggering under his weight, but managing, nevertheless. Considering he outweighed her probably two to one, that was impressive. Not that my brain computed this fact just yet.

"Wait ..." I protested, scrambling to my feet. *"We have to keep moving. I mean, it's not safe ..."*

Kellas still had that dopey smile plastered all over his face, completely free of his usual sarcasm, and I had no idea why. Apparently, my brain had stuck up a blue screen notice and shut down for repairs.

"Soundhs nishe," he slurred.

Knight blustered loudly and stomped his hoof; leaving Kellas with his new admirer obviously suited him just fine. I clenched and unclenched my fists, wishing I could whup the cat man upside the head to fix whatever the dickens was wrong with him ... then abruptly noticed how sticky my fingers were. There was *something* winding around my fingers, so clear as to be barely noticeable. Sunlight glinted along thin strands of something that looked suspiciously like a spiderweb. Looking down, I saw a lot more of the same on the grass around where we stood. I tracked the thread through the grass, right to the woman ...

"You're a SPIDER!" I yelled. Silently of course.

Apparently, she could hear my thought yelling, because the woman's head snapped toward me and she snarled, revealing an impressive set of incisors. Adrenaline instantly cleared my head of confusion. I ran over and grabbed Kellas by the arm, horrified by the sheer amount of web she'd already managed to tangle him up in. I couldn't believe I let myself zone out. What was I expecting?! A normal person to help us in this realm? Get real, girl!

"Bran ... whassamatter?" Kellas wobbled between the spider woman and me, terribly unsteady on his feet. I glared at him; his utter stupidity in the face of our obvious danger was infuriating. That's when I saw the blood trickling down his neck from something that looked suspiciously like a bite.

Spiders bite. They use venom to immobilize their prey ... Yeah. We were in even bigger trouble than I'd realized.

That thought gave me the strength to yank him away from Spider Woman and shove him behind me. She shrieked in indignation, her body warping into a fat round blob, spidery limbs bursting out of her back and lifting her off the grass.

"MINE!" she screeched, grabbing a fistful of her web and pulling hard.

Kellas flopped down on his face in the grass as he was yanked toward her like a rag doll. I frantically clawed at the threads that connected her to Kellas. They weren't hard to cut, but as soon as I broke some, more appeared out of her spinnerets, sticking to me, to Kellas, to everything around us.

"You saved him, but that doesn't mean it's OK to eat him!" I continued to tear at the web being thrown our way in copious quantities. I was getting badly tangled up in all of it. Before long I would be as wrapped up in it as Kellas was. I had to come up with a better solution quickly, or we'd both be spider food. From the crafty look on the spider's face, she knew this, too, and was counting on it. I didn't want to kill Kellas's rescuer, but felt I no longer had another viable option.

I struggled to reach over my shoulder and pulled Fraegarthach free, nearly crying in relief when I managed to do so. The web that had begun to wrap me up in a cocoon broke loose as I transformed into my avatar, the threads shriveling to nothing as the magic blade touched them. Swinging the sword in large looping circles, I drove the spider woman away from Kellas, melting her webs in the process. She clacked her mandibles at me, hissing angrily but staying well beyond the blade's reach, which suited me fine. She was just trying to eat. Just not me and Kellas, if I could help it!

I retreated closer to Kellas, still threatening the spider with my sword should she try to rush me. Calling Knight close, I grabbed Kellas around the waist and tossed him unceremoniously over the saddle, then gathered up our food bag and his clothes where he'd dropped them.

That taken care of, Knight and I backed slowly away from the giant spider until we were far enough out that I felt safe sheathing the sword. Leaping up on Knight's back, I urged him into a flat-out gallop away from the spider, the lake with a white shark weirdly able to live in fresh water, and yet another much too close a call for comfort.

Twenty-Eight

It took hours for the spider venom to wear off, but once it did, Kellas had the mother of all hangovers. It necessitated far slower progress than I would have liked. I was good, though. I did not say "I told you so." I didn't even yell at him for making poor choices. I did admit to feeling a touch grumpy that he'd found a spider more appealing than yours truly, but there was that age gap he'd mentioned, maybe made more apparent by my having de-aged yet another year during this latest disaster so I now looked more like 10 or 11. Phooey.

Knight seemed more than happy to be on the road again, trotting along like he could do it all day. I made him stop frequently to wait for Kellas this time, only too aware of how the cat man had been hot and grouchy after chasing after the horse all morning, and how it had landed us in the spider situation.

We'd managed to escape the spider by the skin of our teeth. I had no way of knowing if her bite had killed *Jaws*, or if the shark had merely retreated for a while to recover. Either way, the two remained in Tír na nÓg and posed a threat to its residents. I needed to fix this somehow, but how?

Then it hit me like a runaway truck. The link between everything was my movie addiction, particularly scary movies. Every single one of the creepies we'd encountered so far had been the cause of nightmares. You'd think I'd have put two and two together and quit watching those stupid flicks ... Wait just one stinking minute!!

I dug my seat bones deep in the saddle and hauled back on the neck rope, pulling Knight up short and eliciting a snort of protest for my less than polite request. Sliding down, I marched up to face the dark horse, going nose to long nose with him.

"You know where the creepies are because the night mares brought them here!" I thought-shouted at him. He blustered in disgust. Apparently, I was a bit dense. Of course, they'd brought the creepies. I'd asked them to! My own nightmares, brought here by the night mares, at my request.

It was a devastating revelation. Fear made real.

Kellas caught up to us and switched into cat form.

"What's going on?" he asked.

"I know what we need to find, now." I wished I had paper and pencil to write down the list that was forming in my head. *"The weres, the mummies, Shen Long,* Jaws, *the spider woman, they all got dumped here from my old nightmares. Which means we need to find ..."* I paused then counted them off on my fingers *"Aliens, all sorts. But the worst ones are from the movie* Aliens, *with Sigourney Weaver. Those guys really freaked me out. Then there is Steven King's* Carrie ... *yikes. Demons from* The Golden Child. *Witches and flying monkeys from* The Wizard of Oz. *And Barney the purple dinosaur."*

"Not the Stay Puft Marshmallow Man?" Kellas remarked drily.

"No, he was just dumb, but the two gargoyles were pretty freaky."

"Can we hope they didn't ALL get through?"

I nodded vigorously. To face every single boogeyman I'd ever been terrified by ... nope! Did not want to go there. Not that I found Barney terrifying any longer. I'd been pretty young. Now I just found him annoying.

I clambered back up on Knight and we continued. I wasn't paying attention to our surroundings any longer, counting on Kellas to keep an eye out for nasties while I desperately tried to sort out the mess I'd caused ... and what I could do to fix it. Would singing work? Like I'd done in my dream back at Nan's when I'd killed off those ghouls? Did I have to fight everything, like I'd done the weres and the mummies, like a real world "video game" where the price of getting it wrong wasn't just losing a game, but my life? What about Shen Long? I didn't want to kill him; he wasn't a bad guy just because I'd been frightened of him in a long-ago movie. Somehow, I needed to just get him back into his own dimension. But how?

A wave of despair suddenly washed over me. I was terribly, horribly homesick. I wished I had my family close-by to ask what I should do. If only this dimension could arrange a video meeting! Or (this thought burst into my brain like fireworks), I could simply arrange a meet-up in that dream dimension I'd visited with Iku last week.

"I need to take a nap! Right now!" I exclaimed enthusiastically, my thought so sudden and strong that Kellas, who had been walking along next to me in cat form, jumped like he'd been stung. Knight shuddered a bit too, as if my thought had taken him by surprise as well. Normally I would have laughed at the cat man's reaction, but my enthusiasm for this latest idea pushed the temptation for glee aside. *"Maybe Nan or Iku will know what I need to do to send these creatures back to their own dimensions. I just need to arrange a meeting in my dreams."*

"In your dreams," the cat repeated, putting a different spin on the old "like that's gonna happen" response. "How are you going to arrange that?"

I honestly didn't know the answer to that one, so I shrugged. *"It just happened, before. Maybe if I lay down thinking about it, then once I fall asleep it'll work?"*

I sensed Kellas's dubious reaction to that harebrained plan. Knight blustered loudly, like he was laughing at me. *"You have a better idea?"* I demanded a bit huffily. The dark horse bobbed his head up and down. Yup, he did. *"And what, pray, would that be?"*

He stopped in the middle of the road and shook himself vigorously, the way a horse does when its back is itchy after a hard workout. It really rattles the brain and shakes your seat. I'd hated it as a kid because it about tosses you off. I'd called it the "wiggle-woggle-itchy" shake.

"Hey! Knock that off!" I protested, and he proceeded to repeat the motion. Dang, horse! *"What's going on?"*

Knight merely tossed his head in irritation. Apparently, I was being dense. He hunched his back and did the tiniest buck. Like he was telling me to get the heck off. Oh! He *did* want me to get off. Man, I *was* dense.

I slid down and stood next to his shoulder. *"OK, now what?"*

He didn't respond. Instead, he gathered himself into a bunch and launched himself skyward ... and disappeared.

"Apparently, he can leave this dimension," Kellas commented and started walking again.

I scurried up next to him. *"He couldn't before, at Taliesin's."*

"You were riding him then," Kellas said, as if that explained everything.

I made a hissing sound through my teeth, and he grinned. Yeah, cats can grin! It's a very smug expression, and pretty darned annoying when you are trying to get a question answered.

He let me hang for a minute, then relented. "Apparently, it's only you who are prevented from leaving," he explained. "The demon spawn can go anytime he wants to. Maybe I could as well, but I won't, because even cait sidhe have standards." The suggestion was that dark horses did not, but I let that slide. Knight surely would not have appreciated the slam. "You said you wanted to take a nap." He pointed at a nearby grove of trees, just off the road we were on. "Would that work for you? I can't imagine the horse will need a lot of time to fetch Amaris or your Iku."

Which is why at mid-afternoon I was curled up in a comfy spot on the ground in a grove of oak trees, doing my best to fall asleep ... and failing miserably. I was simply too excited. This went on for about 10 minutes until I rolled over onto my belly and looked at Kellas , who was sitting nearby. *"It's not working. I can't fall asleep!"*

Kellas made the sneezing sound through his nose that meant he was unimpressed, then he did something entirely unexpected. He came over, stepped up on my back, sprawled out like I was a cat bed, and started to purr. Mind you, Kellas is an unusually large cat, so he weighs a lot more than your normal cat. Initially it was disconcerting to have him plunked down on my back, plus his weight made breathing a bit challenging, but as his purring continued, I started to relax and breathe more slowly and deeply.

I floated down to the ground in the same spot where I'd met Iku in my dream a week earlier. This time I was alone, however. Everything was as beautiful as I remembered it, the land before time completely unsullied by human machinations. The mountains rose high and sharp above me, the trees dark green and vigorous, the stream clear and pure, tumbling over rocks nearby. I settled myself onto a patch of grass that had been mown short by grazing animals. I knew this because I saw something that looked like deer droppings off to one side. I waited ... and waited. And waited some more. Knight! Where the heck are you?

A moose and her calf wandered out of the woods and went to the stream to drink. Despite her size and ungainly appearance, the female moose moved with grace and dignity. Her baby bucked and gamboled about the clearing, clearly enjoying life and the space to mess around. His mother merely looked around, water dripping from her muzzle, then left the stream to graze, her head coming up after each mouthful to watch for possible danger.

She saw it before I was even aware it was anywhere near: a huge grizzly running at the calf, intent on having it for breakfast. The mother moose was in motion immediately, rushing headlong at the bear, which immediately turned tail and ran off. Mother moose did not go far; she wasn't about to leave her baby vulnerable to other possible attackers. The bear didn't give up easily, however. It kept sneaking around, occasionally getting too close, whereupon the moose would bluff rush it again and drive it off. I wondered what she could possibly do to the grizzly if her bluffing wasn't enough. Not that I wanted to find out ... I had always been afraid of bears, unless they were of the stuffed variety made for cuddling up to in bed. How exhausting it must be for the moose, always under attack, always having to be on guard.

I don't know why it took me as long as it did, but I suddenly realized the grizzly was getting closer to where I sat, and I had no mother moose around to protect me! I slowly rose to my feet when I thought the bear was looking elsewhere, backing away toward the edge of the woods, hoping to disappear among the trees before it realized I was there. Gaining the shelter of the trees, I broke into a trot, hoping to put as much distance between myself and the drama unfolding behind me as I could.

Where the heck were Knight and my grandmothers, though? This idea was becoming less fantastic the longer I stayed here. Why Iku thought we'd be safe in this dimension was beyond my understanding … that bear certainly wasn't "safe" by any means. What if there was a cougar or something? What if it were coming after me?

There was a hideous growl from behind me and suddenly there were claws digging into my back and shoulders. I screamed in terror …

Twenty-Nine

I woke up, throwing myself sideways, dislodging Kellas who was still in cat form, his claws ripping holes in my skin. *"Ow, cat man! What was that for?"*

"Company," he thought at me, backing away, a deep growl sounding from his throat. I scrambled to my feet and followed his gaze.

It was the dragon god. He was standing maybe 15 feet away among the trees, one hand resting on his scimitar. His expression revealed nothing about what he might be thinking or his intentions.

I raised my right hand in a tiny wave. *"Hi."* Yeah, like he could hear me!

Yet he nodded as though he could and took his hand off the hilt of his sword. "What is a 'bestie?'" he asked.

Honestly, that is what he said. Could have knocked me over with a feather right about then! I held up one finger in the "wait a moment" gesture, pulled out my lute and strummed a pentatonic chord. "It means a good friend."

"So when you said, "not a bestie, does that mean you are enemies?" He looked puzzled.

I shrugged. "Mostly that we're not particularly fond of each other. Not necessarily enemies, but not buddies either."

"Buddies?" he repeated.

Oi! This was going to get complicated in a hurry if I didn't figure out a way to trim slang out of my language. "Also means 'friend,'" I told him.

"Then why not say so?" His expression turned impatient.

"I did! Never mind," I added hastily, as his hand started moving toward the scimitar again. "Mr. Shen Long, sir, is there something else?"

He made a slight bow and started pacing back and forth. "Before that white witch so rudely interrupted us, you said that *you* were the reason I have been torn away from my dimension into this one. Explain. Quickly. We may not have much time before she catches up again."

"I made a mistake, I was angry at Cerridwen ... that white witch ... and I was playing this," I indicated the lute "... thinking angry thoughts. It just happened. I didn't realize I was working magic. I didn't know I was calling in scary things from my nightmares, it *just happened.*" Dang, there went my voice again. I strummed another chord. "It was an accident." I finished.

He sent me a thoughtful stare. "I am not accustomed to being somebody's nightmare. Where I come from, people revere me."

I winced. "I realize that now, sir. I apologize."

"But obviously here, in this dimension, the people fear me. Why is that?"

I felt Kellas edge closer, lean up against my ankles. I glanced down, but he wasn't looking at me. "In this dimension, people like you ... dragons, that is ... are not nice. They burn down villages and eat people."

He scowled. "That is distasteful to me! I bring the rain so that crops may grow and feed my people. I do not burn anything! I do not kill ... well, not as a usual thing. You must tell these people not to fear me."

Yeah, wow. Like that was going to be an easy task! "How?"

He gestured at my lute. "Sing to them. All people love songs. Sing to them about my goodness and how I take care of them. They will listen." He struck a noble-looking pose. "After all, I am a god!"

Yeah, and people feared gods as a standard sort of thing. Not that I was going to tell Shen Long this! Not if I wanted to keep my head. I bowed, instead. "I will *do my best,*" I said, as my voice failed me yet again. I strummed another hasty chord. "Yes, sir."

He cocked his head as if listening. "She comes. I will go now. Do as I have ordered!" And just like that, he was gone. Poof. Like he had never been there.

Kellas shook himself like a dog. "We need to disappear also," he said. "I smell Cerridwen."

As I could hear her solo violin joining the music that surrounded me, I knew he was right about that. I hastened after him, wondering how Cerridwen must smell given that he was able to smell her at a distance. It must be quite the body odor!

Kellas sneezed violently. "The lady likes her perfume a little too much," he said, and sneezed again. "Hurry up! Where is that ruddy demon spawn of a horse?"

I was caught off guard a moment until I remembered that he could read my thoughts while in cat form. Really needed to be on guard about that little detail! *I don't know. He never showed up in the land before time. Neither did Iku or Nan. Just a moose mom, her calf, and a grizzly bear. The bear kept attacking and the moose kept driving him off.*

"Try calling him, maybe? She's getting way too close for comfort."

I did, but there was no response. Maybe Uiscias had caught him again? I sure hoped not!

Kellas abruptly launched himself off the road, disappearing into a drainage pipe. He popped his head out for a fraction of a second to hiss at me when I didn't immediately follow him. Apparently, I was to join him in the pipe. I jumped down and crawled in on my hands and knees, grumbling quietly at how the water was several inches deep in the bottom and I could not avoid getting soaked from the knees down.

"Shh!" he instructed impatiently. We stayed there, water gurgling past us, until I could hear a carriage approaching, multiple horses' hooves clippity-clopping along at a fast pace. The rig passed overhead and continued down the road without stopping.

We remained in the pipe for what seemed an eternity until Kellas finally squeezed past me out the end of the pipe. I wasn't able to turn around, as the pipe was too narrow, so I backed out, cursing in my mind about the wet and the mud. I got to my feet and bent over to rinse the mud off my hands, but there was nothing I could do about my jeans.

They'd dry out eventually, but in the meantime, they were a muddy, soaking wet, nasty-feeling mess.

"Quitcher bellyaching, buttercup." Kellas was not in a good mood either. He was shaking his paws one by one, also not fond of the wetness. "She's gone for now. We need to get a move on. What did that dragon guy say? Anything helpful?"

We climbed back up to the road and set off in the same direction the carriage had gone. *"He wanted to know what a 'bestie' was. And he wants me to tell everyone how wonderful he is, so they stop trying to kill him."*

"Nothing like another impossible assignment to brighten the day," he muttered.

"Ya think?" I agreed. *"And the trip to that land before time was a total bust, too."*

"Maybe not," he mused. "Perhaps the moose and the bear were sent as messengers instead."

My confusion must have been obvious because he snorted in laughter. "For a Native girl, you sure don't know much about animal symbolism."

"Mom never set much stock in such things."

"Despite being Native herself?"

I thought about that for a bit. When I considered it, Mom seemed to have rejected a whole lot of her Native heritage, like somehow it was beneath her or something. Like how she dismissed Iku's shamanism, calling it "woo woo." How she wouldn't speak the Hidatsa language. How she insisted on my "sticking to the facts" when I tried to tell her about a dream I'd had. Dismissed anything remotely out of the ordinary as my imagination running away with me. Why was that?

"Sounds like something happened to her that she hasn't shared with you," Kellas said, reading my thoughts again. "But let's cut to the chase here, OK? You saw a moose. What about the following makes sense to you? You are the one to make your own choices, or you need to work on your self-esteem ... be proud of who you are. That you also saw a calf suggests we may be catching a lucky break soon. The bear, especially a grizzly, suggests that you are stronger than you realize, that you must claim your power if you are to succeed. And since the bear was attacking our lucky break, you might want to work on all the above in a hurry, or we might not get that lucky break after all."

"Is that all?" I was more than a little overwhelmed.

"Heck no. That's the short version. The long version would take too long, and we need to get a move on."

Which we did. I wasn't happy about having to hoof it, especially since Kellas was pushing the pace beyond my comfort level. Periodically, I'd holler for Knight, as if he were a dog gone off chasing a squirrel, but he never showed up. That meant we were without our food bag again, which was "not my favorite," to put it delicately.

Finally, I hauled up as we were climbing a steep hill at record speed. I leaned over, gasping for air, my hands braced on my knees. *"Where's ... the fire, cat man? ... Gads!"*

Kellas stopped to wait for me, practically bristling with impatience. "You're a ruddy cream puff, you know that?"

"And you're ruddy insane, you know that?"

"Oh, grow up, why don't you?"

"I'd love to ... but there's this little problem I have, maybe you haven't noticed?"

"Oh, I've noticed." A note of worry crept into his voice, tempering the impatience enough that my own crabbiness relented a little.

"How bad is it now?"

"You're maybe eight. Emphasis on the 'maybe.'"

Eight. I was de-aging faster than I had expected, or maybe I had just been hoping I wouldn't. *"Do we even know where we are going?"*

"Someplace where I can hide you until you start getting older again." Again, that note of concern that had the weird effect of warming me to him even while I was deeply annoyed at his pushiness.

"And where is that?"

Had he arms currently, I think he would have thrown them up in frustration. "I have no ruddy idea! Now, can we get moving again before something swoops down from the sky and eats you? Oh, sh..." He began to swear as a giant shadow swept over us and was gone. He switched to man form, grabbed my hand, and dragged me after him into a barn by the side of the road we'd been climbing. "Pterodactyl," he spat out, along with a string of expletives that would have had my mother reaching for her soap.

Thirty

A dinosaur. That one I'd not remembered. Pterodactyls and velociraptors, to be precise. Why not T. rexes, I'm not sure, but my nightmares after watching *Jurassic Park* had featured only those two. I guess I had to be grateful for small favors. Not that it was much of a favor, as both were seriously effective predators.

We sat just inside the barn door peering out for maybe 10 minutes or so while I got more and more antsy and irritable. This wasn't helping! We were getting nowhere, I was getting hangry again, and ... geez!

I jumped to my feet and strode out onto the road, staring up at the sky. Kellas was yelling at me not to be an idiot. *"Hey, you! Pterodactyl!"* Oh, crum. The giant bird wasn't likely to be impressed by my thought yelling. I pulled out my lute and strummed a chord. "Hey, dino! Yeah you, creep! You don't belong here. You're not real, you're just a bad dream. You need to disappear yourself and never come back, ya hear me? Go! Scram!" I glared up at the sky, looking for it, not seeing it and getting even more irritated. "Hit the road, Jack!" Which struck me as an appropriate sort of song to banish things, so I started singing the Ray Charles song at the top of my lungs. Maybe it would help get all these creepy critters out of Tír na nÓg. Worth a try anyway.

Kellas had cautiously joined me out in the road and joined in on the song's repartee.

He had me in stitches. I was having trouble singing my bits. Kellas saw that and started hamming it up.

A giant shadow passed overhead, and a moment later, the pterodactyl landed on the road nearby and folded its wings. We paused, and my lute made a horrible twanging noise. Nope, not a good time to stop playing! I continued.

The bird took a step closer and let out the sort of hideous screech that could turn your blood to ice.

It had the opposite effect on me. I jammed my hand over the strings in one powerful last chord and yelled "GIT!"

The bird exploded in a blizzard of colorful confetti, which the breeze picked up and tossed around in a small whirlwind until dispersing, leaving bits of paper scattered across the road and on the grass nearby.

Kellas and I stood there like we'd been frozen, until he started clapping slowly. "Way to bluff rush the bear, mama moose!"

"Paper," I said, completely baffled. "Why paper? It makes no sense!"

"How does any of this make sense, Brannaugh? You're asking a magical realm to act science based. It doesn't work that way. C'mon." Kellas started off walking again, but I didn't follow. After a moment he realized I wasn't with him. He turned and started walking backward. "Coming?"

My answer was to fold my legs and sit down in the middle of the road. There was something I was missing. Something important. What the dickens was it?

Kellas sighed loudly and sauntered back to where I was parked in the road. "OK, out with it. What's going on in that stubborn wee brain of yours?"

"Paper tigers," I exclaimed, and scrambled to my feet. "What if they're all just paper tigers?" Stashing my lute in its hiding place, I took off walking fast, just needing to move my feet while my brain worked on this latest detail at a furious pace.

Kellas caught up. "OK, so what does that mean? Paper tigers?"

I rolled both hands in an "I'm really not sure" gesture. "What if they just seem scary? What if it's all bluffing, like the momma moose? What if all I need to do is call their bluff?"

"Like *Jaws*? That sure didn't feel like the shark was bluffing. Or those werewolves, either."

"Maybe because we gave them power with how we reacted to them?" I glanced at Kellas to see how he reacted to that bit, saw the Oh! expression cross his face. "Yeah? What if we stopped being afraid of them and started just, well, standing up to them?"

A chirruping sound behind us had us both whirling to see several velociraptors stalking us. Kellas grabbed my arm. "Run!"

"Nope!" I shook my arm free and took a threatening step closer to the dinosaurs. "Git!" I ordered in as commanding a voice as I could manage. Hard to sound commanding when your voice quavers.

They didn't "git." No, they did not. Instead, they crept closer, making that chirruping sound like a gatling of woodpeckers, as if discussing who was going to get the first bite. Somehow, that just really ticked me off. I reached over my shoulder and drew Fraegarthach, transforming with breathtaking speed into my avatar. "I. Said. GIT!" I ordered in that ragged otherworldly voice that was mine yet wasn't.

They got "git," in an impressive explosion of colorful confetti many times bigger than the one the pterodactyl had made. Which made sense after all, as there had been three of them and only one of him. The breezes had a merry old time of it, twirling the bits about in multiple little whirlwinds and eddies until the whole mess was spread far and wide.

As the paper started to settle, Shen Long materialized briefly in front of me, long enough to bow gracefully before he faded away. Oh, good. He was going home, too. As he faded away, so did the confetti, until there was nothing left to indicate anything had been there. All around me, the music took on a triumphant melody, not unlike Beethoven's "Ode To Joy." The nasties were gone. All of them. I was sure of it.

Smiling, I sheathed my sword and shrunk back down to size.

"Dang, girl!" Kellas sounded impressed.

"I know, right?" Couldn't help myself, I was strutting just a little bit as we started off down the road again to lord only knew where. Song welled up inside me like a huge bubble of joy, and I was singing again: Sia's "Unstoppable." Because, at least for now, I was.

Thirty-One

The fine mood lasted the rest of the afternoon until the rumbling of my stomach could no longer be ignored. Knight still hadn't returned. I wasn't sure if I were more irritated at him for having abandoned us or for taking off with our food bag. "We need to find food," I exclaimed after a particularly noisy complaint from my innards.

"I would concur," the cat man agreed. "At the next town we come to, we will get something, somehow."

"And how far is that?"

"No idea."

Swell. I was about to explode in a flurry of nasty comments about the dark horse and selfishness and, and, and ... when Kellas stopped suddenly. He changed back into his man form and turned a frowning gaze on me. "Say that again," he ordered.

"Say what again?" I pressed both hands against my belly as it once again gurgled loudly.

A broad grin crossed his face. "All right! Somebody has her voice back!"

That caught me by surprise. Maybe because Kellas and I had gotten so comfortable with our weird telepathic communication that I simply hadn't been aware that I had been using my voice well after the effects of the lute's magic had typically worn off. "I do? But how? What changed?"

"Who cares? You have it back. C'mon, I'm getting hungry too, and a meal of mouse is not appealing to me right now." He started off.

I jogged to catch up. "But what if it doesn't stay?"

He just shot me a sideways glance that said clearer than words that my fussing was silly. Which in fact it probably was, but he'd not been deprived of a functioning voice box. I proceeded to use that voice, babbling on and on about anything at all, just to hear my own very special lilt. Kellas bore up under it well; perhaps he understood how I felt after all. I was so happy, I started skipping. "Wasn't that so cool, when I said GIT and they went POOF and ... gads, what a mess ... oh my gosh that felt so great! And now I don't have to kill anything! Did I ever tell you how I hate, hate, hate killing things? Even bugs. Well, maybe not biting flies ... especially horseflies, the ones that come in like helicopters ..." Here I demonstrated, making a hideous buzzing noise and running around Kellas in circles. "Buzzing and buzzing and then landing and biting like they have teeth the size of a T. rex ... gads, how I loathe those things. You have to smack them really fast, and then grind down with your hand so you damage them, because if you just slap them, they come back for more, and it drives your poor horse crazy and ..."

At this point Kellas started laughing helplessly. "Slow down, girl! Take a breath, you're fine. It's awesome you've got your voice back, but you don't have to wear it out all at once."

I hopped three times like a rabbit just because I felt like it. "But it feels so good!!!" I started spinning around and around until I got so dizzy I staggered and fell in a heap by the side of the road, laughing like a goof and kicking my heels up in glee. "I have my voice back! Yaroo!! ... Ack!!" That last part was a bit of a shriek, as Knight suddenly materialized, his nose inches from my face. He blew out a massive snort, plastering me with horse snot. "Ugh! Gross, horse! Bleah ..." I scrambled to my feet, wiping my face with the hem of my T-shirt. "That was nasty!" Then I wrapped my arms around his neck in a fierce hug. "About time you got back here! Where have you been?"

Kellas was already untying the food bag from Knight's saddle. "I'm carrying this from now on," he declared, one arm already reaching into the bag.

"Save some for me!" I yipped, reaching out for my share. Note here: I also had a grip on Knight's neck rope, not wanting him to take off who knows where without me again. Not that this would necessarily have stopped him from doing his disappearing act. It was more of a muscle memory thing, from my mustang riding days. Long, long ago, in a galaxy far, far away ...

The thought brought me back to earth with a resounding crash. I might have my voice back, but I was still a long way from where I belonged, and still had no idea how to get back there.

It must've reflected on my face because Kellas paused in the act of handing me an apple. "What just happened?" he demanded.

I scowled. "Nothing." I bit into the apple so I would have an excuse not to elaborate.

That lovely single eyebrow lift he had perfected said everything he needed to say. He knew better, and knew I knew better, but he knew better than to pursue it at this time. "Maybe after your blood sugar is back up where it belongs," was all he said, and went back to rummaging in our food bag for something more than apples.

We started back down the road, me riding again, both of us eating as much as we could stuff into our faces. Hunger is awful, did you know that? It plays nasty tricks on you. Images of starving children crowded into my brain, and I had the grace to feel ashamed of my annoyance over what was merely a temporary lack of food. Kellas was right, though. Once I'd eaten my fill, the dark mood lifted, and I was able to tell him what had suddenly overwhelmed me.

Annoyingly, all he did was nod. "We'll figure that out too," was all he said. Which left only where Knight had taken himself off to. Unfortunately, he was staying mum. The only feeling I got from him was that it wasn't any of my business and I wouldn't understand anyway, me being a puny biped.

A puny biped. Yup. Nice of him, right? But since he was giving me a lift, I had to give that a pass despite being annoyed with him.

Blood sugar restored, my brain started working on our predicament again. Since this was all a product of my childhood fears and imagination, what if the solution, that is, returning home to our own dimension, was just as simple as turning dinosaurs into confetti? Since my movie habits had been the source of the problem, what if they also could be a source of the solution? I searched my memory for anything that might offer ideas, and almost immediately one jumped up to the surface.

"*The Wizard of Oz*!" I yelped, startling both Knight and Kellas.

Kellas gave me the raised eyebrow response. "OK ...?"

"Think about it! Dorothy gets caught up in a tornado that dumps her in an alternate reality, right? Then she has all kinds of adventures on her way to find the Wizard, since she was told he could send her back home ... only to find out he was a total fraud, and she had the solution on her feet the whole time. Ruby slippers! We need to find the ruby slippers and then I can go home."

Kellas greeted that brilliant idea with utter silence.

"Well?" I demanded. "Everything else has been movie related!"

"Not everything," he responded. "Not Taliesin, not that lute. Not getting here in the first place. Just all the obstacles we've faced, other than the gods and heroes who were here in the first place."

"Killjoy," I muttered, seeing his point and not appreciating it.

"But you might have something, after all." He fell silent, not sharing his bright idea, which drove me bonkers.

"Okay! Which means ...?"

He shrugged. "Just that if Cerridwen got you here, she's the only way you can go back. Which means we must go find HER."

I recoiled at the idea. "Heck no! She wants to kill me!"

"You've got your voice back. Those were her instructions when she banished us, remember? Don't come back until you've regained your voice. Now that you've managed that, we can return to her castle and have her send us back."

"But what if I lose it again before we get there?" I said in a small voice.

"Alright, let's think about that some more," he said. "Each time you regained your voice, what was the common denominator?"

Yay. Fractions. Not my favorite. "The lute?"

"Or the sword," he agreed. "Might that be your version of ruby slippers?"

"But then when Knight tried to take me home the first time, we crashed. I had the lute with me, remember?"

He nodded thoughtfully. "True. So maybe it is a combination of things. The lute, or the sword, or maybe you confronting your fears."

"So maybe ..." then I faltered, as the rest of that thought failed to form properly. At Kellas's questioning look, I shrugged. "Lost it, I guess."

Knight settled into a slow jog that matched Kellas's pace as we continued side by side through a countryside that I could only describe as magical. I wondered if Ireland were this beautiful, or if it was only Tír na nÓg's interpretation of it. Green everywhere, stone walls dividing up the pastures and fields in a quilted patchwork. Occasionally a stone house and barns near the road, which meandered up and down over hills and through valleys. Sheep everywhere, a few Kerry cows ... all black, with horns that arced up wickedly sharp from their polls. There were Irish draft horses, too, a few of which trotted over to their fences to call out a greeting to Knight. He invariably called back in a warm, rich nicker, his trot elevating a bit, as if to show off how beautiful he was.

I couldn't help it. Between the beautiful countryside and the rhythmic movement of my powerful mount, the tension that had gripped my body for so long started to ease and fall away. The music soared around me, pure and sweet, no longer the jangled, angry mess that had taken over with the entrance of the werewolves. It wasn't quite Beethoven-esque, but it sure was close. Maybe some composer I had never heard of. Unaware I was doing so, I began humming along with the melody. Words started forming in my mind, made their way to my voice box, and I was singing them in a language I had never heard before. All I knew was I was singing with conviction and joy, and it made my heart soar. Below me, Knight trotted to the beat of the song I was singing, his cadence a perfect match. When the song ended, the music around me stilled and Knight came to a stop.

Kellas started clapping. "Well done, Brannaugh."

I looked down at him, completely puzzled. "What did I do?"

He swung his arm out to indicate our surroundings. "Your music has transported us."

It had transported us ... literally. We had arrived back in Taliesin's clearing. Smoke rose lazily from the cabin's chimney. Eachann whinnied a greeting to Knight from his pasture. As I watched, the cabin door opened and Taliesin stepped out, saw us, and raised a hand in greeting.

"Wow. That's cool ..." I started, and the world went black.

Thirty-Two

I woke up slowly, once again staring through blurry eyes at the sky framed with faces all looking down at me with worried expressions.

"What just happened?" I managed, attempting to sit up and failing miserably.

"You are making a habit of falling off your horse," Kellas supplied. He looked exceedingly grouchy, but I heard the concern he was failing to mask.

"Help me sit up," I asked, holding up one arm for assistance.

"No," he responded. "You're in a good spot."

Taliesin knelt next to me and briefly put a hand on my forehead. "No fever. Can you tell me what you were doing before you rode in here?"

"Singing." Kellas supplied. "She was singing. We were miles away from here, and suddenly we were here."

Taliesin closed his eyes, took a deep breath, and shook his head. "I see. Brannaugh has been overdoing the magic tricks."

"Magic tricks?" Kellas asked.

"Transportation via music is not exactly a beginner's exercise," he said a bit grimly. "There are costs involved, of which you both were unaware, and now we must undo the damage. Help me get her inside."

Once again, I found myself scooped up and carried into Taliesin's cabin. This time, however, I was far too exhausted to feel anything but excruciatingly dizzy and sick to my stomach, and I struggled to keep from vomiting all over the cait sidhe's already filthy shirt. I was settled on a pallet in the kitchen where the pixies took turns fussing over me while I tried valiantly not to embarrass myself by hurling into the bucket they had thoughtfully provided. Dimly aware that both they and Taliesin were applying various smelly poultices on my forehead (which did nothing to help my nausea) I weakly pushed away a spoonful of something or other that the smallest pixie was attempting to get me to eat. Heard Taliesin say something, and the spoon went away. Gratefully felt myself retreating into the darkness of unconsciousness, and then nothing more.

I dreamed. Weird snatches for the most part, then one dream that seemed to stretch on forever. At first, I thought I had awakened, because I found myself in Taliesin's cabin. I needed to go outside, not sure why, but I wanted out. I reached for the door handle and saw my hand go right through it, right through the door, and then I was walking through the door despite it being shut, and out into the yard.

It was nighttime; however, I had no trouble seeing even though there was no moon because everything was glowing. The grass, the trees, the animals … everything. Even the rocks gave off a soft light. The only things that were dark were dead things, like the fence posts, the barn boards. The songs of crickets kept it from being soundless, but nature's orchestra was otherwise sleeping. I could see them too, little dots of glowing life sprinkled throughout the lawn. I knelt, reaching out to touch one, and was shocked to see my own hand glowing, too. I could make out the bones, the blood vessels, the nerves … so much packed into one small area! I jumped to my feet, alarmed, checked myself out … all of me glowed. Well, some of me was covered with a nightshirt, so it didn't glow as brightly, but I could tell I was glowing under that. Oh, man, I was definitely dreaming! I danced around the yard, noticing lots more that was quite impossible: the breezes, for instance. I could see the currents and eddies as they played around the trees and buildings. I could see the flying bugs in the air, millions of tiny specks of light. After a bit, I could see the rainbow hues that surrounded Eachann and Molly and Celeste in lovely bubbles as they grazed peacefully in their paddocks. The trees had them too, and when I bent down to inspect a cricket, the cricket had one as well. Curious, I held my hands out in front of me ... yup! Rainbow hues. What could this be? I walked closer to the barn. Nope, no rainbow halo surrounded the dead wood, but the cabin, where it was made of rock, glowed faintly with the rainbow hues, much harder to detect, however.

Making my way over to the cliffs, I sat with my legs dangled over the edge and gazed out over the twin valleys. There was so much to see, so much going on ... it was impossible to process all of it. What did all this light mean? Too restless to remain sitting for long, I wandered about looking at my surroundings like I'd never really seen them before, placing my feet carefully so as not to step on the critters that scampered around in the grass ... until I discovered I wasn't leaving any imprint where my feet had been. It was as though I had no substance. Well, that was weird! I was dreaming for sure.

"And what if you aren't dreaming, Other World Girl?"

I jumped sideways like a spooked horse, landed many yards away from where I'd started, and looked around wildly for who had been able to sneak up on me so silently.

A dark figure stood motionless where I had been just a moment before.

"Who are you?" I demanded. Tremors ran through me, unbidden.

"You know who I am," the figure responded. "Think."

Sometimes it's good to have a quick temper, because anger can help counter fear and leave you less vulnerable. "How the heck should I know?" But I was beginning to figure it out. Whereas everything else had a healthy rainbow of color, this creature had only a red spectrum. Red, as in blood, and anger and death ...

"Morrigan." The Death goddess. Oh, yay.

"Indeed," she said. She began walking toward me. I could not move, although I tried with every fiber of my being. Wouldn't you? Death was stalking me, and I could not run. It was as though my feet were rooted to the spot. She got close enough that I could see the dark red of her eyes, feel the warmth of her breath on my face. She gazed at me; her expression impossible to read even though the light from my own body illuminated her face. "I find you fascinating," she said finally, and began to walk very slowly around me as I remained frozen in place. "So young and foolish, yet so talented in many ways if you only knew how to access these talents. I have been watching you. Did you know that? You had no idea that you have been repeatedly close to death. Yet my hand gets stayed over and over. Why is that? Is there some purpose to you other than driving Cerridwen into a frenzy? Not that it isn't incredibly amusing to see her galloping around being ineffectual. But to be made thus by a child ... this is rich, and so satisfying to watch. That fire you called up was masterful. The confetti, unexpected and so clever. I would not have thought you capable. And working transport magic! Astounding, really, and so stupid, because it could have killed you then as well, as you were so close to becoming insubstantial. But it merely caused you severe exhaustion. Here you are, in the dark of the moon a week later, prancing about and admiring all the pretty light the creatures give off. You've figured that out, haven't you? Or you will once you think about it a bit."

She stopped in front of me and leaned in, her face once again inches from mine. "You wield the sword of Nuada, child. One of the four magical artifacts of the Celtic pantheon. Even I, when I gave it to Taliesin for safekeeping, would not have thought it would choose its new hero so oddly. Yet here you are. It has never yet chosen poorly. Why you, however? Why, indeed ..."

We stared at each other for a very long time, or maybe it was only seconds. But how long could you manage staring Death in the face? She started laughing then, very softly.

"I like you, so I am going to give you some very important advice, little girl. My sister goddess puts on quite the show of being loving and caring toward those who worship her, but she is not a nice creature. She's given to acts of violence when enraged ... which, I admit, keeps me employed. Yet I would see you survive awhile longer, if only to see what else you might become capable of. So, heed this: if you are to escape Cerridwen's wrath, you must be extremely clever. Use your wits, use your skills, rely on your friends. Running away does not work. You must face your fears. It will take all of you to prevent your untimely death. Remember, I will be watching."

And with that seemingly useless bit of advice, she was gone.

No longer frozen, I sank to my knees, shuddering violently from the aftereffects of the Morrigan's social visit. I was also very tired. Can you get tired in a dream? I know I was having trouble keeping my eyes open. Struggling to my feet, feeling like I was made of lead, I headed back to the cabin where I attempted to walk through the closed door ... and instead crashed into it and fell on my rear with a solid thud.

A moment later the door was yanked open, and Kellas was standing there, staring at me. "Brannaugh! How the heck did you get out here?" He scooped me up in his arms and carried me inside, depositing me on the pallet in the kitchen, pulling a blanket up over me, and tucking it in around my shivering body.

One really nice thing about Kellas is that he never verbally harassed for explanations. He just waited, like a cat, staring steadily until I was ready to spill the beans. Well, perhaps the staring hurries you up a bit, as it is a bit unsettling to be stared at for prolonged periods by one who never seems to blink.

I was too tired to think, but had to know something: "How old do I look right now?"

"About two," he said. There was a note in his voice that I couldn't quite place.

"Ah. Interesting ..." I managed and fell asleep.

Thirty-Three

I woke up some time later, completely disoriented. I was alone. The sun shone brightly through the eastern windows and I could hear birds singing, a lot of them. Like they were competing for attention, which in fact they probably were. I was hungry (What else is new? It seems to be a perpetual state of affairs lately!) Mostly it felt weirdly dangerous being by myself. I threw off the blanket and scrambled to my feet, intending to go find where everyone was, which is when I discovered I was full grown again. Not mini-me anymore. Hadn't Kellas told me I looked about two just before I fell asleep? What the dickens was going on here?

I charged out onto the back porch hollering "Kellas!" in my best hog-calling voice ... that's what Mom calls it, anyways. I call it being able to project. It's not an "indoor voice" for sure. There was a note of fear in it this time, though. Maybe I was just a wee bit panicked? Things were wonky doodle, and I needed my cait sidhe to sort them out. Now, please, before I went into a full-blown panic attack.

He mustn't have been far away, because he came galloping around the corner of the cabin in his full-sized puma avatar shape, ready to take on the bad guys, whoever those might be ... and found it was just me having a meltdown on the back porch, dissolving into a puddle of tears like some delicate wee princess or something.

I dropped to my knees and reached out my arms to him, and bless him for being a good guy; there wasn't any "Where's the fire?" snarkiness. He merely bounded up on the porch and let me wrap my arms around his neck and wail into his fur. How many guys would let an emotional female do that? Not many, is my guess. Most would turn tail and run. Not this cat.

Maybe it was because he was in cat form and we have this weird telepathic thing going for us, but I didn't have to explain a thing to him; I didn't need to tell him why I was in such a state first thing in the morning on a beautiful day. He just seemed to understand why, and simply leaned into me, letting me get his fur all wet and nasty with tears. Dang me if he weren't purring, too, the rumbles from his chest vibrating through my own like a powerful motor.

Maybe that's when I fell head over heels in love with the man. Cat. Whatever. It took a few moments before I realized that (oh, gods!) he could feel this, too. I drew back abruptly, not wanting him to know that bit. I didn't want to endanger our working relationship with what was likely one-sided love.

Kellas morphed back into man form, not giving any indication that he'd felt my sudden emotional shift toward him. "Feeling a bit better now?"

I nodded unsteadily and mopped my eyes on the back of my hands. "It's so disorienting." I indicated my full-grown self. "I mean, I was two when I went to sleep and now ..."

"I see what you mean," he said, and reached down to help me to my feet. "If it helps at all, it's not you. Apparently, the moon goddesses are mucking about with the moon phases, and nothing is quite normal, even for this whacky dimension. It's not your fault," he hastened to add. "Taliesin thinks that Cerridwen and Arianrod are having one of their not-so-wonderful spats again. Which explains your alarmingly fast body changes."

"Why would Cerridwen mess with the moon phases?"

He shrugged. "Maybe she thought you'd be easier to defeat when you are little. Maybe Uiscias could then reclaim Fraegarthach? Thankfully, we have Arianrod, who is a full moon goddess and not about to tolerate anything less than a full moon. It's been very strange this last week."

"Week?" I asked, alarmed.

He nodded. "You've been out of it for that long. We were getting concerned."

I pressed both hands against my stomach, which, as usual, was being a bit noisy about being empty. "So that's why I'm famished. Can we eat?"

He grinned. "There's the Brannaugh I know and love. Food first! I bet the pixies will be thrilled to hear it." He took my arm and led me into the cabin's kitchen where the three pixies were busy making what looked to be an enormous feast. However, it wasn't the food that held me captivated, it was what he'd said: "the Brannaugh I know and love." Love! Oh, my gods. Did he mean it, or was it just a manner of speaking? Must not show anything, Raven. Must be very, very chill.

The pixies dropped what they were doing and crowded around me, chattering to me in their funny scratchy language.

"Oh, thank you!" I answered a bit startled by their enthusiasm. "I'm glad to be back, too. Has everything been quiet for you here? No scary things showing up?"

They exchanged startled glances, then all started talking at the same time.

It made them totally unintelligible. "Whoa! One at a time! I can't make out what you're saying otherwise."

That worked. The littlest one grabbed my hand and started talking rapidly. I was barely able to follow what she was saying, but I got the gist of it. "Cerridwen's been here, and she was yelling at Taliesin. Yup, not fair for sure." More vehement scratchy talk. "She threatened him? So uncool." The littlest pixie smacked a knotty little fist into her other hand, her language becoming even more heated. "I bet you would. Taliesin is lucky he has the three of you to protect him!" Then I burst out laughing, as she described how she and her sisters had jumped onto the goddess and pulled her hair and pinched her ears and generally made her life miserable until she'd run away. OK, so maybe they exaggerated a bit, but the picture they painted of Cerridwen in flight was soul satisfying.

"You can understand them now?" Kellas had a puzzled frown on his face.

Taliesin appeared behind him, looking over his shoulder. "It's the amulet I gave her," he explained. "It can work as a language translator."

I saw understanding flood over Kellas's face. "Kinda like a translator app on a smartphone, then."

It was Taliesin's turn to look confused. "What's a smartphone?"

Kellas and I exchanged knowing looks. "Something from our dimension. Not important."

"Hmm ..." was Taliesin's answer. "Like that movie thing. Magic that isn't magic."

"Science," Kellas and I said together.

"It's kinda the same thing, but isn't," I added.

Kellas groaned. "Not helping!"

The pixies made some noises about needing space to do their cooking, and we were summarily kicked out of their kitchen.

The three of us ended up outside on the porch, Kellas sitting on the railing with his back up against a post, Taliesin and I occupying the two chairs.

"Don't hold anything back," Taliesin urged. "Obviously, you have your voice back and learned a few new tricks in the process of recovering it. Transportation via music is advanced magic."

"Is that what she did?" Kellas asked.

Taliesin nodded. "I noticed several changes in the world music while you were gone as well; was that your doing?"

I shrugged, feeling awkward. "I'm not sure. We had to fight for our lives a few times, and each time things changed."

"Tell me," he said. So, we did.

"Now what?" I asked, once we'd run through our whole sorry tale, right up to the point where we'd shown up in Taliesin's meadow. I was good, I didn't rat Kellas out about the whole spider woman weirdness.

Taliesin was patient, however. "Now what, what?"

"I mean, how do I get home? Now that I have my voice back, and the music sounds like I rid Tír na nÓg of the creepies I let in by accident?"

"I told her we have to go back to Cerridwen's castle, and she didn't like that answer, apparently," Kellas drawled from his perch on the porch railing.

Taliesin considered that in silence a while. Then he sighed, stretched, and grimaced a bit as several of his joints made audible popping noises. "Kellas is correct. You need to face Cerridwen. Beyond that I am unsure."

"There's no other way?"

"None that I can surmise."

Oh, this was great. Just great. Even the wisest man in the world had no better answer for my problem.

"Is there some 'proper protocol' for arranging to visit a goddess in her own castle? Or do I just make some unforgivable screw up and wait for her to come find me?" I demanded. OK, so that was petulant and beneath me, but this whole "go see Cerridwen" was a terrifying prospect. I was compensating a bit. Sue me.

Kellas and Taliesin exchanged glances.

For some reason that ticked me off even more. "OK for you to say, but it feels like I'd be taking myself to my own funeral. Not excited about doing that, thank you very much!"

Kellas grimaced. "It's not anyone's favorite, Brannaugh. But remember what the Morrigan told you ..."

Wait one stinking minute ... how did the cat man know that detail? I hadn't shared my dream with him yet! Not that I had time to ask him how he knew because Taliesin was already talking.

"When was this? You hadn't mentioned it."

"It was last night, wasn't it?" Kellas asked me. "Before you showed up in little-kid form outside."

"More to tell me," Taliesin's voice was calm, but the tension in his body said otherwise.

I relayed my dream. He listened carefully, a scowl deepening on his face the more I described the experience of being without physical form, just made up of light along with everything else. He was silent for what seemed like an eternity afterward as he mulled over what I'd told him, his hands steepled in front of his face.

"It was just a really vivid dream, right?" I asked finally, not sure I wanted to know differently.

He shook his head emphatically. "No. Not a dream. But perhaps in keeping with your lunar tendencies. Like your grandmother Amaris. Also maybe why Cerridwen has been manipulating the moon phases lately. Fortunately, we have Arianrod exerting her own influence, or we may very well be in a bigger pickle that we already are."

We. That was more reassuring than I could say. I wasn't going to be left alone in this ... pickle ... as he put it. "Let me get this straight," I said. "You think Cerridwen is messing with the moon to make me younger? And therefore, less able to defend myself from her?"

"Precisely."

Talk about unfair tactics! Cerridwen had no shame whatsoever. Attempting not to freak out, I asked "Just how much moon was there last night?"

"It was the New Moon."

"So, no moon showing. Which means ..."

"You were without physical substance, although you—that which makes you *you*—is still there. Unable to lift your sword or play your lute, but still alive and vulnerable to attack."

<h1 style="text-align:center">Thirty-Four</h1>

I sat in silence, my emotions warring for the upper hand: terror, horror, and a rapidly increasing fury. Guess which one won out? "I'm gonna gut that useless witch!" I lunged to my feet, fists clenched and teeth bared. "She's gonna be sorry she even thought she could mess with me!"

"That's my girl," Kellas murmured, a smile spreading over his face.

"Not so fast!" Taliesin exclaimed in horror. "You can't just go off the deep end without a plan. Think this through."

"Oh, Taliesin my friend, you know so little about our Brannaugh," Kellas was grinning widely now. "Plan? Heck no. She charges in like an avenging Fury, plans be damned. Wait 'til you see her in fiery mode. It's a sight you'll never forget."

"Nevertheless, it's not a winning strategy, especially against a goddess who cannot be killed," the bard persisted. "Sit down, my dear, and let's figure this out properly." He waited, a patient (or was it long-suffering?) look on his face.

I huffed in annoyance and plopped back down on my chair. "Alright, hit me."

He looked alarmed at that. "Hit you?"

Kellas snorted. "She means tell her what you're thinking. She's full of slang like this and it's gotten us into trouble before."

"Ah." Taliesin nodded. "Very well, I'll 'hit you' then. Our options are limited. You cannot run from her for long before she catches up … my case illustrates that. She's immortal … so she cannot be killed. Therefore, that leaves only one course of action … to confront her with a proposal she cannot resist and hopes she takes you up on it."

My heart sank. "What could I possibly offer Cerridwen that she isn't able to manage for herself?"

"You give her something she truly cannot do herself. In this case, you offer to rescue Rhiannon."

I was floored. Who was Rhiannon and why did she need rescuing? "I don't understand."

"Rhiannon is a Welsh goddess who married a mortal king to avoid marrying the man her father had chosen for her. They had a child, who may have been kidnapped by the former suitor, or perhaps just misplaced by his nannies. The nannies, hoping to avoid punishment for themselves, blamed Rhiannon for his disappearance, saying she had eaten the little boy. Her husband punished her by making her confess her supposed sin to anyone who came to the castle gates and required her to carry them on her back into the castle."

My expression must have said clearly what I thought of that hideous miscarriage of justice, because he nodded. "Turns out the child was found by a farmer and his wife, who took him in and cared for him. Eventually they heard about the doings up at the castle, returned the child to his mother, and the rest is history."

I sat for a moment thinking about this, until the obvious dawned. "If this is history, how can I have anything at all to do with rescuing Rhiannon. She's already been rescued, no? Like, you have already become Taliesin instead of Gwion Bach."

"Rhiannon is a very popular goddess, if a bit of a disaster magnet, as you might have surmised from this story. She's forever getting herself into difficult spots. She's in one right now."

"Maybe she should do a bit of soul searching, then," I scoffed, thinking about the messes I had so recently had to extricate myself from.

Then came second thoughts. I was being uncharitable. I'd had help, lots of help. From Kellas. "Sorry."

Taliesin merely looked amused. "Not a bad suggestion. If goddesses were at all inclined to soul search, which they aren't."

"Tell me she dumped that jerk of a husband at least." How could anyone treat another like that? Inhumane in the extreme! "Did he even TRY to learn the truth?"

He smiled and shook his head. "As to whether he attempted to discover if the nannies were telling the truth, history doesn't say. However, she forgave him, and they lived happily ever after."

"Oh, gag a maggot. Spare me the fairy tales!" I was not impressed. "Did she at least deck him and read him the riot act?"

At his obvious confusion, Kellas explained. "She thinks Rhiannon should have punched her husband hard enough that he fell down, and then yelled at him about what an idiot he was."

That made Taliesin laugh out loud. "Maybe she should have. But Rhiannon is a gentle creature, and besides being a goddess of the sun, moon, and horses, she's also the goddess of forgiveness."

Somehow that just didn't set right. "Forgiveness shouldn't happen in the absence of contrition. That's what my Mom always says, anyways. Otherwise, what's to stop the lousy behavior from happening again, right?"

He just smiled. I huffed in frustration. "Alright. What scrape has she gotten into this time?"

He looked a bit sheepish. "Let's just say it is a matter of the heart, and the object of her admiration is perhaps ... hmm. Not wonderful."

I tipped my head sideways and gave him my best "get real, dude!" eye roll. "You think I should go break up her current love match? Do you have ANY idea what a terrible idea that is?"

"Certainly not taking advantage of your blunt object 'take the adversary out' tactics, is it?" Kellas chimed in.

"Not helping, cat man!" I scowled at Taliesin. "Please tell me she hasn't been being bombarded with well-meaning people instructing her to dump this guy, at least."

The look on his face confirmed my worst fears. "Well ..."

"Sheesh!" This was beyond belief. "Obviously, you have a lady who wants to call her own shots and having everyone gang up telling her she's making a mistake is only going to make her dig in her heels. Gads, how dumb can people be?!"

"Sounds like a job for Brannaugh," Kellas said softly.

"Apparently she knows the feeling," Taliesin agreed. "So how shall we convince Cerridwen that Brannaugh is the one for the job?"

"Who is the guy we're talking about, anyways?" I asked.

"Donn Fírinne, god of Death," he said.

Thirty-Five

"Oh, you have got to be kidding me," I groaned.

"It gets better," Taliesin continued. "Donn and his brothers sought to defeat the Tuatha Dé Danann—and Donn died in the attempt. He was banished to Tech Duinne, a portal to the underworld. He rides a white horse through the sky at night, bringing thunder and lightning with the rain."

"Which is maybe how she met him," I suggested. "A highly charged relationship, shall we say."

Kellas groaned at the terrible joke, and I grinned at him. Taliesin just shook his head in mock despair. "Perhaps the two of you should make your way back to Cerridwen's castle after breakfast."

"Do I have to?" I moaned.

"Do you have a better idea?" Kellas countered.

I didn't, so I just made an awful grimace. "What's to stop her from killing me the moment I'm near?"

The awkward silence that followed my question dragged on. Taliesin finally sighed heavily. "We don't know if she'd kill you the moment you showed up, but you might have a chance if you rode in under a white flag."

"Truce, huh? I grimaced. "A fat lot of good that did my people back in the day." At Taliesin's questioning look, I added "Yeah. The U.S. Cavalry liked to open fire despite a peaceful surrender and slaughter us. Women and children as well. 'The only good Indian is a dead Indian.'"

"Barbaric," he agreed, shuddering at the mental picture that brought up. "I can understand your reluctance."

"What if you rode in as your avatar self?" Kellas wondered.

I shot him a sideways glance. "What horse could possibly carry me when I'm that size?"

"Don't underestimate a dark horse," Taliesin said. "You might have to ride bareback, but I believe the horse himself could manage quite nicely."

As if he knew we were discussing him, Knight lifted his head from where he was grazing nearby and wandered over. I went to him. "What do you think, big guy. You up to carrying around ... this?" I drew my sword, rapidly growing into my warrior self. Far from becoming spooked at the sudden change, Knight merely gave a disgusted snort, and gave his mane a vigorous shake. A moment later, he'd grown to easily 21 hands tall, and not just taller, but wider and beefier as well, like a medieval warhorse. And, yup, his regular saddle would not fit. Bareback it was. Kellas stepped forward and gave me a hand up, groaning with the effort it required.

"Next time, get on the horse first," he grumbled. I grinned evilly at him, and he rolled his eyes.

"You are imposing for sure. However, if I may ..." Taliesin beckoned for us to rejoin him on the porch.

I slid off my warhorse and sheathed the sword, both of us shrinking back to normal size. After a quick pat on his neck to let Knight know his services were appreciated but no longer required at present, I went back to my chair.

Taliesin sat silently for a minute, seeming to gather his thoughts before speaking. "What I didn't have an opportunity to tell you before you had to leave suddenly, is what the sword ... your sword, Brannaugh ... represents. It gives the bearer new and terrible abilities, as you no doubt have discovered on your adventures. It also contains the triple powers of insight, illumination, and creative energy. The wisdom to use, or not use. Maintaining control over its powers is what the sword is all about. You need to decide when to use it, and when to leave it sheathed so that you can resolve disputes peacefully."

"A bit like Teddy Roosevelt, then," Kellas remarked. "'Speak softly and carry a big stick.'"

"Precisely. The idea is to negotiate in good faith but have the strength to back yourself up in case things go wrong, as they sometimes will despite our best intentions. I advise that you request an audience with Cerridwen at her castle, giving her the advantage of being on her home ground so hopefully she will be less reactive. However, be prepared in case she proves ... difficult."

"You're being diplomatic." I probably sounded grim. Well, I was. Everything I'd experienced with that goddess tended to reinforce the "difficult" adjective. "No doubt the Morrigan will be close-by."

"She is never far from trouble," Taliesin agreed.

"Will you be joining us?" I asked him.

Regret clouded his features. "I will not. Despite my overwhelming curiosity, I think it is best if you navigate these waters on your own. You will have Kellas with you, of course."

"Notice how I get volunteered for these outings without being asked," Kellas remarked.

I felt cold dread wash over me. "You will come, though, won't you?" Although, honestly, it really wasn't his fight. I had gotten so used to having him around to support me, the thought of him not being there was terrifying. "I can't do this without you."

Kellas directed his reply at Taliesin. "Can you believe this kid? Have I ever left her? I mean, yeah, a cat like me could get tired of being tossed into one impossible situation after another, but honestly?" He sent me a one-eyebrow-raised quizzical look. "C'mon Brannaugh. Have a little faith."

The relief was so intense, I would have collapsed had I not been sitting already. "Thank you. I know that doesn't sound like much, but ... thank you." I attempted to convey how strongly I felt about that with my tone of voice and the look I sent him, but his only response was a careful nod. It left me feeling just a little lost. Well, what had I expected? A declaration of undying adoration? C'mon Raven. Get real.

Taliesin slapped the arms of his chair. "Well then, that's settled!" He got to his feet. "Breakfast."

We got underway directly after breakfast, with me up on Knight and Kellas carrying our food bag. The littlest pixie had supplied us with a large square of white cloth to attach to a stick once we got close to Cerridwen's castle. She'd looked at me with a such an expression of anxiety on her little face that I'd knelt down and given her a gentle hug. She'd wrapped her stick-like arms around my neck and sobbed, clinging to me like she would never let go. Taliesin carefully peeled her off me and cuddled her like a small child while she continued to wail. It didn't exactly make leaving any easier.

It was a bit better once we got underway, though. As I'd discovered before, doing something, even if it wasn't particularly well planned, was better than sitting around stewing in one's own juices. The music around us was cautious but playing in a major key, which helped. If nature's orchestra could find a positive note in all this, perhaps I wasn't doomed to an early death after all. At least that was what I kept telling myself as we retraced our steps.

Taliesin had told us of a better path by which to return to the castle, one that didn't require crashing through the woods as we'd done on our way to his place the first time. It did require descending a series of heart-stopping switchbacks along the side of a steep mountain, however. Knight had no difficulty stepping around the sharp corners, but the dizzying drop-offs had me squeezing my eyes shut to avoid focusing on how very far down it was should I fall off. I think we all breathed a sigh of relief once we came to the bottom and could stride out normally again. We had not gotten too far when the music warned me we were being watched.

I reined Knight in immediately. "I think it might be a good time to find us a stick."

Kellas nodded. "You felt that too, did you?" He held up a pole about eight feet long and an inch thick. "I've been keeping an eye out for one. This do?"

"Perfect." I dug out the cloth the pixie had given me earlier and Kellas fastened it to his stick. He handed it up to me and I held it with my right hand, balanced on my foot. The flapping fabric didn't seem to perturb Knight in the least, which was good because it was large enough to snap impressively in the breeze. In motion once again, I listened closely to the music to see if anything had changed. We were still being followed but not as threateningly, almost as if our unseen company were taking a wait-and-see approach now that we rode under a flag of truce.

The flag presented a bit of difficulty as we rode through the forest, as I had to maneuver it under and around overhanging branches, so it was a relief when we finally broke out into the open. Like the road we'd taken away from Cerridwen's castle, this was also rutted dirt not much wider than a single wagon. It soon joined a wider boulevard that was level and smooth, much nicer for traveling on, but very exposed. I could only hope our white flag would keep some archer from picking us off from a distance.

The closer we got to Cerridwen's castle, the less we spoke. Our unseen escort(s) remained with us. We never saw them clearly, just caught glimpses of motion from time to time. Kellas trotted steadily nearby, his face an unreadable mask. He didn't volunteer and I didn't ask what might be shadowing us ... it seemed irrelevant. It was unnerving, however. Even Knight seemed twitchier than normal, and he was not known for his sangfroid, which was saying a good bit. Balancing the ruddy flag and sticking his increasingly elevated trot was taking all my concentration and strength. When I couldn't handle it any longer, I reined him in, dropped the pole, and slid off. He stepped around nervously, obviously unhappy we had stopped.

"Hey!" I tugged on his neck rope. "I understand your reluctance to go in there," I nodded at the castle, "so I'm not going to ask you to carry me any closer. But when I call you, I need you to come immediately, no hesitation, no *mañana*, do you understand?" I shook the rope to show him how important this was. "Do you agree?"

His response was a gusty bluster and a half rear. I released the rope, and he disappeared in a swirl of darkness.

I picked up the white flag, but Kellas took it from me. "Might be good if you had your hands free. Come on." He gave me a little push toward the castle, and on we went.

A half hour of steady walking brought us to the drawbridge. It was up when we arrived, but shortly afterward it lowered for us with a great deal of rattling of chains and groaning of hinges. As we stepped onto the wooden deck, our previously invisible escorts materialized around us ... a full dozen of heavily armed, unfriendly looking warriors each of whom would make at least two of me.

Kellas's face took on a pinched look. He took a hold of my left elbow, pulling me closer to him. "Cerridwen's home guard," he muttered in my ear. "You should be honored. She must find you very scary." He guided me as I stared at the guards until he gave me a little shake. "Face forward! he hissed.

I faced forward but found it very difficult to keep moving my feet. It's hard to move when you are scared silly.

We were escorted through the seemingly abandoned town. Just once I caught a fleeting glimpse of scared faces peeping through a window. We were escorted up the impossibly long and wide set of stairs that led to the goddess's castle, across the beautiful courtyard with the fountain, to the gigantic front doors I had nervously zipped through what seemed like ages ago. The doors swung wide open as we approached and we were hustled through, straight back into an enormous hall.

Thirty-Six

It was gorgeous. Think medieval cathedral and you'd be close. Everything was built of stone and heavy dark wood. The ceiling arched over our heads a hundred feet or more. Huge, fluted stone pillars on either side of a wide central area held the heavily ornamented ceiling where it arched down, and there were lower areas to either side of the central corridor, where ribbed vaults did their share to hold up the massive ceiling. Windows along the sides were narrow, arched things, the glass glazed with leaded diamond-shaped panes. The floor was a dark colored marble heavily streaked with greys and whites, polished to a mirror shine. I would have stood still and stared, given my druthers, not that I was given the opportunity.

We were hustled down the long expanse of rather slippery floor to where several figures sat on massive thrones set upon a raised dais. Our escort had crowded even closer as we approached the gods.

"That's close enough," one growled, reaching out to grab my free arm. "Kneel, human!"

I shook his hand off. "Stop invading my personal space, you troglodyte!"

Kellas clutched my left arm even tighter, hissing through his teeth. A warning. I shook him off too, but kept glaring at the fae bodyguard, who bared a mouthful of razor-sharp teeth at me. I bared mine back at him and gave him as nasty a face as I could muster. I'd worked with wild horses. I knew intimidation techniques when I saw them, and they just tended to infuriate me. I also knew he was unable to back up his nastiness right there in front of the Celtic pantheon, so I felt relatively sure he wasn't able to follow through with his threat anytime soon. Later? Who knew.

Kellas nudged me with an elbow. "Psst." He nodded toward the dais.

I dutifully faced forward and focused on the gods.

Cerridwen sat on the right throne. A very large bear of a man sat on the left one.

"Tegan, Cerridwen's husband," Kellas whispered in my ear.

Tegan was flanked to his right by another man so dark, twisted, and odd, he looked like he had stuck in the middle of metamorphizing into a huge black crow. To Cerridwen's left stood a woman so impossibly beautiful, she might have just stepped off Pygmalion's pedestal.

"Morphan and Creirwy," Kellas supplied. "Son and daughter. And you know the other one."

Indeed, I did. The Morrigan had left a lasting impression on me. I was unlikely to forget who *she* was. She stood next to Creirwy, in sharp contrast to the young woman's blond, white-clad incandescence, projecting a disconcerting magnetism of unmistakable power. The others seemed to brace themselves against her energy, not ignoring her exactly, but very, very, circumspect.

Cerridwen spoke first. "You presume a great deal, human, coming here uninvited."

I dragged my gaze away from the Morrigan. Cerridwen had a haughty, sour look on her face. I wasn't sure if it was because she'd eaten a bad apple and had indigestion, but it was not a look that would wear well over time.

"You've been trying to have me killed." I think I was as startled at what came out of my mouth as the gods were. But oh well. Since I had started, might as well plan the rest of my funeral. "You have been playing games with the moon to make it easier for your pet, Uiscias, to murder me. Not honorable, Cerridwen, and not, may I stress, anything I appreciate. You need to stop, NOW."

From the corner of my eye, I saw Tegan stir just slightly, and a scowl furrowed his forehead. Oddly, the glare was being directed at his wife. Hmm. Maybe a possible ally?

I continued. "I admit I was guilty of bringing a whole slew of unpleasant characters into this domain. It was an innocent error, and I took it upon myself to fix that mistake. Being relentlessly pursued by your assassin—who, quite honestly, is an arrogant, overprivileged jerk—did not make my job easier. However!" I spoke forcefully, preventing her interrupting me, "I am prepared to do you a favor in return for my safe passage back to my world."

Cerridwen's face had taken on a dark red hue. She was NOT happy with me. "What favor could you possibly render me that I cannot do for myself?"

Exactly what I had demanded of Taliesin not long ago, but since then I had been thinking how Cerridwen had unsuccessfully fought the Chinese dragon, yet I had managed to send him home. How Kellas and I had rid Tír na nÓg of all the fantastic beasts I had unleashed. How Fraegarthach had chosen ME to be its new bearer after a millennium of hiding in lute form. Cerridwen must have a very limited imagination indeed, if she could not acknowledge what this puny human had managed in a very short span of time. Not that I intended to disabuse her of her narrowmindedness. Her problem, not mine.

"Rhiannon is enamored of Donn Fírinne. It is my understanding that this alliance is not of your liking. I can change that."

The sour look changed to disbelief. "And how might you, a mere child, manage that when the gods themselves have been unable to?"

I had no idea. Really, truly not a clue. Not that I was going to admit it. This was the magical equivalent of a Hail Mary pass in the final minutes of a game. "My secret. You don't need to know."

Cerridwen lunged to her feet, her energy surging in moonbeams around her. But she still did not unleash those at me; why, I had no idea. "You are insolent."

I nodded slowly. "Yes, I am. And I would be ashamed of me if you weren't such a petulant pain in my behind."

Like pouring gasoline on a fire ... yet she still held back. The other gods and goddesses were exchanging startled looks at one another, all but the Morrigan, who was smiling widely, although not at all in a nice way.

Cerridwen stalked toward me, every step as liquid as a tiger on the hunt, stepping gracefully down the stairs from the dais, until she and I stood practically toe to toe. She glared down at me. I was doing my level best to stare coolly (I hoped it looked "coolly") back up at her. Didn't help that she was a head taller than I, drat it. "Impertinent little brat. Everything you are you owe to me. I could take it all away," she snapped her fingers "like that."

I frowned. "Really? Because I thought I got all my brains and good looks from my parents."

She hissed in fury and raised a hand to slap me, but I blocked her arm with my own like I was channeling Bruce Lee and felt my body morphing upward into my avatar body. "Don't start what you can't finish," I growled in that ragged voice that was mine but not mine. I was dimly aware that the fae guard drew back rapidly in alarm. Geez, I hadn't even drawn my sword yet and they were practically tripping over themselves to flee. Hey, how was that, anyways? Didn't the drawing sword/growth spurt usually go together? Something to figure out later. Right now, there was still this goddess to deal with.

She had fallen back several steps when I'd changed, although we continued to glare at each other. However, there was a subtle shift in her energy, as if she had started to reconsider her attitude toward me somehow. The glare was being replaced by a calculating look. "You have matured somewhat," she said at last. "Taliesin has managed to teach you a thing or two."

Thereby completely dismissing anything I'd managed to figure out on my own. What a grade A jerk she was.

"Perhaps you might be able to assist us with our ... little problem with the Death God after all."

Death God. Eek. Forget that for now, Raven! "In return for dealing with the Death God, you will grant Kellas and me safe and immediate return to our own dimension," I said firmly, feeling myself slowly downsize as the threat she presented diminished. "And you will not interfere in any way with my efforts with Rhiannon, nor send anyone else to do so." I heard Kellas grunt in approval at those clarifications.

"You say you have a plan."

"Which will remain a secret."

She grimaced. Obviously, she didn't like others to keep secrets. Never mind that she probably had a boatload of her own.

"I cannot risk my plan being revealed to Rhiannon in advance," I explained. "Also, I may have to change it up in the middle of things. Best if I kept it to myself. But I must have your sacred vow that if we complete this quest, WHEN we complete it, you will give us safe passage back to our own world with no further requirements or dithering." I knew I was pushing hard, but please, please, let this work!!

Cerridwen studied me for a beat. "You are in no position to make such demands." She turned her back on me and stalked back to her throne, relaxing onto it, every inch the haughty queen. She didn't say it, but she might as well have: "Whatcha gonna do about that, sistah?!"

I pondered the situation for a prolonged period, until I felt Kellas stirring uneasily next to me. Taliesin had warned me about the powers of my sword and knowing when to draw it and when to be diplomatic. Tempting though it was to draw Fraegarthach and light into Cerridwen, it wasn't the best solution to my current problem. "Well, then!" I exclaimed in as jolly a voice as I could manage. "Time to celebrate, eh? How about a dance?" Reaching over my left shoulder, I pulled out my lute. "Anybody have a request? Oh, never mind, I have just the thing here." I checked the tuning swiftly and started to sing.

"When I was at home I was merry and frisky,
My dad kept a pig and my mother sold whisky ..."

"The Irish Washer Woman" was a bouncy, happy jig tune I'd sung time and again with my Dad when we went for long walks, so I knew all the words and the effect it had on you. You could not help but skip, jump, and sing along to it. Which was what I was hoping would happen. Might the magic catch them up and keep them dancing until they begged to stop? I was going to find out.

The guards were the first ones to succumb to the music, and began dancing around us like men possessed (which, to be honest, they were.) Creirwy and Morphran were next, then Tegan and Cerridwen were compelled from their thrones, dancing a jig around the dais. A snarl from Kellas let me know he too was drawn in. Only the Morrigan was able to resist the music, gazing down at me with a slight smile on her face. She approved of my tactics! I felt my heart swell just a little bit. Odd that I should find her approval gratifying. Maybe it was the same thing as finally getting an A from an extremely strict teacher renowned for handing out Fs.

The jig was a short tune, maybe a minute and a half long, but I repeated it over and over until my audience was clearly staggering from exhaustion. Yet Cerridwen continued to dance, her face set in a furious scowl, her lips drawn back from clenched teeth as if keeping back the words she knew I required to stop the music. Two could play this game, however. I gradually increased the tempo, just because I could.

It took Tegan, red-faced and puffing with the effort to keep jigging, to finally force the issue. "Cerridwen! Give the young lady what she wants. This tune with be the death of us!"

When her offspring added their voices to Tegan's, she relented. Not that she wanted to, obviously. "Fine!" she spat, as if the single word tasted like bile on her tongue. "We have a deal."

I inclined my head graciously toward her and stopped the music mid-phrase. The guards tumbled to the ground, Morphan and Creirwy sank to their knees, and Tegan collapsed with a gusty sigh upon his throne. Cerridwen managed to control her descent onto her throne so that it wasn't quite as obvious that she was worn out, but I could tell that she was.

Nothing happened for a space of about a minute while everyone attempted to catch their breath. It was a weird tableau, gods and warriors panting and glaring, me clutching my lute and trying not to panic. What if they all attacked once they caught their breath? But I should not have worried. The Morrigan started clapping, slowly, just a bit mockingly, but still ...

"Well done, Earth Child. Clever, and effective, and without causing irreparable harm except, perhaps, to the pride of some individuals. I am willing to wager that you may well be able to rescue our intrepid colleague from her own foolishness. You, dear sister," she sent Cerridwen a pointed look "would be well advised to send the bard and her protector on their way immediately and thank your lucky stars she did not wreak more damage than she already has."

Cerridwen, still unable to draw a full breath, merely glared even more darkly, but she made a dismissive wave of her hand. "Go. Just go. Don't return until Rhiannon has dismissed the Dark Lord."

I bowed, swung the lute over my back, grabbed Kellas's hand, and walked swiftly away from the gods, through the doors and into the sunshine outside. We didn't slow down until we were well away from the castle, at which point I stumbled, collapsed to my knees on the ground, and just stayed there, my fingers digging into the dirt as I struggled to steady my heartbeat and slow my breathing to normal levels.

Kellas stood by patiently, waiting for me to regain my equilibrium. "The Morrigan was right, by the way. That was well played, Brannaugh. Had me for a bit there when it looked like you were trying to get us spitted with your snarky ways, but it worked. Nicely done."

I huffed a bit, still trying to get a grip on the aftereffects of our little adventure. I sent him a glance up through a curtain of hair. "Thanks. Sorry about the jig, though."

He shrugged. "I survived." He waited a little while longer, then patted me on the shoulder. "C'mon. We need to get going. Call that dark horse of yours and we'll take on our next impossible mission."

Gratifyingly, Knight materialized the moment I called him. I told him who we needed to go see, and off we went to meet our destiny with Death. Or something. Whatever.

Thirty-Seven

It was a great distance to Rhiannon's castle, too far for one day's travel even with a horse to help me along. As Tír na nÓg was nearly as rainy as Ireland, we decided to take our chances with an overnight stay at an inn. Like most inns, the one we settled on had a bar on the first level where you could get food and drink. Which was good as we were tired of the solid but uninspiring victuals our food bag served up. Mindful of the last time we'd stopped at a bar, we were particularly careful not to attract attention, which for me meant disguising myself. I braided my hair and tucked it under my hoodie and slouched along like Kellas's shadow. He ordered for the two of us while I stuck to the shadows, keeping quiet and doing my utmost not to attract attention. The people in the pub were a different sort altogether from those in the last one, much quieter and not at all interested in a couple of trail-worn travelers. It helped that there were tall wooden dividers between tables that did a very nice job of increasing privacy. However, the dividers didn't stop us from overhearing the discussion taking place at the table next to ours. I didn't pay much attention until one of the men mentioned Cerridwen and then cursed her for being a meddling idiot.

Kellas and I exchanged startled looks, and he pointed a fork in their direction and whispered "Listen!"

I leaned back against the tall seat back and tuned in, not in the least ashamed that I was eavesdropping on their conversation. Had they wanted to keep it private, they were in the wrong place.

"What's our moon goddess been fiddling with now?" one of the men asked, his voice a bit muffled as though he was talking with his mouth full.

"Och, she went to milady's castle and was bossing her about, telling her what to do and who she could see. That's not how to manage our Rhiannon, no! The lass dug in her heels and announced she would marry that bounder Donn Fírinne Tuesday next, that she would, and that would be that. If Cerridwen had just kept her yap shut, I might have had a chance to make Rhiannon see that I was the better match for her, despite her meddling son Pryderi announcing to anyone who would listen that she was to marry *me*, without asking her thoughts on the matter at all. We all know how it went the last time, when her Da tried to marry her off against her say-so. Dang and blast, we men are slow to learn, eh?"

"If you'd just taken my advice and run off with her the moment Donn started hanging around, we'd not be dealing with this," the first man said.

"Something tells me kidnapping the girl and running off with her wouldn't make her any fonder of me, my friend."

"So what? Nobody cares what females want anyway." The friend must have taken another gigantic mouthful because he was nearly impossible to understand again. The dismissive misogynistic attitude came across loud and clear, however. My face must have reflected my fury, because suddenly Kellas was gesticulating wildly, like he was afraid I'd jump over the divider and light into the jerk.

"Na, na, McDougal. Not in these modern times we live in. Women are to be cherished and their input sought on things that matter to them."

"Harumph," was McDougal's response. "Who'd have thought the great Manawydan fab Llŷr would have become a man who gives a care what a skirt thinks! You've become soft, man. A disgrace to our sex."

Manawydan must have been a very patient fellow indeed, for his only response was a soft laugh. "Time will tell, McDougal. Time will tell. However, if you keep stuffing your feed in like a pig at the trough, you might choke and never get the opportunity to see tomorrow."

McDougal's response was another "harrumph," and that was the end of that topic of conversation. We waited to see if they would leave before us, which they did. As the lighting was poor in the pub, I could only get an impression of the two, and guess who was who. Both were tall, strongly built men, but one seemed kinder, gentler. Thoughtful, in the way he chuckled as they passed our booth, clapping his friend on the shoulder as an affectionate response to something the other had said. It was just the briefest glimpse, but I was already convinced that here was the solution to our Rhiannon problem. Perhaps if Rhiannon could be helped to see the advantages of a mate who was considerate of women ... well, at least now I had something to work with.

We started off on the last leg of our journey after a decent night's sleep and a breakfast hearty enough that it sat like a lump of lead in my belly. Rhiannon's castle was not that far away, and a great many others were going the same way. Apparently, Rhiannon's impending wedding required not only many guests but also others who would work behind the scenes to make it spectacular. We saw various groups of entertainers among the heavily laden carts carrying the food, extra help, and all the whatnot required of a massive shindig. Kellas struck up a conversation with one bard who was walking alone.

"What's all this about, my good man?" he asked, feigning total ignorance of the situation.

The other shot him an arrogant look. "You must be from far parts if you haven't heard. Our lady Rhiannon is getting married, and we are all summoned to be a part of the festivities. Why, later today, she will hold auditions to decide who will perform music at her wedding. It will be a great honor and privilege to be among those chosen."

"And not unduly harm their reputations as musicians either, I'll be bound."

Another disdainful look. "How plebian an attitude. Are you a bard?"

Kellas snorted. "No, but my friend there is one." He jerked a thumb in my direction. "Sings like an angel."

I kept my face hidden behind my hoodie, merely fussing over

Knight and pretending I hadn't heard their conversation. There was a brief pause as the man tried to size up the competition he might have from me, then he merely grunted. Kellas said his goodbyes and trotted over to join me. "There's our opportunity, lass. Join the bards chosen to play, and we're in."

"You're assuming I'll be chosen."

He sent me a disgusted look. "No one would refuse you, Brannaugh. Just listen to your lute, play like our lives depend on it, and we're golden."

"No pressure, then."

"No pressure," he agreed, and sent me a smile that would have melted the frozen hearts of a legion of women stronger than I.

We traveled the rest of the way to Rhiannon's castle in silence, where we were directed through the main gate and up to a large courtyard where auditions were being held. Kellas trotted off with Knight, ostensibly to find the horse stabling, but mostly to find an unobserved spot where the dark horse could disappear himself without causing alarm. I got in queue for my turn at an audition.

We all could hear our fellow competitors as they sang, played, and danced with conviction for the chance to be included in Rhiannon's marriage celebration. The more I heard, the less confident I felt about the whole idea. There was no doubt in my mind that only the best musicians had gathered here today. My own feeble efforts were not going to measure up, and I would be dealt a humiliating dismissal. The decisions were being made by a trio of judges who took careful notes, then either dismissed the auditioners or waved them farther into the castle. The line in front of me shrank steadily, one song at a time, until finally it was my turn.

I bowed to the judges and made my way on trembling legs up onto the makeshift stage, my lute clutched to my chest like a security blanket. I could feel it humming in excitement, louder all the time. Seating myself carefully on a stool that had been provided, I bent my head over the strings. Any thoughts I had entertained as to what to play fled. I sat frozen in fear. My lute lay silent in my arms.

There was a stirring in the crowd of musicians still waiting their turn, then a shout: "Play, or get off the stage!"

Still nothing. The crowd grew more restless. "Please!" I begged the lute in a whisper, but still nothing, not until the crowd started stamping their feet demanding I leave. Then my hands moved unbidden. A chord crashed outward from my lute, impossibly loud for an unamplified instrument, drowning out the crowd. Then a series of notes, my fingers flying over the strings as if possessed, intricate, liquid, rising to a high note that lingered, quivering for several heartbeats, then I was singing full out in a language I had no idea what it was: fierce, proud, defiant.

I sang the first verse by myself, but when I reached what must have been the chorus, I was joined by several other musicians playing tin whistle, a fiddle, and a different sort of bagpipes than I'd even seen before. Kellas was among them, playing a handheld drum that bore a distinct resemblance to one my Iku played when doing her shaman duties. The music soared out and upward, carrying me away with the notes until it finally faded away to nothing, leaving me feeling empty ... until the applause about knocked me from my seat. I jerked my head up and looked around in confusion. Kellas gripped my arm and pulled me to my feet. "Bow," he ordered out of the corner of his mouth. "Thank you, thank you," he called out to the crowd, then he was pulling me from the stage and away, leading me to where the judges sat. "Are we in?" he demanded without preamble.

One snorted in disgust. "Are you in?" he repeated and pointed upward to where a glamourous looking lady stood on a balcony overhead, clapping enthusiastically. "What do you think?"

Kellas glanced upward, then nodded. "Good, then. Where do we go from here?"

The judge waved us away. "Follow the servant there, he'll direct you."

As we went to follow the servant, the other three musicians joined us. "Are we in?" one asked. Kellas nodded, and he whooped softly. "Lucky for us when we met you earlier!"

"Who ...?" I began, but Kellas hustled me away, the others trailing behind us like ducklings.

"I'll fill you in soon. We must get out of here quickly. Uiscias was in the crowd ..."

Thirty-Eight

Mentioning our bardic nemesis had the desired effect of hurrying my footsteps. Our castle guide took us up a flight of stairs to a long hallway punctuated by several doors. He stopped at the first one, pushing it open. "This will be the young lady's room. The men will be across the hall. Please make yourselves comfortable. If you need anything, just pull the service bell rope and someone will assist you." He gestured to an intricately woven rope hanging just inside the doorway. "Once you've freshened up a bit," he said (he was being diplomatic; we all stank from the long journey), "someone will come to guide you to dinner."

With those instructions, he left. I stood in the doorway of my room, unsure of the next step. Kellas came to my rescue. "A wash-up first, introductions afterward," he assured me. "I'll come knocking when we're ready … it'll take us longer, being the four of us." He rapped a distinctive pattern on the door. "Only if you hear this, Brannaugh. Don't open your door for anyone else."

Because that made me feel better! I just nodded, backed into my room, shut the door, and used a massive key to lock it.

It wasn't an enormous room, nor was it fancy, but it felt pleasant, nonetheless. Stone walls (it was a castle after all!) two tall, narrow windows with leaded glass panes, a single bed with a warm-looking coverlet, a table with a pitcher of water and basin, soap, towels. Oak floor with a simple rug. And that highly decorated service bell pull rope by the door.

I was suddenly struck by a very real problem. I could wash up, but I had nothing to change into. The pixies had cleaned the only clothes I had while I had slept for a week, but since then I'd added layers of dirt and stink back. Hardly the sort of clothing I should be wearing to play for a queen! Perhaps I could request some new attire?

I reached for the bell rope to call, then hesitated. How would that be greeted by her majesty's servants? A scruffy musician demanding fresh clothing because she hadn't thought to bring her own? Not that it was my fault. Cerridwen ...

A gentle knock at the door interrupted my thoughts, and the voice of the servant who'd brought us up here, albeit muffled by the thickness of the oak door, came through. "Miss? I could not help but notice you had no luggage. I have clean clothing here for you, if it pleases you."

Disregarding Kellas's warning about not opening the door for anyone but him, I immediately unlocked the door and pulled it open. The servant stood beaming at me; his arms heaped high with clothing. "If I may ..." he indicated bringing the items in. I backed up to let him pass. He stepped by me and gently laid the clothing on the foot of the bed. "With the compliments of our lady goddess. She wishes to inform you that your music has pleased her greatly, and she looks forward to hearing more very soon." He bowed and left as swiftly as he had arrived, closing the door gently behind him.

Such service! Merely think of a need and it was met, although I had to wonder at the speed of it all. Had Rhiannon ... she had to have been the glamourous lady on the balcony earlier ... possibly noted my shabby appearance and arranged all this as I made my way to my room? Possibly. Which would put her in a whole different category of goddess-ness than Cerridwen and the Morrigan ... that is, likeable.

There were several different outfits in the pile of clothes, and I held each up for inspection. The basic dress was a simple off-white linen shift that would cover me from neck to toes, its long sleeves very full and dramatic. Two different overdresses, one ruby red, one emerald green, looked like they laced up over my torso. Below the waist they were open at the front, letting the white dress show out through. There was underwear the likes of which I had never seen; even so, a fresh pair was a welcome sight. No bra ... not that I'd had one the whole time I was here. Fortunately, I was on the small side in that department. Finishing off the offering was a pair of ultrasoft leather shoes that bore more of a resemblance to slippers than shoes.

I went to work scrubbing off road dust and sweat, and even managed to wash my hair before attempting to don the unfamiliar clothing. Once again, as had happened way back when at Nan's house, I had no sooner slid something on than it changed to fit my frame. Such a handy trick! I hesitated a bit before choosing the green overdress, slipping it over my arms and laboriously doing up the lacing. Fortunately, it was more demure than some I'd seen outside at the auditions, covering my breasts instead of pushing them up front and center, as if for inspection. I'd seen how some of the men had ogled the women dressed like that, and it made me extremely uncomfortable. I tightened the strings around the neckline of the underdress to make sure there were no gaps.

I brushed my hair and carefully did it up in a French braid, tying the end with a ribbon I found in the pile of clothing the servant had brought in. There was no mirror in the room, so I had to hope that I looked OK. By then I'd been close to an hour dolling myself up and was beginning to wonder what was keeping Kellas, when he knocked his special pattern on the door.

He too had been given fresh clothing and was dressed in a white linen shirt that was open at the neck, a closely fitted dark colored vest, and brown pants. His hair was wet and slicked back out of his eyes, not that it was staying that way. One lock had fallen forward and curled down over his left eye. It wasn't fancy clothing by any means, but it suited him to a T. He was, in a word, gorgeous.

He noticed my wide-eyed stare and immediately misinterpreted it. "What? Do I have a booger hanging off my nose or something?" He swiped at his nose. "Better?"

I rolled my eyes at him and hastened to cover up my feelings with a neutral "You look nice."

"You look nice, too. Very traditional." His eyes twinkled, so I knew he was being his normal stinker self.

"And what's that supposed to mean, buster?"

"Just that you look very nice," he deflected. "We're to go down to the dining hall now, if you've finished primping and preening."

I glared at him and pushed past into the hall, where the three other musicians waited. They also had cleaned up and donned outfits very similar to the one Kellas wore. One swept a low bow when he saw me. "Behold, the lovely young lady! You grace us with your presence."

"Hold on, Romeo, you'll get her expecting flattery at every turn," Kellas interrupted, herding me along in front of him. "Liam's a *póg mo thóin*," he muttered in my ear. Not that I had any idea what that meant, but I gathered it wasn't complimentary.

We descended a set of stairs and followed our ears to where a huge throng of people were gathered in a huge dining hall. Think Hogwarts dining hall from the *Harry Potter* movies and you get the idea. The noise was deafening, everyone talking at once, half yelling to be heard. I shuddered and stopped in my tracks. Kellas gave me a gentle shove. "I know, it's awful. Let's just eat fast and get out."

I let him hustle me along to a less crowded table where we sat down. Servants immediately came over, offering platters of different foods. I chose a few items that looked somewhat familiar, declining something that looked a bit like brains mixed with eggs and some other things I couldn't identify.

"Smart move," Kellas muttered in my ear. "Those were calf brains. A great delicacy to many, but very nasty in my opinion."

"Waste not ..." I muttered but was very glad I had not taken any. Somehow it just seemed revolting. But then, I didn't like liver or tongue or other things like that, either.

We were joined by the other three musicians who had aided my audition. Declan, Seamus, Liam, and I spent dinner getting acquainted and planning possible further collaboration. Kellas was right, Liam was a bit of a kiss-up, but the other two seemed thoughtful and pleasant to be around. They had come to the castle along with another man who had almost immediately abandoned them to join up with another group. He'd been their bodhran player. After his defection, they had been desperately trying to get any drummer who would listen to join their group, which is how Kellas had happened across them. Declan had snagged him as he'd returned to the audition courtyard after helping Knight disappear. Seeing the possibilities of us helping each other, Kellas had dragged them up front when I'd been called up.

"You very nearly gave us a heart attack when you didn't start playing right away," Seamus said. He was the one who'd played the odd-looking bagpipes. I'd learned they were called uilleann pipes.

I sent him an apologetic glance. "My brain stuck."

"Stage fright is real enough! And that was a tough crowd," he assured me around a mouthful of calf brain.

He meant well, so I tried to ignore that he was chewing with his mouth open. They all ate with their elbows square up on the table, their forks held in a vise grip as though they were hammers, shoving food into their mouths as fast as they could, as if fearful it might be snatched away. I kept my eyes down on my own food, as it was better not to watch. I heard Kellas chuckling softly next to me. When I glanced up, he cocked his head slightly toward our tablemates and winked. I grimaced back and did my best to eat more, but it was all tasting a bit like sawdust. I finally set down my fork with a sigh.

"Are ye gonna finish that bit?" demanded Declan, stabbing in the direction of my mostly full plate with his fork. When I shook my head, he beckoned. "Shove it over here, then. No reason to waste good food."

I complied, trying not to let it show how weird that felt to me. He made short work of it, then pushed the empty plate away with a happy sigh. "It feels good to be full for a change." He belched loudly, a contented smile on his face, unaware that his lack of manners did not particularly endear him to me.

Leaning over to Kellas I whispered. "Is this normal? All the belching and eating like pigs at a trough?"

Kellas cough-laughed, then looked thoughtful. "I wonder ..." he mused aloud, then refused to share what he was thinking. One of his less wonderful tendencies!

Someone banged on a drum for attention and announced that after our meal we would be gathering in the throne room to serenade the happy couple, meaning Rhiannon and Donn Fírinne. Kellas shot up from his seat like he'd sat on a tack. "Be right back," he said before disappearing like a wisp of smoke on a windy day.

Thirty-Nine

The dining room was emptying quickly as musicians returned to their rooms to gather their instruments. I followed the three men as they hastened after theirs, even though I never went anywhere without my instrument, not that they knew that. I had to maintain appearances. Liam promised to bring Kellas's borrowed bodhran along. I popped into my room, pulled the lute from behind me, and was back in the hall before the others had managed to collect their own instruments. Kellas ran up then, panting heavily but looking triumphant.

I gave him a stern look. "What have you done now, Kellas?"

He gave me a cat-ate-the-canary grin. "You'll see."

Since there was no chance the cat was going to reveal his secrets before their time, we tromped off to the throne room along with what seemed like hundreds of others. How all of us could possibly be needed for one wedding was beyond me, but then, I wasn't a goddess. What did I know of pomp and circumstance?

Rhiannon's throne room was very much like Cerridwen's, although far less dark and threatening in aspect. There were lit candles every-where, hanging aloft in large candelabras. Torches jutted at angles from every available spot, and wood burned merrily in fireplaces set into the walls at regular intervals. If it hadn't been for all the people milling about, I might have found it a pleasant place. As it was, the nervous energy the other musicians exuded was overwhelming and unpleasant. I huddled as close to Kellas as I dared, hoping the proximity would help alleviate some of the threat I was feeling. A moment later, he laid an arm around my shoulders. "I got you, Brannaugh."

Declan leaned close to him and whispered in his ear. Kellas shook his head. "She'll be fine," was all he said.

Up front on the dais, a member of the goddess's court was telling us how the evening was going to proceed. "Her highness will tell you want she wants to hear from each of you, and you will perform that song and none other. She will then decide if your services are still required. Please line up in an orderly fashion, no pushing or shoving, you will all have an opportunity to perform. Anyone fighting will be summarily dismissed."

I wondered if the man ever managed to speak without looking down his long nose at others. It didn't set particularly well, but no one else seemed to mind. Everyone was jostling about to get as far up the line as possible, our companions among them, but I hung back. When Kellas shot me a questioning look, I just shook my head. I really did not want to be crowding in with everyone just then. When we didn't join them, Declan came looking for us. "We're up the line quite a way, come on!" he urged.

"Brannaugh has some claustrophobia issues, mate. You'll have to join us back here at the end of the line."

He groaned but left to let the others know. They all joined us soon afterward, looking unhappy but resigned to the situation.

"What will we do if I don't know what she asks us to play?" I whispered to Kellas.

"What you always do: ask your lute. It's never let you down yet."

"But what if it doesn't?"

"You fuss too much."

"Something the matter?" Liam asked.

"No," we said in unison, then shut up and listened.

Our fellow musicians were all extremely talented. Better than *America's Got Talent*, although I could not figure out Rhiannon's decision-making process of who got to stay and who was dismissed. I felt sorry for the ones who were dismissed, as they were obviously disappointed to have made it this far then told to go home. The tension among those remaining kept climbing as we waited our turn to perform. Whispered conversations grew more and more urgent, to the point where I finally stuffed my fingers in my ears and hid my face against Kellas's shirt front. He just pulled me closer and let me be a nervous wreck. Thank goodness for my cait sidhe ally.

Our turn eventually arrived. Only the chosen musicians remained in the hall, a silently superior bunch quietly appraising our little band as we set up in front of the dais.

Rhiannon leaned forward on her throne, fixing me with a kind smile. "You're the one who sang a fighting song earlier, aren't you?" she asked. "A very different choice for wedding material. Why that one?"

I sent a desperate glance at Kellas, who continued to face forward, a small smile on his lips. Guess this was all up to me! "Um, I'm not sure," I managed softly. When she indicated she couldn't hear me, I added more loudly, "I really don't know. It seemed the right choice at the time, I guess."

She smiled. "It was an excellent choice. That song has been my strength in hard times. I should like to hear you sing it again, if you would be so kind."

"Yes, ma'am." I glanced around at my fellow bandmates, and nodded 1, 2, 3, 4, then struck the opening chord, only to be interrupted by an enormously loud fart. I looked up, startled, the chord dying under my hand.

"Whoops! Sorry." Donn Fírinne apologized, but the look on his face was more "wow that was a good one!" than apologetic. It must have been a smelly one, too, because Rhiannon's face wrinkled a bit and she leaned away from him. He grinned and waved the air, as if pushing the smell her way.

Rhiannon indicated I should try again. Again, 1,2,3,4 and the first chord ... Another massive gas eruption, this one louder than the one before, and apparently even smellier, because the goddess leapt to her feet, pinching off her nose. And that wasn't the end of it, either. Donn kept off-gassing loudly, the sound vibrating off his throne and echoing off the walls. Barely suppressed giggles gave way to guffaws, as no one was able to contain their amusement any longer. Poor Rhiannon was well within the fume cloud and started gagging from the smell, waving at Donn to leave the dais. He seemed entirely amused by the episode, threatening to embrace Rhiannon to prevent her from leaving. Things went quickly downhill from there, with the goddess fleeing the throne room, Donn in pursuit, cackling maniacally.

Once they'd left, Kellas bent over and roared with laughter. When he finally managed to catch a breath, he'd developed a side stitch and had to hold his side, gasping in agony while he continued to giggle help-lessly. "That was a good one!" he finally managed, wiping tears from his eyes. Our fellow musicians also were gradually getting their own laughter under control. They weren't alone, either. Most everyone else had tears of laughter running down their faces. I seemed to be the only one who hadn't found the episode remotely funny.

"Tell me you didn't have something to do with that!" I demanded.

"Then I'd be lying, wouldn't I?" he wheezed. "Ow ..." He tried to stretch his side stitch out.

"So you did!" I accused. "That was mean. Poor Rhiannon!"

"Might make her reconsider, won't it?" he retorted.

"A gas attack would stop a wedding?"

"Sure could. Make her think: 'What if he cuts one of those in bed,' eh? He'd pull the covers over their heads for sure. He's the type."

I sent him a horrified look. "That would be awful! Who'd do such a thing? That's disgusting!"

He indicated the dais. "Obviously, Donn would. You saw how he tried to keep her from leaving."

I wrinkled my nose at him. "Gross."

He grinned at me. "Entirely! OK, that's that. I am going to assume we're "in." Time to return to our rooms and rest up for whatever gets thrown at us tomorrow. I shall have to plot my next undermining activity."

I was shaking my head in dismay as we filed toward the exits, our musicians once again trailing behind like ducklings, all chatting among themselves about the evening's excitement. I was tired and more than a little overwhelmed, wanting to go somewhere I could collect my thoughts, to attempt to wrap my head around things, when our serving fellow came rushing up, all out of breath.

"Apologies!" he gasped, struggling to get his breathing under control. "Her highness sends a message ..." he gulped and must have swallowed wrong, because he immediately started coughing violently.

Liam jumped forward and started thumping the poor man on the back until Declan pulled him off. "Not helping, Liam."

The servant held up a finger, asking for a moment to compose himself before finally managing to wheeze out his message, while he looked directly at me. "Her highness wishes for you to perform at her wedding itself, not just the celebrations leading up to it. She feels your path and hers are intertwined." He looked a little awkward repeating that last bit as if it were too airy fairy for his way of thinking.

I nodded solemnly, not knowing what to say to that.

"So, you agree?" he pressed, and I nodded again. "Then you must meet with her highness tomorrow to discuss possible songs and participate in all activities planned leading up to the ceremony itself. Agreed?"

I nodded once again, feeling a little odd and uneasy about the whole thing. After all, here I was trying to prevent that very thing from happening!

"Very well, then," he said, very business-like now that his breathing was finally under control. "You will be summoned to her highness's chambers for a consultation at some point after breakfast. You will come prepared."

"Yes!" shouted Liam, hugely excited.

The servant sent him a stern look. "You are not invited. Just the young lady here, although you may bring a chaperone if you wish?" He was looking at me.

Still acting like the cat had gotten my tongue, I indicated that would be Kellas.

"Very well, then. The two of you will be ready when I come to get you tomorrow morning."

"But, what about us?" Liam blurted; his disappointment readily apparent.

"What about you?" the servant responded.

"I might need their help," I heard myself saying, then added "if the music our goddess chooses requires them."

He nodded. "In that case, acceptable." I heard the others breathe sighs of relief. "But only you and your escort need attend her highness tomorrow." Again, the men's disappointment was palpable, but less intense than before.

He left after wishing us a good night, and we made our way back to our respective rooms. I was very happy to close and lock my door behind me, shutting out the craziness of the day.

Except, it didn't.

Forty

I had no sooner locked the door than I realized I was not alone in my room. Swinging around in alarm, one hand reaching back for my sword, I scanned the small space but saw no one. Someone was there, though, I could hear it, a very quiet, high-pitched note as though someone was holding her breath.

"I know you're here. Show yourself!" My voice may have quavered a bit, but wouldn't yours? "I have a weapon and know how to use it!"

"Don't do that!" A woman's voice, alarmed, followed by scuffling sounds as someone slid out from under the bed on the far side from where I stood. She stood, brushing dust bunnies and cobwebs from her hair and clothes.

Rhiannon. The lady of the castle was hiding under *my* bed. Oh, my gosh.

We stared at each other for a very long and awkward moment. Finding my voice finally, I blurted out (intelligently, I am sure you will agree) "What are *you* doing here?"

She straightened a bit, trying to regain some fragment of her dignity. "Hiding, obviously."

"Hiding?! From whom? Why?"

She looked discomfited and shrugged. "You know ... him." When I obviously appeared not to know who the heck she was referring to, she added "You were there. In the throne room. Him!"

"Donn Fírnne?" OK, color me completely floored by that one.

She nodded. "You saw how he was."

"Yes, but … Aren't you marrying him in just a few days?"

I wasn't expecting what happened next. Rhiannon threw her hands up, plopped down on the edge of the bed, and burst into tears.

Uh-oh.

What to do? It seemed unkind to just stand there doing nothing, so I eased myself down on the bed next to her and put an arm around her carefully, like she was made of glass. Awfully familiar of me, comforting a goddess of her stature, but somehow it seemed the right thing to do. She leaned into me as though she welcomed it, though, so I just stayed there, letting her cry, and feeling like the most awkward creature on the face of the planet.

The sobbing took some time to diminish, but it did eventually, and she fumbled around in search of a handkerchief. I popped up and grabbed the only thing available: a hand towel I hadn't used earlier. She blew gustily into it and wiped her face as well before giving me a watery smile. "Thank you."

"Feeling better?" What do you say to a goddess under the circumstances?

She nodded a bit jerkily, and then patted the bed next to her, indicating I should sit down again. "I need someone to talk to, and you are the only one from far away, so I feel I can confide in you and no one else need be the wiser. I can trust you not to tell anyone?"

I nodded, not knowing what to say, and sank down on the bed next to her.

"I have changed my mind. About marrying Donn."

O… K … that wasn't what I expected. I managed another nod.

"Ugh!" She bunched her hands up in the towel like she was trying to throttle it. "I just want to be my own person!" She sent me a sideways glance. "You know, people always trying to tell you what to do and not giving you a chance to say what you really want?"

I grimaced and nodded. It's a universal experience, I think.

"My son, Pryderi, was pushing me to marry this hero, Manawydan fab Llŷr. I barely know the man! And then Donn showed up and was so much fun, and doted on me so … But so many came forward and forbade me to see him, said so many negative hurtful things that I just wanted to protect him … so when he asked me to marry him, I said yes. But since the wedding has been planned, he's changed somehow. He acts like he owns me, even. He's jealous and unreasonable, and then he does things like he did tonight that are just humiliating!! Why? Why would he do something like that?"

What would I know of such stuff. I'm 16! But I think she was asking a rhetorical question, so I just shook my head and shrugged. "Guy stuff?"

She rolled her eyes and groaned. "No kidding." She was quiet for a little while. "Somehow," she started, then stopped and sighed. "Somehow, I must get rid of him yet make it easy for him to save face. But how?"

I gave her an incredulous look. "Why is that on you?"

She turned and looked at me like I'd grown a second head. "What do you mean?"

"I mean, he's a grown-up, yes? He's a god, a death god, even. What makes you think you must coddle him like an overgrown toddler? Why is it on *you* to protect any man's precious little ego? Why would you put up with bad behavior from anyone even for a second? You're a goddess, a much-loved goddess. Act like one! Tell him to shove off, and don't let the door hit him in the butt as he leaves. You need to grow a backbone, lady!"

Holy crap, where did that come from? I sent her a sideways glance to see if she was about to smite me for my little rant, but she was merely looking at me with astonishment that was slowly changing into something very different. Like she was taking back her own power, somehow. The frantic energy that had been evident from the moment she crawled out from under my bed was dissipating; she seemed to grow taller, stronger. She abruptly stood up. I jumped to my feet, too.

"You are absolutely correct. I don't have to put up with any of this!" she declared with some heat. "I don't have to marry anyone if I don't feel like it, either. I will make the announcement in the morning." She marched to the door and opened it, before turning and smiling at me.

"Thank you. I won't be needing your musical services anymore because the wedding is off. Kindly meet me in the morning as arranged, however. I would like to speak to you before you go."

I managed a nod because what could I say to that? "Yes, milady."

She left. I collapsed on the end of the bed and tried to make sense of what had just happened. It was all so unreal … a goddess hiding under a bed to get away from another god who was being a jerk to her? Wasn't that human stuff? And where did that "grow a backbone" line come from? Who did I think I was to chastise Rhiannon like that? I flopped back and stared up at the ceiling without seeing it, my mind whirling in confused circles.

I woke up some time later, cold and crampy from lying with my lower legs hanging off the bed. It was still dark out. I was barely awake enough to crawl under the covers, where I shivered for a few minutes before drifting off again to a night filled with disturbing dreams that made no sense.

Forty-One

I was very glad when morning daylight started banishing the shadows. When Kellas knocked on the door, I was ready to go. We went down to the dining hall, arriving before most of the rest of the castle's inhabitants were awake. I snagged a couple of pastries and headed outside, feeling claustrophobic. Kellas followed suit, a bit put out not to be partaking of something more solid, but apparently understanding that something was going on with me and he needed to just go with the flow. Once we were far enough away from people overhearing anything, I relayed what had happened last night.

"Well, that puts a different spin on things, doesn't it?" he said. We sat with our backs against the castle wall, on a thin strip of grassy verge that overlooked a steep drop-off to the sea. It had been a scramble to get here, but with so many people about, it was one of the few places I felt was private.

"Any ideas?" I stuffed the last of my pastries into my mouth and licked the sugar off my fingers. "I mean, can we just shove off the minute we say goodbye like she asked, or do we have to hang around?"

"I think we have to make sure she doesn't change her mind again, don't you?" he countered.

"After last night? You'd think she'd do that?"

"I think a lot of things could have happened between last night and this morning."

I groaned. Why couldn't this just be simple for once?

Kellas just snorted in agreement, grabbed me by one hand and levered me to my feet. "C'mon. This isn't gonna get easier by putting it off." He led the way back along the castle wall to the door hidden at the base of one tower that we'd come through. We'd just stepped inside when we heard voices down the corridor ahead of us. Kellas put a hand on my arm, stopping me. "Sh." Like, he felt that was necessary! He closed the door softly, putting us in shadow.

"I was just saying, m'lord, that demonstrations like last night do not put you in a favorable light with her ladyship's people. You will need to be more careful!"

"Ask me if I care! As soon as we are married, I will use this place to launch a new campaign to unseat the Tuatha Dé Danann from power. I shall succeed this time because none will stand against their favorite goddess's husband. After all, she chose me, why would they stand against me?"

I gripped Kellas's arm. Donn Fírinne was using Rhiannon in an effort to take over Tír na nÓg? Last night's stupidity was mere elementary school nonsense. This, however …

"We must tell Rhiannon!" I whispered right by Kellas's ear. He nodded and put a finger to his lips.

"I would agree, sire, but you must …" The rest was lost in the ether. The others were moving away from us, their voices becoming more muffled. Kellas took my hand again and hurried me to where the corridor met another one at right angles, then we hastened in the opposite direction from Donn and his companion. We didn't stop to catch our breath until we had regained the upper hall.

"Close one," he said. I nodded. "Let's go to Rhiannon now. No point in waiting." No argument there! But where to? "Dining hall. Maybe we can find someone who knows where to go."

I took off at a run, turning into the dining hall and crashing full speed into a very large man, bouncing off and landing hard on my rear on the stone floor.

"Are you all right?" The large man was bending over me solicitously, a concerned expression on his face.

"Ow ..." I managed, then forced a weak smile. "Sorry. Wasn't watching where I was going."

Kellas helped me to my feet. "She's a bit disaster prone," he started, then realized who we were talking to. "Manawydan fab Llŷr, sir! Our apologies. We need to find milady Rhiannon immediately. Can you help?"

Manawydan's gaze narrowed. "And why might this be so necessary that you go charging about crashing into people?"

"Donn Fírinne." I stammered. "He's planning a coup against the Tuatha Dé Danann. He's using Rhiannon."

"And you know this how?"

"We overheard him talking."

"This way," he said, and took off walking fast. I had to jog to keep up. He led us up a long set of stairs into a corridor lined with floor-to-ceiling arched windows. Striding to an enormous oak double door, he knocked urgently, and waited.

His knock resulted in raised voices inside, and then Rhiannon's tremulous call to "come in" accompanied by an angry exclamation from Donn Fírinne.

Manawydan charged in like a crazed bull. I started after, but Kellas grabbed me by the arm. "Caution," he muttered, and pushed me behind him before easing into the room, not proceeding too far from the door. I peeked around him and saw Rhiannon on the far side of the room near a large ornate window, her arms clasped around her as if warding off a chill. Donn Fírinne loomed nearby like an angry ostrich, all ruffled and irritable.

Manawydan strode over to the pair. "My lady, is something the matter?"

"Nothing's the matter! exclaimed Donn, waving one hand in the air as if chasing off an irritating fly. "Rhiannon and I were discussing a matter of importance that is of no concern to *you*. State your reason for being here, then leave immediately. You are interrupting us."

Rhiannon's expression said otherwise, her distress obvious. "No, please stay."

Manawydan merely kept his gaze on Rhiannon, awaiting further instruction. There was a vibrating tenseness to his posture, as though he could explode into action in whatever direction needed. It was intimidating. I was grateful to be on the far side of the room from him, and wondered how Donn Fírinne would respond. I didn't have to wait long.

"You are impertinent, sirrah! Begone at once."

Manawydan turned his gaze on the death god. So glad it wasn't me! Even Donn took a half step backward. "Milady bid me stay. I will stay."

"She and I are to be wed on the morrow ..."

"No, we are not! I told you." Rhiannon exclaimed.

"We shall," he countered.

"Shall not!"

This would have devolved into an endless loop, if not for Manawydan. "If milady does not wish to marry, that is her choice, and a man of honor should accept her wishes." He stepped between Donn and Rhiannon. "You should leave." His voice took on a hard edge, and the threat in it was unmistakable. "Now."

Donn's response was to draw a dagger and lunge at Manawydan, who blocked Donn's arm, then grabbed it and twisted it behind the god's back, forcing him to drop the weapon. Manawydan kicked it away and gave Donn a hard shove toward the door. "Leave!"

Donn staggered several steps, nearly falling before regaining his balance and wheeling around to face his opponent. "I shall not!" he snarled. *"Eirich agus dean seirbhis do d' mhaighstir!"*

For those of you who wonder what he was saying, it translates to "Arise and serve your master." Which is exactly what happened. Things started coming out of the floor, the walls, the ceiling ... things that I hesitate to describe because they were an awful assortment of dead creatures in various states of decay. The stench was unbearable.

Kellas swore, shoved me out of the room, and transformed into his puma avatar. I would have happily left, but there were people in that room I cared about, even if only recently so, and Kellas, whom I definitely cared about (remember my crush on him, right?), so I didn't do as ordered. Instead, I drew Fraegarthach and charged into the fray.

And a fray it truly was. Manawyden had drawn his sword (these fellows never get dressed without one) and was hacking and thwacking about, chopping the dead things to small bits of stinky stuff, trying unsuccessfully to reach Donn Fírinne. Rhiannon was throwing what looked like small golden moons at the creatures, which made them to go up in smelly clouds of smoke. She had terrible aim, not that it mattered with so many nasties to dispose of. Kellas was doing his thing, ripping and tearing with teeth and claws while gagging at the terrible grossness of biting into rotting flesh. I waded in, swinging my sword with a skill I did not know I possessed, happy to let the sword do what it knew how to do. I think I was saying something as well, but dang me if I knew what that was, because honestly? I was thoroughly grossed out by the whole thing.

Once, my Iku had made me help her clean a dead chicken, having me shove my hand into its body cavity and rip out the still-warm guts. I'd puked all over the floor before she relented and let me off the hook for that one. I swore I'd never eat meat again, which lasted exactly 5 hours until the bird reached the table as roast chicken. I'm truly fond of roast chicken, but I've never eaten meat again without being very aware that a living creature had died so I could eat. It changes something in you, makes you far more grateful and humble about food.

Weird, the odd bits that come up in your brain while doing something unrelated. What could cleaning the entrails out of a dead chicken possibly have to do with chopping undead things into small parts? Which Fraegarthach was doing with deadly efficiency. Or undeadly efficiency, I guess, because these things had already died. Unfortunately, Donn had an endless supply of the things, because no sooner had we dispatched the closest ones, more came crawling out to replace them. I began to realize we had to reach the death god if this fight was going to end. To do that, I had to reach Manawydan first. Someone had to guard his back while he fought the death god, or he would be overwhelmed from the rear.

However, I needed my back guarded as well, and for that I needed Kellas. I chanced a quick look about and found him also attempting to reach Manawydan. "Great minds," and all that. Fraegarthach responded to my thoughts, and we made our way to Kellas's side, chopping to bits an undead thing that had just latched onto the puma's back. Together we worked our way over to Manawydan. I backed up to the man, now head and shoulders taller than him (although he was very large to begin with) and with Kellas to one side of us and Rhiannon on the other, Manawydan pressed Donn with increased ferocity.

I wish I could have stood back and watched them fight, because it was a master class in swordsmanship, which I truly could have benefited from. However, even my rudimentary grasp of the art was doing what was required of it, and the bits and pieces of dead things were really beginning to pile up, requiring careful foot placement to avoid slipping on the squishy bits. I was gagging from the smell, trying not to let it turn into a full-on vomit, grateful for my sword and not having to use my teeth to fend off the undead, as poor Kellas was doing.

"Send them away!" I heard Manawydan yell over the clamor of yipping and squealing undead. "Yield!"

There was a slight hesitation in the creatures around us, as if echoing what must have been Donn Fírinne's own at Manawydan's command, then,

"*Till air ais gu do chuid eile a dh'Alba*," I heard Donn spit angrily. Which roughly translates to "return to your rest." There was a moment where nothing moved, then the undead things melted into the floor, even the chopped-up bits, leaving behind only the ghastly smell of rotting flesh. I turned cautiously to face the two men, just as Manawyden lowered his sword.

Snarling, Donn lunged at him, too fast for the other man to raise his sword to defend himself.

Fraegarthach reacted with lightning speed, whipping up and around, dragging my right arm with it, connecting with Donn's neck with deadly force. I watched in horror as Donn's head separated from his body, hitting the floor with a sodden thump. His body followed shortly thereafter. There was a moment when nothing happened, nobody moved, then Donn's parts simply melted away, oozing into the floor just as those of his minions had.

Rhiannon screamed and threw herself at Manawyden, who wrapped his arms around her, holding her tight. I turned and vomited my breakfast ... because being nasty like that is normal for me, I guess. Not that I hadn't reasonable cause. Kellas transformed into human form and made a dash to where a pitcher of water was sitting on a table nearby, using the entire contents to rinse his mouth over and over, dry heaving the whole time.

Helping myself to a lovely white napkin on the same table as Kellas's water pitcher, I carefully wiped down Fraegarthach's blade before sheathing it behind my back and shrinking down to my normal size. The napkin would never be the same, but I figured Rhiannon wouldn't mind, considering we had just rescued her from marrying a zombie. Interestingly, the rotting odor was abating rapidly, as if Donn's melting away had taken the stench along with him.

Nobody said anything for what seemed like a very long time. We all just stood there shuddering. Manawyden recovered first.

"We are fortunate that the sword of Nuada has returned after so long an absence, and that its new champion has shown up at a most opportune time," he said. "We are indebted to you, miss ...?"

"Brannaugh," Kellas interjected, before I could forget myself and spit out my real name.

I merely nodded. "Yup! That's me." Oi! Way to sound dumb, girlfriend!

Rhiannon released her death grip on Manawyden and stepped back, smoothing the rumples from her dress. "You are a surprise, Brannaugh. I would never have thought a songbird could transform into a warrior. I am so grateful."

They were ignoring Kellas, though, and that felt wrong. "Umm ... Kellas helped too," I pointed out timidly. The pair merely glanced at the cait sidhe.

"Of course we are grateful for the fairy cat's aid as well," Rhiannon said a bit stiffly.

What is it with these people and cait sidhe? I bristled at the cool reception offered Kellas, but he merely laid a hand on my shoulder. "We must be off immediately, milady. We are needed elsewhere. With your leave?"

She inclined her head regally, adding "But first, name your reward."

I must have looked completely at sea, being presented with such an offer. It felt like she was buying us off or something. Kellas was not so shy and had an immediate answer. "A boon, to be fulfilled at whatever time we have need of it, milady. Should you feel this is appropriate, of course."

She looked a bit crabby at that. Maybe she was more used to people asking for gold or land or something, neither of which we had any use for right now, but after a moment's hesitation, she nodded. "Of course." She took a ring off her index finger and handed it to me. It did not escape me that she handed it to me, not Kellas. "When you have need of me, you will know how to use this."

I accepted it with as much grace as I could muster, still upset at how they were treating Kellas as if he were infected with some nasty disease. Also, more than a little put off by how it felt like they were trying to get rid of us as fast as possible, without calling in the guard to escort us out. Kellas grabbed my hand, and bowing, we left as quickly as we could without running.

Forty-Two

We stopped by our rooms and changed into our own clothes (which had been laundered, a kindness for which I was very grateful) then quickly exited the castle. Minutes later, we were on the road, jogging away from Rhiannon's castle. Once we were hidden from the castle, I called for Knight. He appeared after a few anxious moments on my part, and I gratefully climbed aboard. I was exhausted. So was Kellas, bent over, hands braced on his knees as he struggled to regain his breath.

"Let's not waste time here," he managed, straightening up and gesturing at the road ahead.

We walked in silence for a while until I couldn't contain myself a moment longer. "What in the name of all that's holy is *wrong* with those people?" I demanded. "You fought for them, and then they treat you like a nasty insect or something."

Kellas shrugged, but I could see it bothered him as well. "There's a long history you aren't familiar with, Brannaugh. My people have not always been ..." He hesitated, struggling to find a word. "Kind."

"But to hold that against you when you were doing your utmost to be of service. Heck, you saved their backsides! It's just wrong. No one should be judged by what others have done, good or bad!"

"That would require a level of emotional intelligence that many people apparently lack." He shrugged again. "It is what it is."

I huffed my frustration. "Well, it's wrong."

"Not getting an argument from me, kid," he responded. "But you need to let it go. Being angry about something you cannot control only eats you up from the inside."

I gritted my teeth but tried to do as he suggested. It sure wasn't easy.

We walked for hours until simply unable to go any further, then made camp, such as it was. A small fire to ward off the darkness. A meal from the pixies' never-empty food bag. Curled up on the hard ground hoping sleep would take over while Kellas took the first watch. Cold, so cold ... shivering and teeth chattering. Pure misery. A blanket, smelling strongly of horse sweat, laid over me as gently as a parent soothing a restless child, then when that wasn't enough to warm me, Kellas in puma form curling up close, his back pressed against mine, purring in a steady reassuring rumble that vibrated through my body, shaking loose the tension that had gripped me for so long. I slept.

I woke to full daylight, disoriented, until I realized I'd slept all night, leaving Kellas on guard duty. I lurched up guiltily, only to discover the cait sidhe, now in man form, passed out where he'd cuddled up next to me last night. Knight stood nearby, head up, alert, watching over us like he was a herd stallion.

I carefully freed myself of the blanket so as not to wake Kellas and went over to Knight. I just stood there, not offering to pet him or anything, until he drew a long breath and let it out gustily, then turned his head and nuzzled my hair, puffing warm breath into my face. Only then did I lean on him, letting my gratitude seep from every pore, knowing somehow that this was the best way to let him know how much his acceptance meant to me.

This was how Kellas found us once he finally pried his eyes open and sat up. Like me, it took a few moments before he managed to pull things together, then he groaned and flopped back down. "My bad," he managed, before sitting up again. "I screwed up."

"It's OK. Knight stood guard all night for us." I stroked the dark horse's neck. "Hungry?"

"Starving, actually." Kellas rolled to his feet and shook the dirt and dead grass off Knight's saddle blanket, folding it carefully back into its normal dimensions.

As "starving" fit my own situation, we didn't waste any time digging into the never-empty food bag before setting off for Cerridwen's castle. Knight hit a slow jog that matched Kellas's own, and we made good time, reaching by early evening the now-familiar outer edge of the large field where you could finally see her castle rising on its hill on the other side. That is as far as we got, as we were suddenly surrounded by Cerridwen's home guard, all bristling with weapons, all pointed at us. Not the reception I had been anticipating given our agreement with their boss.

Kellas was incensed. "What's the meaning of this nonsense?" he demanded.

In answer, Cerridwen herself, mounted on a tall white horse, came up behind her guardsmen. She was flanked by Tegan and Morphran, each on dark bays. She had that haughty better-than-thou pout on her lovely face, which did nothing to improve her looks or our moods. "Well?" she demanded, as if we should be able to read her mind as to what that "well" was all about.

"As if she didn't already know," Kellas muttered out of the side of his mouth at me.

I, however, was not in the mood for coddling goddesses, not after the time I'd had with all of them since turning 16. "Deep subject!" I spat. Which, as I'd hoped, had the effect of rendering her completely puzzled.

She gave herself a tiny shake. "What kind of answer is that?" she demanded crossly.

"You said 'well,' and I responded, 'deep subject.' Wells tend to be deep, you see," I explained as snottily as I could, and I can be plenty snotty. "Instead of being all imperious and aloof, how about you very kindly ask how our mission went, and then we will say 'We succeeded nicely, thank you very much. Donn Fírinne is banished back to his lair, averting a certain war with the undead and leaving Rhiannon free to make better choices ... hopefully, but with her, who knows.' Then you say, 'Oh, that's wonderful and thank *you* very much,' and then, 'Oh, by the way, let's arrange your voyage home to your own dimension immediately' ... since that is what we agreed upon as the reward for managing what you couldn't do your own self ... and we'll be off immediately. Because it's about time we went, don't you think? Before you demand somebody else commit suicide as payment for your so-called services?" I gradually got louder and angrier as I spoke, until I was shouting at the top of my lungs, standing in my stirrups, shaking with rage and something else even deeper and unnamed until I realized that tears were pouring down my face.

Kellas had grabbed hold of my ankle in horror. The look of shock on all the gods' faces was a sight to see, not that it gave me a bit of pleasure. Tegan was looking at his wife as though he was seeing her for the first time and wasn't liking what he saw. I was beyond giving two shakes what any of them thought, one way or another. I wanted to go home. I wanted my family. I wanted my own place in time and space and if Cerridwen wanted me dead, well, too bad, so sad. I'd murder the lot of them first, I would, and not give a second thought about it. Done and done.

"I. Want. To. Go. Home. NOW!" I bit out, the anguished growl that came crawling from my throat nearly unrecognizable as my own. "You PROMISED!"

Cerridwen was white with some emotion or other, who only knows what. Like I cared. She drew a deep breath, struggling to regain her composure. "I never demanded anyone's death in return for a favor," she managed.

Wrong thing to say. "Oh, yeah?" I urged Knight forward, pushing past the guards like they weren't there until we were stirrup to stirrup with the goddess. "What about my great grandmother, huh? What about her?' I was so angry, I was spitting, and the droplets were hitting the goddess in the face, making her flinch back. "To save her child, MY NAN, you required a sacrifice of the greatest order. Obviously, you meant that for you to save her child, she had to sacrifice herself. You killed my Nan's mother, you, you ..." I struggled to find the right word. "YOU PHONY!" And, yeah, I was crying uncontrollably now. Knight was slowly backing up and Kellas was there, somehow having climbed onto the dark horse's back. He wrapped his arms around me, pulling me close as I sobbed my heart out. "I ... just want ... to go home," I choked out.

Tegan spoke. "You demanded Olivia's suicide to save her child?" he asked, his voice shaking.

"I didn't mean that; she took it to mean that." Cerridwen's voice was tremulous. Her face was crumpling as though she too were about to cry. "It was a mistake. A terrible, horrible mistake that I have regretted ever since."

Tegan scowled. It was evident that he and Cerridwen would be having a serious talk later, but it was me he addressed now. He rode closer and laid a gentle hand on my shoulder. "It is evident that you have had far too much to manage during your time in Tír na nÓg. But for your efforts, we thank you from the bottom of our hearts. We shall open a portal for you to cross back to your own dimension. All you need to do is ride your horse through it, and you will be transported to a location as near as possible to your place and time. It's not perfect, so please forgive me if we're off a tiny bit. Are you ready?"

I managed a shaky nod, sniffing heavily to keep snot from running down my face. He patted my shoulder and turned his horse away. Pointing to a spot nearby, he murmured some words, and a shimmering doorway appeared. Beyond the portal, all I could see was darkness. He looked back at me. "*Filleadh abhaile i síocháin.* Return home in peace."

Kellas had taken over Knight's neck rope and wasted no time in urging him forward toward the dark doorway, from which echoed the faint sounds of people chanting. Understandably fearful, Knight balked. Understandably impatient, Kellas gave him an angry boot in the ribs. Also understandably, Knight's response was to do one of his disappearing-into-thin-air acts, dumping the pair of us unceremoniously onto the ground. Kellas got the worst of it, as I landed on top of him. Kellas was (understandably!) less than overjoyed, and we had a bit of a go-around getting disentangled from each other and attempting to get back on our feet. I am sparing you the specific details because there was a lot of hissing and spitting and bad words involved. Mostly from Kellas.

Morphran dismounted and came over to help us up, a faint smile playing across his homely face. It made him far less fearful-looking. My amulet had fallen out from beneath my T-shirt, and he noticed it straightaway. "An interesting piece," he said quietly, not that he had to lower his voice, as his parents were loudly arguing nearby. He sent them a sideways glance that clearly conveyed his annoyance at their public confrontation.

I touched it. "A gift from Taliesin. It ... translates. I can speak different languages."

His smile widened the tiniest bit. "It does far more than that, but that is for you to discover. If Taliesin gave it to you, he holds you in very high regard. I shall have to make my brother a new one."

"You made this? It's beautiful!"

Now his face was wreathed in a lovely smile that totally transformed it. He bowed slightly. "Thank you. But you must be off before the portal closes. Don't worry about the dark horse; he can transport anywhere, any time he pleases. He gave me a gentle push. "Go on. I promise it's safe." He glanced at Kellas. "And thank you for your invaluable service, cait sidhe. *Dul i síocháin*: Go in peace."

Kellas nodded in response, then grasped my hand tightly. "To make sure we stay together," he whispered.

I squeezed his hand to let him know I'd heard him.

"On three," he said. "One, two ..." On three, we walked through the portal. Together.

We crash-landed in the dark. Literally *crash*-landed ... it was like we'd been dropped from a tree or a low-flying airplane. I lay on the ground stunned, my cheek pressed against rough pavement. I could hear Kellas nearby, cussing and spitting, not unlike his cat self, although it was words, not growls, and not the sort for delicate ears.

"Brannaugh?" He was next to me now. I groaned, and he gave my shoulder a reassuring pat before helping me up to a sitting position. "Anything broken?"

"Don't think so." I struggled to my feet, wincing at a spike of pain in my ribs. "Oh, that hurts."

"The landing was none too gentle," he grumbled.

I looked around. We were in the middle of a deserted city street, streetlamps punching pools of light at intervals. The buildings seemed to tower over us in the low light, sleek and almost weirdly uniform in comparison to Taliesin's hut or the hills of Tír na nÓg. In between lay shadows that could have hidden anything.

"C'mon." Kellas took my arm. "Before a car comes along and flattens us." He guided me over to the sidewalk.

I leaned against a lamppost, still trying to draw a deep breath. "Where are we?"

He glanced around. I swear, even though he was in his human form, it was like he could flick his ears forward and backward as he examined our surroundings. "Ithaca, close by the Commons. At least we're not in some random place, but it'll still be a hoof and a half to get home."

"What's that sound?" I was gradually becoming more aware of my surroundings, and what I was hearing made me uneasy. "It sounds angry."

Kellas turned his head in the direction the sound was coming from. "It *is* angry. Chanting. Maybe a protest." It seemed to galvanize him, because he grabbed my arm again and started leading me away from the source of the noise. I wobbled along beside him, feeling worse than I'd ever had after being offloaded by a bucking mustang. There would be bruises, for sure. "I wish you'd learned your spell of seeming already. You look about 10 or 11, not exactly an age to be gallivanting around at midnight in the city with someone like me. I'd rather not get arrested." Despite the flippant way he said that he tugged me a little closer before pulling my hoody up over my head. "Stick close."

I saw movement in the darkness farther down the street. There was something not quite right about it. "Kellas ..."

He saw them too. A group of people had just come into view out of the shadows. They were dressed all in black, so they blended into the darkness, nearly invisible except for their motion. As they came under a streetlamp, I could see they were men wearing riot gear, carrying shields and long batons. There was an eerie quality to the blackness that surrounded them, however, one that swallowed up their faces, concealing them like phantoms. They saw us almost as soon as we saw them, and as of one mind they spread across the street, blocking our escape in that direction. They marched intently toward us, completely silent except for the sound of their booted feet, focused.

Like a herded sheep, I turned and bolted. Stand my ground? Not this kid! The laughter that followed us was mocking, malicious, and grated like thousands of tiny shards of glass.

I am so grateful for ...

My niece Eleanor, who shares my love of writing and made many excellent suggestions that greatly enhanced the narrative.

My grand girls Abby and Josie, who corrected my outdated kid slang and substituted their own (probably already outdated) kid slang.

My grand girls McKenzie, Aislynn and Evelynn, who bugged me unrelentingly on weekends for what I had written that week and suggested song after song for Raven to sing ... and then played them ad nauseum on my computer.

My friend and beta reader Holly who very gently told me the first version of this story read like two different ones, and that I needed to cut it in half and write a new ending. It was very sage advice.

My friend and beta reader Stasia, who over many years has kindly taught me all I know about horses, *and* read all the versions of this story *and* loved them all.

My copy editor Brendan, a wonderful find who not only fixed my mistakes and made suggestions that improved clarity, but left uplifting comments that invariably made my day.

My cover and interior designer Betty, a kindred spirit and a joy to work with.

My Friday brass ensemble, who share my fascination with classical brass music, made all the sweeter by sharing dessert and conversation.

And last but far from least: My hiking partner/husband Charlie, who makes sure I get out on the trails every single day, no matter what the weather. Inspiration abounds in nature.

About the Author

If it involves caring for plants, animals, birds, bees, and butterflies; playing with color and composition; being ready to explore; craving peace and quiet; enjoying music and magic; and spending time with kiddos, family, and close friends, I am all for it. Wandering in unfamiliar woods and wide-open spaces holds no fear for me, but I am a fish out of water in urban environments, in crowds, and in heavy traffic.

www.ingramcontent.com/pod-product-compliance
Lightning Source LLC
Chambersburg PA
CBHW022126310726
48972CB00007B/2211